Being Bold

Tactical Operations & Protection

Blye Donovan

ISBN: 979-8-9867683-9-7.
Imprint: Independently published.
Cover designed by Angela Haddon.

OTHER TITLES BY BLYE DONOVAN

Rolling Brook Protectors

Hunted at Whiteford Farm
Gifts from a Stalker
Small Town Frame-up
Condemned by Secrets
Marked as Queen of Hearts

Stand-alone Novels

Undercover Santa
Blaze of Glory

Texas Heat Shared Series

Wait for You

TOP Security

Going Rogue
Being Bold

To Mary and all the wounded warriors out there, do not give in. You are someone's rainbow.

CONTENT WARNING

This book contains profanity, violence, and mature sexual content. It also includes survivor's guilt, and mentions PTSD, parental death, cancer, and loss.

Being Bold

A TOP Security Novel

Blye Donovan

CHAPTER 1

Bo

Everett "Bo" Larson's earpiece crackled before a voice spoke three words that promised to ruin his day, "Suicide bomber threat."

He gave the signal for 'message received' and kept moving. His team was on a routine reconnaissance mission in Kandahar—or had been. That information just changed everything.

Fan-fucking-tastic.

Instead of scouting for an urban security op, Bo and his teammates had a new objective—neutralize the threat.

Blaring car horns warred with the hum of generators as he walked the busy city street and waited for further instructions. His special warfare unit had been in Afghanistan for the past six months. He knew the work they did was important, but if he was being honest, he was ready to leave the country because of shit like this.

There was beauty here, though. A harsh, rugged one. Everything seemed to have sharp edges—the buildings, even the mountains—and the dry landscape left everything a shade of brown, never green. Like the sky. When it was blue, it still wasn't clear. A layer of dust, pollution, and smoke permeated the air so that the days passed in a haze. It lingered above the stores he walked by, drifting out to settle over the mountain peaks like a dingy shawl surrounding the city in the distance.

These mountains were more like hills compared to the Rockies he grew up with in Bozeman. Glancing at them now, Bo thought of home. Of Montana.

Too long.

A frown tugged at the stern corners of his mouth. He'd been away too many years. Over the last half-decade, the Navy had sent him all over the world, but he'd avoided his namesake.

"Bo" was short for Bozeman. During initial training, he'd earned the nickname when his instructor thought the city sounded made up. What had started as "Boze's Man" had been shortened to "Boze" and eventually became just "Bo" the day he'd earned his SEAL pin.

A shopkeeper called to potential customers in Pashto, pulling him out of his reverie. The exuberant man fell silent as Bo approached. Sometimes, he said hello in the Afghans' language. Other times he chose to ignore their guarded stares. Today, he didn't have time to win hearts and minds.

The spring sunshine warmed his broad shoulders as he followed ten feet behind his teammate at a leisurely—unthreatening—pace. Plain clothing and the beard he'd grown out disguised Bo's true identity. Still, people crowding the concrete walk in front of the shops moved out of his way. He couldn't hide that he was an outsider here. Not with his auburn hair and sunburned skin, but he hoped his look said, "European expat" and not "Navy SEAL."

Being the trained operator that he was, the news about the bomber had still tightened every muscle in his body—and there were a lot of them. You didn't make it in his line of work without being in the best shape of your life.

"Confirmed sighting. Martyr's Square."

Well, fuck.

A traffic circle surrounded the square. It made Bo wonder if they were dealing with an SVBIED. A suicide vehicle-borne improvised explosive device would be a lot tougher to eliminate than a person on foot.

His teammate's shoulders tensed in front of him. The younger man had earned the nickname "Nugg," short for golden nugget, because of his propensity to point out a lesson learned for any situation. Afghanistan was Nugg's first deployment, but Bo had mentored him for the last year. They'd become close as brothers. Growing up, Bo didn't have any, but he'd found his family with the SEALs.

When Nugg cursed, probably wondering the same

thing as Bo, he spoke, knowing Nugg would hear him. "Not our first rodeo, man. Stay cool."

This wasn't the first time their unit had tangoed with an extremist intent on blowing themselves up. While that should have made things easier, an unfamiliar worry gnawed at Bo's gut. Adrenaline surged through his veins, but he couldn't shake the feeling. Good thing he was used to setting emotions aside to focus on the mission.

Ignoring the gloom dragging at his heels, he listened to the information coming through his communications device. He and Nugg were the closest to the location intel claimed the bomber would be. Not that they needed the instruction, but their commander ordered them to respond to the situation. They'd both already changed course for an intercept.

Bo started to scan the crowds in earnest as information flooded in.

"Female. Black hijab."

A grumble moved his chest as the feeling in his gut broke past the barrier he'd erected. He hated that extremists used female suicide bombers. Not only was it ten times harder to pull the trigger on a woman, but that description was useless. A black hijab described every female in this country. They all wore scarves of some sort that covered their heads and necks. He quickly glanced across the square and counted over fifteen women in his general vicinity who met that description.

"Have to do better than that," he muttered, but

kept walking. He'd made it halfway around the square when he realized Nugg had pulled his disappearing act. The guy had an innate ability to blend into the background in any situation, almost like a ghost. Normally, it impressed Bo, but at a time like this, it annoyed the hell out of him.

He was about to ask for his location when Nugg's voice filled his ear. The words echoed from Bo's eardrum to reverberate throughout his entire body. "Tango identified. Eleven o'clock. Corner pharmacy."

Go time.

A fresh surge of adrenaline heightened his senses. When he spotted Nugg's terrorist, the woman's face was visible, but the long, black head scarf concealed her hair, shoulders, and upper body. She *could* be wearing a suicide vest with a bomb underneath it, but how could they know for sure? He couldn't— wouldn't—take her life unnecessarily.

Inching forward, his hand hovered at his belt, ready to grab the pistol in the IWB he used on these missions. The inside-the-waistband holster sat by his appendix, leaving his weapon easy to reach but hard to see. "I've got eyes on her. Nugg, confirm target is hot."

Nugg didn't respond right away, and the closer Bo got, the clearer he could see the woman's face. Tears tracked down her cheeks while the crowd of shoppers milled around her without sparing her a glance. He was ten paces away across the roundabout exit when her gaze met his. Something desperate shone in her eyes, and it liquefied his gut.

"Help me," she mouthed in Pashto.

A car drove by. The wind from its speed blew her hijab aside enough for him to see the vest she wore underneath. His gun was in his hand. Still, he hesitated. She might be wearing a bomb, but he didn't believe she wore it willingly.

A flicker of light drew his eye, and he spotted Nugg close behind the target, weapon lifted and ready to fire. Before he could say or do anything to stop him, the woman disappeared in a cloud of smoke, and the world exploded.

The car that had just turned in front of Bo helped shelter him from the blast, but its force still picked him up and tossed him into something solid. His back connected first, then his head. The breath rushed from his lungs, and he struggled to pull more in as his ears rang and his vision swam.

A cloud of smoke and building dust darkened the sky. Beneath it, everything was chaos. It raged around him as he attempted to sit up. Hot pellets of pain showered his body with the movement. When his eyes cleared, he found his left leg trapped under a flaming car door. The sight of the fire sent a flood of adrenaline coursing through his veins to wash the shock from his body.

Frantically, he worked to shove the metal off. The slightest movement sent lances of heat shooting up his leg.

"Arrgh!" A piercing howl left his throat as the fire

ate at his skin.

Gritting his teeth against the excruciating pain, he kicked the door off with his right leg. He thought he'd been in pain before, but the effort it took to move that door left him in agony so acute he couldn't fight against it. A blackness swallowed him, and he crumpled to the ground.

With a gasping breath, Bo shot upright on the couch. His heart hammered in his chest as his head swiveled, taking in his surroundings.

Cabin. Home.

Not that horrible day four years ago.

A tortured sound—half groan, half sob—escaped his throat. He'd had the nightmare again. Only it wasn't just a nightmare. It was his past. A past that haunted him relentlessly.

Dropping his head into his palms, he squeezed his eyes shut against the images from that day. He'd lived through torture as a SEAL, but this torment was slowly driving him to the edge of insanity. Death waited at the bottom, and it was getting harder and harder not to give in and jump.

Not that he'd take his own life, but he felt dangerously close to doing something stupid like BASE jumping at night without any lights.

After the explosion left him with a fractured tibia and third-degree burns, he'd spent nearly a year recovering. He'd regained full use of his left leg, but scars mottled the lower half. Though he could've remained a SEAL, he hadn't been able to face his unit.

Instead, he'd gotten out of the Navy and found a new team at Tactical Operations & Protection.

TOP, as everyone in the business called it, was a leading security firm. He'd been with the company as an operator for the past three years. They did everything from personal protection to private military operations.

Maybe he'd ask his team lead, Victor, for a solo op. Something he likely wouldn't come back from. At least then, his death might mean something. If he died helping someone, maybe it'd make up for the lives he hadn't saved.

Even though he'd recovered from his physical injuries, part of Bo never healed. Deep in his chest, a gaping pit loomed. When the nightmares came, he stared into the pit's abyss, guilt threatening to pull him into its depths.

Because he'd lived, but Nugg hadn't.

His teammate had not only been a friend, he'd been the younger brother Bo never had. He'd respected the hell out of the guy. Nugg had been smart, loyal, and too damn good at his job for it to be over so soon.

If anyone should've survived that blast, it should've been him.

Bo felt moisture on his cheeks and shoved to his feet, swiping at his face with both hands. "I need a fucking drink."

Anything to dull the pain he felt over the memories.

The wind whistled outside as he headed for the

whiskey in the cabinet over the sink. He didn't have far to go. His cabin maxed out at 632 square feet. It only had three rooms plus a loft, with a bed he rarely slept in. The loft sat above the kitchen and bathroom, the only room in the home that wasn't left open to everything else. Like the cabin's construction, the kitchen's cabinets were made from hand-peeled logs. Their light-blonde color helped bounce the moonlight shining in from the undressed windows. It'd be full in a few days. Because of that, it provided enough of a glow to light his path as he padded across the braided oval rug separating the living and eating area.

Despite the wool socks covering his feet, a chill shuddered over his sweat-slicked skin. Bo noticed the cold for the first time since he'd woken up. It was winter in Montana, which meant nighttime temps in the mountains dropped below zero. The corner wood-burning fireplace was dark. The flames from the fire he'd stoked before falling asleep on the couch had long since burned out. He'd have to relight it. *After* he had a drink.

With a grunt, he pulled the stopper out of the whiskey bottle and poured a couple of fingers of the amber liquid into a glass. Knocking it back, he let the burn warm him up. Without the fire's crackling, the air within the confines of his cabin remained still as a tomb, but he didn't mind the quiet. He'd bought this place because of it.

His little cabin sat an hour south of Bozeman. Buffers surrounded the property, contributing to its isolation. He had the Lee Metcalf Wilderness to the west, and to the east, a national forest kept everything but animals away.

Exactly how he liked it.

He kept people at a distance, which was easy to do when his closest relatives were already dead and gone. He'd lost his parents to an avalanche at a young age, and the grandmother who raised him died shortly before he joined the Navy.

Bo poured another shot of whiskey when the phone he'd left charging on the kitchen counter buzzed. Setting his drink down, he picked up the company-issued cell phone. He wouldn't have one if he didn't need it for work. He'd disconnected from anything in his old life three years ago.

Nugg and his SEAL team had been his family. Until he'd let them down and couldn't face them.

Without anyone left to talk to, he'd hardly needed a phone. As it was, he'd had to install satellite comms out here to keep in touch with TOP. When he'd found Tactical Operations & Protection, he'd appreciated the opportunity to be part of something that didn't care about his past. Even if they didn't see each other outside of work, he trusted his team members to have his back when needed, just as he'd do for them.

Another grunt rumbled his broad chest. It was one a.m., and a string of text messages littered his screen. A quick scroll showed what he already knew. The team was giving him shit for missing Crane and Rogue's marriage celebration. The couple eloped months ago, but the unconventional wedding in a hospital meant the rest of their group had missed out on the event. The two newlyweds had agreed to throw a party to make up for it once Crane had fully recovered from the gunshot wound a traitor on their team had given him.

Bo set down his phone without responding and went back for the whiskey in his glass. He was happy his TOP teammates had found love, but he couldn't handle a party. Not when guilt would eat at him the whole time because Nugg deserved to find that kind of happiness, but couldn't.

I *definitely don't fucking deserve it.*

His mouth went sour, and his hand tightened around the glass. He'd replayed that day so many times. If he could go back and do things differently . . .

The cabin door crashed into the wall, interrupting Bo's inner turmoil. He jerked at the sound, and his half-empty tumbler flew from his grasp to shatter on the kitchen floor. The cold blew in with a fierce howl, leaving the door hanging wide open.

What the hell?

A woman dressed in black stood on the threshold. Wet snow glistened on the crown of her head. Strands of dark hair gusted around her face with the howling wind, looking like a . . . like a black hijab.

His nightmare had come to life.

He couldn't speak. Unsure if the vision before him was another hallucination or reality.

"Help me." Foreign and melodic, her voice flowed

to him across the whistling wind like a siren's song, the words trapping him in a flashback of the Afghan woman.

While he stood frozen to the floorboards, the vision stepped inside, lifted a hand to her head, then collapsed in a dead faint.

CHAPTER 2

Ten Hours Earlier

Selene

The wind fought to steer Selene's trusty RAV4 off-course as she turned—or, more accurately, *slid*—into the parking lot of Saber Tech. She was twenty minutes early for her three o'clock shift because she'd given herself an extra hour of travel time in this weather. Driving in snow was not her forte. Up until four months ago, she'd been a SoCal girl. The only snow she'd been used to was the kind at a ski resort, where she didn't have to drive in it. But at some point, she'd lost her damned mind and moved to the mountains of Montana.

Okay, so she hadn't made the move heedlessly. Selene liked to make lists, specifically pros and cons. She'd done her research, made her list, and the move had made sense on paper—the pros outweighing the cons. Of course, it was one thing to write "driving in snow" on a con list and a completely different thing to experience it firsthand.

"Eeeeeek!" she squeaked when her tires lost traction in the packed precipitation, pulling her car to the left. She gripped the wheel at two and ten as if her life depended on it. "Please don't let me hit anything," she prayed as she finally found the grooves in the snow made by other cars.

She inched forward at five miles per hour until she located an empty spot in the parking lot where she could pull in without the risk of hitting another vehicle. When she put the car in park, she let out a sigh of relief. At least she didn't have to do that again for another eight to nine hours.

She would've rolled her eyes, but seeing a salt truck with a plow improved her mood considerably. "Please let that last until I get off work." She hoped the road back to her apartment in Big Sky would be plowed, too, or she'd have to put on her big-girl panties and figure out how to put chains on her tires.

Sighing, she adjusted the radio station. The words "heavy" and "snow" piqued Selene's ears. Her stomach cramped as she turned the volume up.

". . . snow coming down. We can expect eight to sixteen inches of snowfall, with more accumulating in the higher elevations. Watch for periods of blowing and drifting snow starting around six o'clock this evening and continuing into the overnight hours with lows dropping below zero. I'm Cindy Weiks from the Eagle Weather Command, Montana's weather leader."

Selene let out a groan. "Great, Cindy. Just what we need—*more* snow."

Not thrilled with the meteorologist's prediction, she turned the radio volume back down. If this job didn't pay what it did, she'd be on the first plane back to Southern California. She'd taken the position of translator for the technology company because she wanted a change. Her job in Santa Barbara had grown stale. She loved being near her parents, but the routine of an office job had started to wear on her. It was a new concept for her.

The first part of her twenties, she'd lived in different parts of the world, moving every six months to a year. Her life had been one grand adventure after the next, using her language skills to soak up different cultures in countries across the globe. But then she'd turned twenty-five, and her dad got cancer. She'd spent the last two years in the city where she'd grown up, taking care of her family. Now that her dad was in remission and doing better, he'd urged her to follow her dreams.

Only, she wasn't sure what those were, except to travel. Something this job had promised but not yet delivered. Thinking about it, she drummed her fingers on the steering wheel. At least her dad understood her wanderlust. He'd joined the Navy and spent his twenties traveling as much as possible. It was how he'd met her mom.

A smile softened Selene's face as she thought of her parents. Still in love after nearly thirty years. Her dad had been stationed in Souda Bay when he met her mother. Selene was born two years later in Crete. Her first language was Greek, then English, German, and French. She had a natural knack for languages and had mastered all those by age seven. Even though they'd moved to Southern California after that, she'd continued studying and adding new ones to her repertoire.

An alarm beeped on her phone, reminding her she had fifteen minutes until her shift started. She shoved her fingers inside her GORE-TEX gloves and stared at the office building through her front windshield.

This Saber Tech location was only a couple of years old. They'd gone modern for the construction. It boasted five stories but sported one sleek concrete face, broken up by tall glass windows with unadorned metal frames. The pale concrete almost blended into the snowy scenery.

Perhaps that had been the architect's aim since the company was the most secretive she'd ever encountered. She understood protecting intellectual property and not disclosing proprietary information, but Saber Tech took those concepts to the extreme. She signed no less than six non-disclosure agreements before they even gave her the job.

Once she'd fastened the snow strap on her gloves, she grabbed the wool beanie off the passenger seat. Just getting dressed to go outside here was a chore. You needed so many layers, and even then, she knew she'd be freezing before she made it the fifty feet to the front entrance. Grumbling about the weather, she turned the engine off and braced herself to step outside.

A blast of icy wind assaulted her as soon as she closed the car door. "Holy mother of God." She raised her eyes skyward. "Eighteen degrees wasn't bad enough on its own? You had to add in the wind chill?"

Teeth chattering, she picked her way across the slippery parking lot in her still-new snow boots. She had work flats in her bag that she'd change into as soon as she reached her desk. She'd learned the hard way that there was no chance her feet wouldn't wind up wet and freezing if she wore them across the lot.

Her face was half numb by the time she made it. Double glass doors opened automatically to a vestibule with heated air curtains. The vaulted space was as warm inside as it was cold outside. She shivered and soaked in the warmth before stepping into the modern glass revolving door to enter the central part of the building.

The entrance gave the illusion of openness. A long hall stretched half the length of the building. It was wide enough to support five glass retractable wing turnstiles, which controlled access to the interior offices. Below them, wall-to-wall nylon carpet in a muted gray and blue pattern reduced the noise of foot traffic. To the right, a low security desk in stained bamboo added a bit of imposing authority but didn't block the view through the space. The open plan extended to the upper levels, where a curved balcony wrapped around the wall to Selene's left.

"Hi, Henry." She waved to the older man who was always on duty during her shift.

He looked up from his computer monitor and smiled, bright white teeth shining against his chocolate skin. "Afternoon, Ms. Selene."

Stopping in front of the turnstiles, she tugged off her right glove with her teeth. Then began the struggle of digging her access badge out of her coat. She was paranoid about losing it, so she kept it on a lanyard around her neck. Only now, it was buried under multiple layers of clothing. Lifting her chin, she used her ungloved hand to unsnap the closures at her throat. With those free, she tugged at the zipper. It didn't budge.

She heard a chuckle from Henry, who watched her daily struggle with amusement. Giving him a mock stink-eye, she freed her other hand and used both to unzip the outer shell of her coat. Next came the fleece inside liner. That zipper moved a lot easier. Past the outer layers, she patted the lapel of her dark blazer for the lanyard string she wore over a flowy blouse she'd tucked into black dress pants. She'd almost found it when someone cleared their throat behind her.

Turning around, she automatically stepped aside, assuming they needed the gate she blocked. "Oh, sorry. You can . . ."

Something about the lean Asian man staring her down stole the words from her mouth. A primal alarm bell went off, sending wariness buzzing along her skin.

Gulping, she moved further away from him while he continued to assess her silently.

"Miss Coleman?"

Confused why he knew her when she had no idea who he was, she answered, "Yes?"

He extended a manicured hand. "Gang Dao. I don't believe we've been introduced yet, but I make it a priority to know all my employees."

Surprised, Selene blinked her light green eyes at him, then accepted his hand. "Mr. Dao, oh, um"—*stop stumbling and say something clever*—"pleased to meet you," she finished in Mandarin and managed a smile.

He levered one back at her and spoke in his native tongue. "Your tone is impeccable for a non-native speaker." He gave her hand a squeeze, then released it.

His touch gave her the urge to wipe her palm against her coat. To stop herself, she used it to push her shoulder-length ebony hair behind her ear.

"I see my team's trust in you is warranted."

What a weird thing to say.

"Thank you." Cupping her hands together, she kept her smile in place and hoped he'd move along. Surely, the head of Saber Tech had more important things to do than creep her out.

With another long stare, he nodded at Henry and breezed through the turnstile.

Watching her boss's bosses' boss walk away, she asked, "Is he always so . . ."

"Perceptive?" Henry supplied.

"I was going to say intrusive," she muttered under her breath, but she nodded at the security guard.

The ever-cheerful man grinned. "I don't suppose you make it to his position without being a little . . . *direct*."

"Hmm," she hummed in agreement and worked to put the meeting out of her thoughts.

Grasping her access badge, she swiped her way through the turnstile, absentmindedly told Henry to have a good afternoon, and headed for her desk on the second floor.

She had three documents to get through today, one she hadn't even looked at yet because it'd been dropped on her desk late last night. As far as she'd gathered, she was one of two linguists at this location. So far, she'd translated everything from correspondence to business manuals. Saber Tech had locations across the world with its main hub in China. A lot of what landed on her plate came straight from there. Even if the tech material was rather dry, she loved that she got paid to read.

"Whoo." Gripping the metal railing, she paused halfway up the winding stairs. She wasn't out of shape, but her body still hadn't adjusted to living at the higher elevation. At least, that's what she told herself. By the time she'd made it up the flight of stairs to the second floor, she was overheating in her heavy coat. Usually, she froze. In her experience, office buildings rarely turned the thermostat above 65 degrees.

Must be some unspoken rule.

When she entered the room, several people she shared the office with popped their heads up and called out, "Hey, Selene."

She waved greetings and made her way to what had been dubbed the 'translator's corner.'

Her daytime counterpart sat hunched forward, nose inches away from the computer screen.

Setting her bag down, she stripped out of her coat and said, "Alright, Stu. Time to make a run for it."

"Huh?" He stopped staring at his computer and pushed his glasses up his narrow nose to look at her. "Oh, hi. What did you say?"

"You're sprung. Time to head for the hills." She smiled with the joke, but his facial expression told her he clearly didn't understand. Inwardly, she sighed. Stuart was a nice guy, but he had no sense of humor. "Nevermind. I'm here. You can go home."

"Oh, right. Thanks." He saved his progress and logged off the computer they shared. As soon as he stood up, she draped her jacket over the back of the desk chair.

Before she could sit, Yumi appeared. The willowy Japanese-American had become her friend over the last few months. She worked in the office down the hall. Their paths had first crossed when Selene was tasked to translate one of Yumi's technology guides. She'd tried to explain it to Selene, but at 'hypertext pre-processor' and 'application program interface,' her eyes had glazed over.

She might work for a technology company and know what to call a particular product, but her expertise ended in interpreting words. She had no idea how they worked. Coding and programming? That was Yumi's language, not hers.

Her friend held out a steaming mug. "I made coffee."

Selene accepted it with an exaggerated, "Thank God for you. I know I'll need it."

A grin flashed across Yumi's lips. "Anything for my work wife."

That made Selene chuckle. She took a sip of the coffee and tried not to cough. Yumi liked to brew it strong. "Don't we have to have husbands to be work wives?"

Her friend raised a dark brow with a smirk. "Let's work on that. You want to go out tomorrow night?"

She wasn't sure she was ready for a husband. Not when she didn't know where she'd be in twelve months. If this job didn't send her traveling soon, she might start looking for a new one. Her wanderlust had returned with a vengeance after the last two years in Santa Barbara.

Taking a seat, Selene deliberately set her coffee out of reach. "As long as it's not to that dive bar you dragged me to last weekend."

Yumi made a face like she was offended. "Scissorbills is way more than a dive bar, *Miss California.*"

"You're right. I'm sure I misjudged it by the plastic

pitchers hanging from the bar or the wall of slot machines," she deadpanned.

The older woman, who Selene knew was thirty-three but looked barely twenty-two, stuck her tongue out in response.

Ignoring the look, she logged into her computer and then turned to ask while it booted up, "Hey, have you met Mr. Dao?"

Caution replaced the humor in Yumi's eyes. "Yes. Why?"

"He's here." Her friend tensed at the news as she added, "I met him this afternoon and . . ."

"And?" Yumi pressed when she didn't finish.

A thoughtful frown created a line between Selene's brows. "I don't know. Strange vibes."

"'Strange vibes?' What are you, forty?" Yumi laughed, but tension underlaid her words.

She scowled at her friend. "I have work to do, Ms. Nakano." For dramatic effect, she spun her chair around to face her computer, turning her back on the other woman.

Unlike Stu, Yumi understood the value of comedy. She gasped. "Yes, ma'am!"

When Selene heard her leaving, she called, "Text me later!"

"I will!"

The hours ticked on as she became engrossed in her work. She'd managed to get two full multi-chapter documents read and translated by the time she came up for air. Leaning back in her chair, she yawned, then rolled her shoulders.

"Ouch," she muttered as her muscles protested. She'd been hunched forward like Stu. A bad habit that would likely make her creaky before she reached thirty.

Glancing at her phone, her eyes widened, surprised to see it was eleven o'clock. She'd be off work in half an hour. The last document she'd worked on had been much harder to slog through than expected. Her stomach growled. She'd forgotten to eat dinner because she was so focused on finishing it.

Too late to eat now.

With a sigh, she picked up the folder she'd received the night before. The translations they were tasked with usually came via email, but this file had appeared in her physical inbox when she'd been on a break yesterday. Opening it, she started to page through it. She'd only glanced at the first sheet when the overhead lights flickered.

Please don't let us lose power.

Selene was the only one in her office who worked 'til nearly midnight. She'd seen other souls wandering around the building this late, but there weren't many. It hadn't been her first choice to work second shift, but she'd taken what was available. Since the company's headquarters were fifteen hours ahead, she understood the need to have workers on later shifts.

When the lights flickered again, a groan escaped her lips. She turned to look out the wall of windows behind her, but couldn't see anything through the glare of the overhead fluorescents. Taking the file with her, she wandered closer to see if it was snowing like the weather forecaster had predicted.

Cupping the folder around her head to shield her eyes from the glare of the office lights, she pressed her nose to the glass. "Damn!" Snow had completely covered the tracks of vehicles and foot traffic in the parking lot. Flurries continued to fall, swirling around the lampposts on either side of the buried pavement with the wind.

"Maybe I'll just sleep here," she grumbled as she walked back to her desk.

Plopping down with a sigh, she picked up her phone intending to text Yumi for advice on snow tires. In her hasty grab, she knocked the file folder to the floor. Papers scattered, but what caught her attention was a tiny piece of tech that tumbled out.

What the heck?

Crouching on all fours, she retrieved the device from underneath her desk, scooping up the papers as she went.

"And just what are you?" Sitting back down, she twirled what appeared to be a tiny microchip, trying to decipher its purpose. It had no markings to give her any clues.

Yumi might know.

Thinking about asking her friend, Selene set the piece of technology on top of the manila folder and snapped a picture. Opening up her text messages, she sent the image to Yumi.

Selene: Any idea what this is?
Yumi: You still at work?
Selene: Yes
Yumi: Bring it over for a better look.
Selene: K

Right when she tucked the microchip into her blazer pocket, the lights gave up their battle and plunged her into darkness.

"Just great." With a sigh, she turned on her phone's flashlight.

Shouldn't this place have a generator?

You would think a technology company had the ability to keep its power on during a storm. The thought crossed Selene's mind as she navigated to Yumi's office down the hall.

When she made it to the room where her friend worked, she nearly tripped on the base of a chair someone had knocked over. Righting it, she skirted the wall of partitions that made her friend's office a veritable maze. She knew her way to Yumi's desk, but traversing it in the dark slowed her down.

Halfway there, she halted her steps at the sound of voices. "Where is it?" Selene didn't recognize the speaker. Something in his tone sent a tingle of fear down her spine, though, and she wondered if she should turn around.

"I told you. I don't know what you're talking about."

That was Yumi. Was she in trouble?

Hearing her friend, Selene abandoned her thoughts about leaving. She switched off her flashlight and crept closer.

"I know you took the model, Miss Nakano." Oh! That was Mr. Dao. "Now, kindly tell me where it is."

Selene reached the end of the walkway and peered around the partition. Yumi sat in her desk chair while a large man in a black suit stood behind her with crossed arms.

"I don't have it," she directed her response to Mr. Dao, who faced her from his perch on the edge of her desk.

The CEO smiled. He was clearly playing the good cop in this scenario. "Then tell me who does."

Selene's mind raced with questions. *What had Yumi gotten herself into? Did she take something from the company?*

If she was working some sort of corporate espionage, Selene wanted no part in it. Still, she didn't want to abandon her friend. She stood frozen, unsure if intervening would make things worse.

"The translator."

An audible gasp left Selene's lips at Yumi's words, and three pairs of eyes darted in her direction.

Shit! She ducked behind the partition and listened for footsteps. Why would Yumi say that? Had she misjudged her that much?

Why throw me under the bus?

Oh my God! Her hand closed around the tiny tech

in her pocket. They couldn't mean this, could they? What could this microchip-looking thing be a model for?

Someone shined a light in her eyes, blinding her. Lost in her panicked thoughts, she'd missed their approach.

"Well, Miss Coleman, it seems I misjudged you."

She lifted her palm to protect her vision, but it didn't do much good. "Wha-a-at?" She was so confused that she stuttered on the question.

Had she fallen asleep at her desk? Because this had to be a nightmare. She'd been caught eavesdropping, sneaking around in the dark like some, some—

"Felix, you can lower that." Mr. Dao's command cut off her mental breakdown.

The behemoth of a man in the dark suit lowered the flashlight so that it shone past her.

When she'd blinked the spots from her eyes, words poured from her mouth. "I was just, um"—she caught her lip as her heart pounded in her chest—"let me apologize, Mr. Dao. I was coming to see Yumi after the power went out, and when I heard voices, I wasn't sure I should interrupt. I had no intention of eavesdropping. I'm very sorry." Her throat felt as scratchy as a cactus. She swallowed and waited.

Please don't let me get fired.

"I'm sure you didn't, Selene." His expression churned her stomach. "Can I call you Selene?"

"Su-u-ure." What was wrong with her? For

someone who prided herself on the ability to speak multiple languages, she was having an unusually hard time forming words.

"Well, Selene. Ms. Nakano"— Mr. Dao waved at Yumi, her friend's arm caught in one of the bad cop's meaty paws—"seems to think you have a piece of company property in your possession. Is that the case?"

"Perhaps she meant this?" Selene pulled the technology she'd found from her pocket, holding it in her palm for Mr. Dao to see.

He stepped toward her, blocking most of the light, and she lost track of the other man and Yumi.

"It was in a file that was placed on my desk. I thought it was part of the translation package, but perhaps it was put there by mistake?" She managed to keep her voice even over the hammering of her heart because she needed Mr. Dao to see that this was all a mix-up, and no one meant to hide anything.

"Ah, I'm sure it was." When he took the tech from her palm, she prayed that was the end of this mess.

Forcing a smile, she took a step backward. "Okay, then. I'm glad we could clear that up. I'll just head back to my desk."

"Miss Coleman?" Mr. Dao stopped her before she could bolt like a rabbit.

Fighting her body's urge to run, she asked, "Yes?"

"I'm afraid I can't let you do that."

Before her brain processed what he meant, she felt someone behind her.

"Felix?" Mr. Dao's gaze moved beyond her head.

Selene spun around, or she would have, but something had pricked her in the neck.

Where's Yumi? That was her last thought before her consciousness slipped away.

CHAPTER 3

Bo

Bo blinked the past from his eyes and zeroed in on the woman lying at his threshold.

Shit, that was real.

Skirting the glass littering the floorboards, he rushed to the cabin door and fought the wind to close it. The icy bastard whistled in protest as he threw the latch. They didn't need to lose any more heat before he could light another fire. Turning on the overhead lights, he prepared to attack the next problem. All five feet seven—*maybe eight*—of it.

Where the hell did she come from?

He lived in the middle of nowhere for a reason. Mainly—isolation. He'd never seen another soul on his property. There were hiking trails in the forest to the east, but just getting to them from his home was nearly a full day's hike.

Crouching next to the prone woman, he brushed

the short strands of hair off her face. Her profile was classically beautiful, the symmetry of her forehead and chin highlighting a natural balance between her features. Her hair was as black as the night sky. The flurries caught in it even glistened like stars under the overhead lights. More snowflakes coated the long, dark eyelashes resting against the apple of her right cheek. When he smoothed them away, his fingers grazed her skin. It was pale and cold to the touch.

Not a good sign.

He remembered how she'd clutched her head and knew he needed to assess her for injuries. Had she been on a hike and fallen? She had to be lost to have wandered so far off the trails. Reaching for her shoulders, he carefully rolled her onto her back. She certainly had an attractive face, exotic even. Younger than he'd thought. His eyes took in her black parka, the snow-crusted boots, and . . . *work pants?*

Bo frowned. It looked like she was wearing suit pants under her coat. That's not what you wore to go hiking in the forest. He tested the cloth. The black wool was soaked through, making him swear. She was probably on her way to being hypothermic. Unless he wanted to drive her to the hospital in this weather, he had to get her out of the wet clothes and into something warm.

"Miss? Your clothes are wet. I'm taking them off you to prevent hypothermia, okay?"

The woman didn't respond. Not that he'd expected her to, but it seemed like a good idea to try before he stripped her naked.

Bo scrubbed his hands down his face and blew out a breath. Rocking back on his heels, he pushed to his feet. Before he undressed her, he needed something warm to clothe her in. He headed back toward the kitchen, climbing the ladder to the loft above.

The space wasn't tall enough for his six-foot-two frame to stand in, so he crouched as he reached for the piles of clothes stacked next to his bed. If you could call it that. It was literally just a mattress on the floor. Grabbing a hoodie, sweatpants, and a pair of wool socks, he shuffled back to the ladder. When he turned around to climb down it, he knocked his head on the ceiling.

"Dammit!" Grumbling because he did that more times than not, he chucked the clothing to the floor and placed his hands on the rungs. He swiveled to check on the woman, but she hadn't moved. Worry made its way into his chest. The nearest hospital was over an hour away in Bozeman. He hoped she didn't need it.

Once he'd descended, he retrieved the clothes he'd tossed and knelt by the woman again. He started with her boots, undoing the laces. When he pulled the first one off, he cursed. She wore only thin dress socks, and her feet were blocks of ice.

Removing the other boot, he set the shoes by the front door. Next, he gently lifted her feet, removed her thin socks, and put his too-big pair on her. With that done, he needed to get her wet coat off. Bo moved closer to her waist and lifted her into a sitting position. When her head lolled to the right, he noticed the gash above her left ear.

That's a fucking bullet graze.

His jaw set, and he ground his teeth together as surprise bled to anger. Who would shoot at this woman? And exactly what level of danger had fallen into his lap?

Sporting a not-atypical glower, he lifted her hair out of the way to get a better look at the wound. It had stopped bleeding, but the torn skin would probably swell. Thankfully, the nearly two-inch abrasion wasn't very deep. Releasing a breath he hadn't realized he'd been holding, he decided on clothes first, then he'd tend to that.

Getting her out of the rest of her garments wasn't an easy task, but he managed with a lot of lifting and twisting. He'd broken a sweat by the time he had her in his hoodie and pants. Wiping his forehead on the sleeve of his henley, he glanced at the fireplace. He had to get that going next. She might be dry, but she was far from warm.

Slipping one arm under the woman's shoulders and another in the crook of her knees, he lifted her. Staring down at her face, his heart did a weird half-skip in his chest. Thoughts of how well she fit in his arms followed the strange sensation.

What the fuck?

Needing her out of his grasp as fast as possible, he lowered her onto the couch. With purely clinical movements, he pulled the hoodie around her head to trap in warmth, then propped a pillow underneath it.

She looked . . . peaceful. He wasn't sure if she was sleeping off the shock of whatever she'd been through or if the mild hypothermia was the reason for her slumber. If he let the back of his hand linger against her cheek, it was only to check her temperature, which was still too cold.

Pulling the blanket from the top of the couch, he covered the woman with it, tucking it around and underneath her sides and feet. When she still didn't stir, he had the urge to ensure she was breathing, but glancing at her chest, he could see it softly rising and falling beneath the covers.

Satisfied, he shuffled the few feet to the corner fireplace. Kneeling on the stone surround, he grabbed a couple of logs from the stack he'd piled this morning and added them to the grate. After he stuffed some kindling between them, Bo lit a match and touched it to the pile. The logs ignited. As he watched the flames build, he thought of another fire and glanced at his leg.

The sweatpants covering the mottled skin didn't stop him from thinking about how he got those scars. He had a love-hate relationship with fire. Being close to it made him uncomfortable. His left leg would twitch, and sometimes his stomach rolled with nausea. A flicker out of the corner of his eye pulled his attention away from the hearth.

What Bo saw forced him backward. He fell on his

ass with a thump, his throat squeezing as he choked out, "Nugg."

His dead teammate leaned against the back of the couch. Tilting his head toward the woman, he asked, "What's your take on her? Whoever shot at her's going to want to finish the job."

Bo swallowed. He knew his friend was only a hallucination, but it didn't make it any easier to deal with. The first time it happened was a few weeks after the bombing. He'd thought Nugg had been a dream, but then he kept seeing him. For months. It was another reason he knew he had to leave the teams. How could he be a SEAL if he'd lost his fucking mind?

He couldn't remember the last time he saw Nugg, though. At least a year. He'd been doing better with TOP and having missions to focus on. Every person they saved and every Tango they took out helped him rebalance the scales. Not that he'd ever make up for not stopping the bombing, but at least it was something. Something to keep him going. Like helping the woman passed out on his couch.

He didn't answer Nugg, knowing the sooner he ignored the hallucination, the sooner it would disappear. Instead, he glanced at the woman. She remained unconscious.

"Her temperature's still too low."

Bo glowered at Nugg's comment, but then he thought of something.

Hot packs!

Remembering the heated compresses in the first

aid kit, he trudged to the bathroom, glaring at the glass he had yet to clean up on his kitchen floor. Opening the door, he switched on the light. The enclosed bathroom was wide enough for a corner vanity along the exterior wall, along with the toilet and a shower tall enough for Bo not to have to duck under the spray. Across from the vanity, a little alcove held shelving for linens above a combination washer-dryer.

I've got to remember to put her clothes in there.

Planning to do that after he cleaned her head wound, he crouched and opened the corner cabinet to retrieve the first aid kit. When he stood back up, he snagged a washcloth and ran water over it. Cleaning the wound would probably hurt and wake her up. At least, he hoped she would wake up soon. If not, he might have to rethink that hospital trip.

Carrying the red bag of supplies and the cloth, he returned to the living room. Nugg had disappeared. With a huff of relief, Bo set everything down on the coffee table. It was a solid block of wood with a live edge, giving it a unique shape. He'd cut it himself from a fallen tree on his property. Which is why he knew it was sturdy enough to hold his weight.

Sitting on the table's edge, he opened the first aid kit and took out what he needed. Then he pushed the hood out of the way and tipped the woman's face so that he could get to the graze.

A soft whimper escaped her lips as he cleaned the wound, but her eyes didn't open. When he dabbed antiseptic over the abrasion, her eyelids fluttered, and she jerked away from his touch. "Yumi. I have to . . ."

"It's okay. You're safe." Bo reacted, stopping her from rolling off the couch, but she was out again before he even had a chance to wonder what color her eyes were. With a sigh, he settled her back against the cushions.

Her voice had held a faint hint of an accent, but he couldn't place it. Wondering about it, he finished dressing her head wound.

Where is she from? And who's Yumi?

He hoped whoever the woman was worried about wasn't outside in this weather. If they were . . . he didn't want to think about that. Not when there was nothing he could do about it without more information. Especially when she didn't seem able to give him any.

Pulling the hood back over her head, he tucked her hair across her ears, trapping body heat wherever possible. The strands felt soft like the smoothest fabric. Satin or silk, maybe? He didn't go in for anything fancier than flannel or denim, so he was hardly an expert on that sort of thing. He leaned back and noticed her lips seemed to be returning to a more normal color, no longer tinted with cold. Her bottom one was big and full, tinged pink in the center. Though thinner, her top lip curved in a perfect bow shape.

He forced himself to stop staring at her mouth and grabbed the first aid kit. It had two hot packs inside. Figuring she needed them both, he activated the packets with his palms, then tucked one in the hoodie pocket and the other under her back. With her as warm as he could make her without—

When his thoughts turned x-rated, he shoved to his feet. The whiskey must've gone to his head because there was something fucked up about fantasizing over an unconscious woman. Giving himself a mental dressing down, he cleaned everything off the coffee table, then scooped up her clothes on his way to the bathroom.

He could admit it'd been too long since he'd been with a woman. Close to a year, actually. But that didn't give him the right to wonder what this one would taste like or how those curves he'd seen would feel moving underneath him. When his dick woke from its long slumber, he forced himself to put those thoughts out of his mind.

You're seriously fucked up.

He shoved her sweat-and-snow-soaked clothes into the washing machine with more force than necessary. Being a SEAL made relationships difficult, so he hadn't even tried. Since he'd been with Tactical Operations & Protection, he'd stuck to one-night stands with women he'd picked up at bars. A night of mutual release, nothing more. He couldn't even call it pleasure. Not when he barely remembered what that felt like. And relationships? Those were for people who deserved them.

Bo scrubbed his hands through his short beard as if he could scrub the past away, then turned the washer on. Next problem to tackle? The kitchen floor.

With another glance toward the living room, he pulled a short broom and dustpan from one of the kitchen cabinets and swept up the pieces of glass he could see. Despite keeping his hands busy, his mind returned to the woman passed out on his couch.

What the hell am I going to do with her?

CHAPTER 4

Approximately One Hour Earlier

Selene

Selene woke up slowly, her brain sloughing through a veil of grogginess. Her ears alerted her to voices, but she couldn't make out the words. An irritating itchiness radiated from a spot on her neck. Still, confusion settled over her senses like a fog. It weighed her eyelids down, making them difficult to lift.

Where am I?

While she struggled, something jostled her body enough to shake her fully awake. Her head rolled into a hard object, and she opened her eyes to find she was in the backseat of a vehicle. Tan leather separated her from Mr. Dao, who sat diagonally to her in the front passenger seat. The man he'd called Felix drove.

Where are they taking me?

She glanced out the window, where she'd knocked her head. Moonlight bounced off snow, lighting the world around them almost as bright as if it were daytime. It stretched for as far as she could see. A mix of fir, spruce, and pine trees surrounded either side of the road. If you could call the path the SUV traveled that. Her bottom left the seat as they hit a bump. She couldn't see any buildings or any lights in the distance. Wherever they were, it seemed rather . . . isolated.

If she had to get out of the car in this, at least she had on her heavy coat and snow boots. A frown twisted her mouth as she listened to the wind battering the window. Her different attire meant they'd dressed her after they'd . . . *knocked me out!*

Selene's mind stuttered on the thought, then she registered that her left arm was handcuffed to the door. The drugs in her system had been keeping panic at bay, but as her situation became clear, her chest constricted. She fought the urge to tug against the cuffs, knowing that wouldn't do her any good. When her breathing wanted to hitch, she swallowed hard to keep quiet. They still hadn't noticed she'd woken up.

"We're almost there."

Almost where? Her mind screamed.

"Excellent, Felix." Mr. Dao turned in her direction after the statement, the seat leather crackling with his movement. When their eyes met, he said, "Well, look who woke up." His smile chilled her blood into an icicle. "That makes things easier."

What have I gotten caught up in? And where the hell is Yumi?

Selene worked to quiet the voice inside her head that screamed in panic. She cleared her throat and asked as calmly as possible, "Where's Yumi?"

His eyes clouded, but he only said, "She'll be following you soon enough."

Whatever the hell *that* was supposed to mean.

"Following me where?" She clenched her hands into fists when they wanted to shake. Her mind had already jumped to too many horrifying conclusions, but she refused to believe them.

"Isn't that an interesting question?" His teeth flashed in a grin like it was normal to have this conversation when she was handcuffed. "The great beyond? Heaven? If that's what you believe, or maybe back here to earth, if you put your trust in rebirth."

Halfway through his musing, she'd reared back in her seat, a violent combination of shock, disgust, and terror suffusing her limbs. She could feel herself vibrating from the force of it.

This can't be real.

Surely, she was having a nightmare because the CEO of Saber Tech was talking about killing her.

He shrugged with the nonchalance of a man without a care in the world. "I don't put stock in any of it. We get one life to live, so I intend to live it to the fullest." His eyes gleamed with a sinister light. That or it was just the reflections from the dash. "No matter the consequences."

Mr. Dao turned back in his seat, and silence filled the cabin. Outside, the crunch of snow under the car's wheels grew louder as they headed up an incline.

She barely recognized her voice, strangled with fear as she asked, "Where are you taking me?"

Dao's hand clutched the dashboard as the tires slid before grabbing purchase. He gave Felix a sharp look, then answered without looking at her, "We're in the national forest." His head swiveled in her direction, and he added, "Plenty of trails here for a hiker to lose her way on."

So that's why they'd dressed her in snow gear. His plan was to drop her in the wilderness and hope she succumbed to the elements.

Her stomach jumped at the possibility she'd live through this. Until her brain weighed in. She had zero survival skills and had never been outside in this weather longer than it took to ski down a hill in the snow. Without any gear or something to navigate with, they were right. She'd die in the forest.

Mr. Dao spoke, breaking her out of her thoughts. "I've been doing this a long time."

Feeling extra morose, she barked, "Doing *what*, exactly?"

"What's that phrase Americans like to use, 'covering my tracks'?" She detected actual glee in his voice. When he turned around with a quiet chuckle, any hope of appealing to his character shriveled in the cold air. They were going to kill her. And for what?

"Why are you doing this?" Selene challenged. If she was going to die, she deserved to know why.

"Oh look, we've arrived!" he exclaimed, ignoring

her question.

The vehicle crunched to a stop in the middle of nowhere. If there were hiking trails nearby, she didn't see any signs for them.

"We'll have to walk from here," Felix announced.

A sliver of hope that she might get away fluttered to life in her chest. As much as she didn't want to step outside into the frosty night air, she wanted to escape from Mr. Dao more. She had every intention of bolting as far from them as she could as soon as they uncuffed her because she'd rather take her chances with the forest.

Felix opened her door, dragging her out by her attached arm. The temperature felt colder than it had earlier in the day. It stole her breath with a cutting gasp, sneaking in through her open parka, and chilling her to the bone.

"Uncuff her."

At Mr. Dao's command, her body flooded with adrenaline, warming her up. She was ready when Felix released the cuff from around the door handle. With a jerk of her wrist, she took off like a track star.

She made it maybe ten feet before she got stuck in waist-deep snow. The ground was like powder. With every step she'd taken, she'd sunk a little more. Behind her, she could hear Mr. Dao's roaring laughter.

Before she could climb out, a hand gripped her shoulder and held her in place.

"Stupid woman." That was the first time Felix had

spoken directly to her.

Praying he'd be more sympathetic than her crazy boss, she turned in her hole and begged, "Please, let me go. I'll leave. I'll go back to California."

The beast of a man huffed. His coal-colored eyes held no remorse.

"I don't know anything!" Tears flooded her eyes, and her breath sobbed out. "There's no need to do this, please."

Mr. Dao appeared through her blurry vision. "Put these on her and make her get moving." He dropped a set of snowshoes into the powder next to her. They didn't sink. Blowing into his cupped palms, he said, "It's too cold to stay here long."

Felix grabbed her underarms and lifted her out of the ground like she weighed no more than a doll. His strength scared her, but not as much as the gun he pulled from inside his trench coat.

Pointing it at her, he commanded, "Put them on."

With shaky fingers that had turned red in the cold, Selene struggled to snap the snowshoes around her boots. When she could stand, Mr. Dao shoved two hiking poles at her.

"May you have a good journey," he said in Mandarin, his tone ripe with false sincerity.

"Go to hell," she told him in the same language.

The sociopath grinned at her. She'd never hit anyone in her life, but she had the sudden urge to beat him to a pulp.

Before she had a chance to act on it, Felix shoved

his gun in her back. "Move."

Selene stared at her feet and took a deep breath. She'd only used snowshoes one time in her life. Her dad had cajoled her into trying something new on a skiing trip to Mammoth Mountain in California. She'd never gotten the hang of it.

Picking up her right foot, she trudged forward as fast as she could. The gun at her back *was* a good motivator.

By the time they'd gone a hundred feet, she sweated with the effort of constantly kicking snow off the shoe deck. Her leg muscles burned worse than any workout she'd ever done. Her breaths formed puffy clouds in the freezing air, while Felix and Mr. Dao didn't seem to have the same issue. She wanted to stab them with the ends of her poles, but the sight of Felix's weapon stayed her hand.

"That's far enough."

At Mr. Dao's announcement, her inner voice simultaneously said, "Thank God" and "Oh shit." Would they leave her now? Or, and she hated to acknowledge the thought . . . would they shoot her?

I don't want to die!

"Give her the sedative."

What? At that moment, what they intended to do to her became very clear. If they knocked her out again, she'd surely die from exposure.

Her unconscious body would be buried in the snow as she slowly froze to death.

It would look like an accident. The precipitation

would literally cover their tracks. When, or *if*, someone found her in the spring, she'd be just another statistic, one of the hundreds of people who underestimated their abilities and perished in the wilderness every year.

I don't think so!

As Felix reached for her arm, Selene slung her pole and knocked the syringe from his hand. The brute grunted, falling to his knees when his center of gravity shifted. While she had the advantage, she kicked up her legs and ran, not looking back.

The only problem?

In her desperate attempt to flee, she'd forgotten about the gun.

Amidst Mr. Dao's maniacal laughter, a shot whistled by her ear. It sounded as loud as a freight train in the quiet night.

Shit, shit, shit!

A sob escaped her as she pushed her legs harder, hurdling through the snow that tried to slow her down with each step. She needed to reach the tree line if she had any hope of escaping. It was only twenty feet away.

The next bullet grazed her head, and she stumbled, crumpling forward into the snow. The initial bite of the bullet faded as shock suffused her body. Something warm seeped into her left ear while she lay there, stunned.

"It's always more entertaining when they fight." Mr. Dao's commentary floated to her from a distance.

She couldn't tell if they were getting closer or not. Dizziness made it hard to focus.

"But you weren't supposed to shoot her, Felix. What if someone heard that?" The question was clearly rhetorical as he snarled, "Time to get the hell out of the cold."

"What if she's not dead?"

"The spatter of blood would suggest otherwise. And if she's not, the elements will finish the job."

Selene stayed very still, determined to make them think she was already gone.

"Should I shoot her again to be sure?"

No, you should not, Felix! Her flight response triggered, and she nearly leapt to her feet.

"No! You've already ruined my plan." The scorn in Mr. Dao's voice slowed the adrenaline pumping in her veins. "The best we can hope for is they think she ran afoul of a hunter. There will be no possibility at all of it looking like an accident if she's riddled with bullet holes."

Felix grumbled something about hunting weapons in response that she didn't catch, but what she did hear was the crunch of snow under their shoes as they walked away.

Thank you, baby Jesus!

Her face had gone numb, pressed against the frosty ground. Whatever had dripped into her ear made its way down her neck, but it was no longer warm. She refused to shiver. No matter how cold she felt, she wasn't going to move until their car drove away.

Several too-long minutes later, she heard the roar of the Range Rover's engine. She could've wept with relief, but any tears would've frozen. The chill had seeped past her bones into the very marrow. If she made it through this, she was going to take the longest, hottest shower ever.

Another couple of minutes and the crunch of tires on snow receded into the distance. She waited a few more minutes to be safe before pushing to her feet. The movement made her wince as pain pierced her head, but she couldn't let herself worry about what that might mean.

Avoiding the direction Mr. Dao traveled, Selene forced one foot in front of the other as she made her way to the tree line. The falling snow seemed to multiply, coating her eyelashes. She blinked against the moisture and pulled herself forward with her poles. With every step, the wind bit at her bare hands, but she kept moving. As if salvation lay in those woods.

The snowfall slowed when she made it under the cover of the pines, but so did her pace. She was so cold. She had no idea where she was or where she was going. What chance did she really have to survive this?

But what about Yumi?

Thinking of her friend sent a spike of fear through her spine. If she lived, she could save her. Warn her somehow that Mr. Dao would be coming after her. Selene still had no clue *why* he wanted her dead. What had she stumbled into? What was that model for? How could it be important enough to kill her over?

Questions plagued her as she trudged through the woods. The crisp, earthy smells of winter filled her nose as she ducked and pushed branches out of her way. The blanket of snow made her crash through the foliage, deafening, scaring any creature brave enough to be out in this weather. When the ground started to slope upward, she dug in her poles and crampons, determined to see what lay over the rise.

Maybe there'd be a house. Or a campsite. Or at the very least, a road.

Because she had to live. To warn her friend.

If she could get somewhere with a phone . . . for a moment, she paused, flushed with hope, patting her pockets for her cell phone. But no, of course they hadn't given it back to her. They hadn't brought her work bag either. She didn't even have her wallet.

A bitter thought twisted her gut. *They couldn't make it too easy to identify the body.*

If—*no, when,* she corrected herself—she lived through this, she *would* figure out a way to save Yumi. But that wasn't all she'd do. A darkness she'd never felt before stirred to life in her heart, demanding she make Mr. Dao pay. Because if she'd gleaned one thing, it was that she wasn't the first person he'd done this to.

He wouldn't get away with murder. She wouldn't let him.

By the time she topped the rise, her leg muscles

were on fire. She paused, taking in the idyllic scene below. Moonlight glinted off snow-covered slopes, which bottomed out to a clearing cut by a wide, currently frozen creek. It was long, winding, and narrow, but the land leveled enough to host a rustic cabin before reaching the opposite slope. She didn't see any smoke coming from the chimney or any lights within, but maybe there'd be a phone. Or at the very least, a dry place to rest.

Renewed energy surged through her veins. Riding that wave, she half slid, half hopped down the slope to the dark little cabin. When she made it to the log building, she dropped her poles, unlatched her snowshoes, and climbed the two steps to the front door. She reached for the handle and prayed it wouldn't be locked.

As she turned it, the wind rushed in, blowing the door out of her hold. It slammed against the cabin wall with a loud knock. Inside, she saw a man, backlit by moonlight streaming in from the kitchen window.

Oh! Thank God someone's here.

"Help me," the words rushed from her half-frozen lips.

The wind kept blowing, wrapping her hair around her head wound. The man didn't respond, but she wasn't deterred. Not when he was her last speck of hope, glimmering like a beacon of warmth after the icy hell she'd endured.

Relief wanted to make her weak, but she thought of Yumi again. Stepping inside, Selene lifted her hand to touch the stinging in her head. Pain coursed down her neck, followed by a wave of dizziness that swept over her and sent her crashing to the floor.

CHAPTER 5

Bo

The woman woke with a noisy gasp of breath, scaring the shit out of him. He'd been tucking the blanket tighter around her shoulders, but he jumped backward in reflex as she reared up into a sitting position.

"Ouch!" She clutched her head with a grimace and shut her eyes.

While his heart rate settled, he asked in as soft a voice as possible, "Do you want something for the pain?"

Her eyes popped open, and their color struck him, making his heart flip-flop. They were so pale a green as to be almost gray. Like fog rolling over an aquamarine sea. He'd never seen anything like them.

While he stared, she grabbed at his arm. "How long have I been here?"

Heat raced up his skin straight for his heart, and

he blinked, too stunned to respond.

She glanced around as if the answer were in the air somewhere, before those soul-stealing, gray-green eyes landed on his.

Lost in her gaze, he couldn't help but ask, "Where are you from?"

"SoCal."

His brow knitted in confusion. That didn't seem true. "Originally?"

"Oh. No, I was born in Crete."

"I've never been there. What's it like?"

"From what I remember, it's beautiful. And *warm*." The hint of a smile tipped her lips up. But there was a sigh behind it. Like she wished he'd skip the small talk. Then her eyes widened, urgency slipping into her melodic voice. "I need a phone."

He cleared his throat and forced himself to focus on something other than her mesmerizing face, looking down at her grip on his arm when it tightened.

"May I use yours, please? My friend is in danger, and I have to warn her." The agitation in her tone ratcheted up a notch as she begged, "Please, I need to warn Yumi."

Bo nodded, ignoring the little voice that did a fist pump on learning Yumi was her friend and not a significant other. "Let me get it."

"Thank you."

Uncomfortable with her gratitude, he rose and walked to the kitchen to retrieve his phone from the counter. He still didn't know what happened to her, and instead of finding out, he'd asked her where she was from. If this had been a TOP mission, he would've failed. Where the hell was his head at? In his ass? He had better get it out of there if he was going to be of any help to her.

After giving said ass a swift kick, he filled a glass with water, snagged some painkillers, and took everything back to the woman. Who he still didn't know the name of. Another thing he should've asked immediately.

Such a fucking idiot, Bo.

She'd moved into a sitting position with her feet on the floor, her gaze taking in his home. As he approached, a shiver racked her frame.

"Here." He set everything he carried on the coffee table and pulled the blanket around her shoulders. He rubbed them for warmth until she stiffened under his hold.

Realizing what he'd done, he dropped his hands and moved to the opposite end of the couch. Instead of acknowledging the overly intimate gesture, he swept a hand toward the table with a grunt. "There's water and 500 milligrams of acetaminophen."

Her quiet thank you had him squeezing the back of his neck, avoiding eye contact.

Just fucking apologize. It couldn't get any more awkward than he'd already made it.

"I'm sorr—" he said at the same time she started recording a voicemail.

"Yumi, it's me—" she paused and glanced at him.

Bo said nothing else, but the cabin was suddenly too warm. His skin heated from the inside out.

She turned away and finished her message, "It's Selene. Mr. Dao, he . . ." Her delicate throat bobbed on a swallow.

Selene.

Bo liked her name. It was exotic, just like her.

"You're in danger. When you get this, call me back at *this* number. Please. And go somewhere safe."

He wanted to put a hurt on Dao for the fear he heard in Selene's voice. Bo blinked but couldn't shake the feeling. It was irrational. He didn't know this woman, yet he felt extremely protective of her.

Her sea-churned gaze met his. "She didn't pick up." Her hands fiddled nervously with the phone, clearly worried for her friend.

"Why don't you text? In case she sees that first."

"Good idea."

He watched her fingers fly over the keyboard and wondered who Mr. Dao was.

Is he the guy who took a shot at her?

Bo's nose flared, his jaw flexing. If Dao were the one who'd hurt her, he'd make damn sure he didn't get another opportunity.

When she hit send, she met his gaze. She didn't say anything, just studied him with those piercing eyes. As a SEAL, he'd been on his share of ships. The colors in her irises reminded him of waves crashing against the hull at dusk, the green blending with the gray.

Shifting in his seat, he cleared his throat. "I'm Everett. But you can call me Bo."

She handed the phone back. "Thanks for your help, Bo."

He set it on the coffee table. "We'll leave it here in case your friend responds."

She thanked him again, and the words started getting to him. He didn't deserve her thanks. It made his skin burn like coming in contact with a hot brand.

Before he growled at her to stop, he got down to business. "Where did you come from?"

She shook her head. "I have no idea where we are, but I live in Big Sky."

Big Sky was at least a half-hour drive from here. "Why were you in the woods wearing clothes better suited to an office?"

At the mention of her clothing, she glanced down at herself with a gasp before her gaze shot back to his. Outrage colored her voice as she demanded, "Where are my clothes?"

"The dryer." He scrubbed at the side of his face and suppressed a groan as he explained, "You were borderline hypothermic when you got here. I had to put you in something warm and dry fast."

"You, you . . ." she spluttered.

He rushed to add, "I acted purely for the purpose of saving your life," before she did something he probably deserved, like slug him in the face.

She dropped her head in her hands, then winced when she tapped the bandage over her wound. "I can't believe this is happening," she muttered.

"What *did* happen?" When she lifted her gaze, he added in what he hoped was a non-threatening tone, "I know that's a bullet graze." He tried to talk to people as little as possible, and his skills were rustier than a shipwreck.

Her eyes glazed over. "My boss tried to kill me."

"Mr. Dao?"

She nodded in response.

"Why would he want to kill you?"

"I don't know." Anger tightened her features.

Bo grunted. There was something she wasn't telling him. "That's hard to believe."

* * *

Selene

Okay, sir.

Selene didn't appreciate his insinuation. She stared the guy down while the petulant part of her wanted to cross her arms and turn away. But since she wasn't wearing a bra, she didn't need to draw any more attention there.

O-M-G!

Her stomach took off on a rollercoaster every time she thought about it. He'd undressed her. And not down to her bra and underwear.

Full. On. Naked.

She was mortified. Prior to this, she could count

the number of men who'd seen her naked on one hand. Okay, three fingers, but relationships had never come easily for her. Somehow, the con list usually outweighed the pro list.

Now, this man she didn't know had seen her in her birthday suit. Although out of everything that had happened to her in the last twenty-four hours, that was hardly the worst of it.

She was lucky to be alive.

And if that wasn't a sobering thought, she didn't know what was.

But grateful or not, she could do without the bite in his tone. She wasn't lying about knowing why Mr. Dao wanted her dead. It might have something to do with the technology she'd found, but she didn't know that for sure. He'd conveniently not told her.

Besides, her head was debating whether it wanted to split in two, she was worried something bad had already happened to Yumi, and she'd barely been awake long enough to get her bearings.

Selene exhaled a frustrated breath and asked, "How long have I been here?" It looked dark outside, but she had no clue if it was the same night or a new one.

"Since last night. You slept most of today." Bo glanced at the phone she hadn't thought to check. "It's seventeen forty-two, that's—"

"Five forty-two."

His eyes narrowed at her, almost like he was . . . suspicious? "You know military time?"

She couldn't help the arch look as she told him, "It's the 'twenty-four-hour clock.' More than just the military uses it."

When his expression turned apologetic, she internally sighed, feeling bad for being bitchy when he'd helped her. Backpedaling, she explained, "My dad was in the Navy. He taught me."

A ghost of a smile flitted across Bo's stern features as if they'd forgotten how to form that expression. It was so brief she nearly missed it.

Oh, wow.

When he smiled, Bo was rather attractive.

"I was Navy."

His umber hair matched his eyes, except the closer she looked, she noticed gold striations running through the brown of his irises and streaks of red in the short strands atop his head. His nose was strong and broad with a slight curve. He'd likely broken it before. His mouth . . . the rusty-colored beard accented the fullness of his lips.

Actually, really *attractive.*

Selene let her gaze travel from the rugged features of his face down the corded muscles of his neck, shoulders, and geez . . . the henley he wore highlighted every contour. And this man had a lot of them. She was used to seeing beefy gym rats in SoCal, but something told her Bo's body hadn't been hardened in a gym.

Wonder what he looks like without the clothes.

A smirk crossed her lips. It seemed only fair since

he'd seen her without hers.

Before she could do something stupid like ask him to strip, her stomach growled loud enough to shake the cabin. Feeling heat fill her cheeks, she placed a hand over her middle and reverted to her default politeness. "Can I trouble you for something to eat?"

Instead of answering, he grunted and rose to his feet, making her wonder if that was *his* default response. When her stomach protested again, she stood up. Her body wobbled, and she gasped, involuntarily plopping back onto the couch. She closed her eyes and leaned forward, trying to stay upright instead of pitching to the floor. She was light-headed. From her head injury or lack of food, she wasn't sure. How long had it been since she'd eaten?

Lunch yesterday.

No wonder her stomach had sounded like a freight train. She hadn't had any food in over twenty-four hours.

"Are you all right?"

She lifted her head and focused on Bo. He'd knelt beside her, and one of his hands extended toward her as if he weren't sure he should touch her.

"Sorry. I felt light-headed."

He rasped, "Let me help you, then."

She nodded, and he slipped his arms around her, lifting her to her feet while she tried not to think about how good it felt to have his hands steadying her.

When she was standing, he asked, "Okay?"

"Yes," she managed to get out as the breath caught

in her lungs from his nearness.

He backed away, watching her to ensure she didn't fall, probably. Determined not to, she took a step and then another until she was sure of her feet.

With a curt nod, he turned away. Blowing out a breath, she stuffed her hands in the pocket of the navy hoodie and followed Bo to the kitchen. He rummaged through cabinets, muttering something she couldn't make out.

A small table with two chairs graced one side, and she hovered by it, asking, "Can I help?"

He spun around, looking surprised to find her there, his eyes widening slightly. "No. Got it."

His gruff response threw her off guard. "Oh, okay."

Was he mad that he had to feed her? She knew she was imposing, but what choice did she have?

Frowning at his back, she slid into a chair. Her life was a mess, but at least she still had her life.

What am I supposed to do now?

She had to go to the police, right? Calling them probably should've been her first thought. Shaking her head, she went to retrieve his phone from the living room.

Back in the kitchen, she approached Bo as he stirred something on the stove. The scent of tomato hit her nose, and she could've moaned. She didn't care what he made. She would eat every last bite. "That smells good."

He visibly stiffened, so she paused a couple of feet away. "Tomato soup. And I'll make grilled cheese."

A genuine smile tilted her lips up. "That's one of my favorite combos."

When he grunted again, she focused on the reason she'd walked over here. "Do you know the local police number? I didn't want to dial 9-1-1 when it's not an emergency, but I have to report what happened."

His muscular shoulders moved with a sigh before he turned around. His face was set in stoical lines, and he scrubbed at the back of his neck. "You probably don't want to hear this, but I don't think they'll be much help. Unless you have some sort of proof, it's your word against his."

Annoyed, she pointed at the bandage on her head. "Isn't this proof enough?"

"That someone shot at you, yes. But they'll need more than that to hold your boss." His eyes were regretful as he added, "If they haul him in for questioning based on your report, he'll be out in twenty-four to seventy-two hours. Then, he'll know you're still alive and could try to finish the job."

She actually felt her face blanch. All the blood in her body seemed determined to flow elsewhere, leaving her head a little woozy. She must've looked like she would faint because Bo stepped toward her and caught both of her arms.

"Whoa there, ocean-eyes."

Selene blinked and shook off a wave of dizziness. "What did you call me?"

She might not have noticed the slight pink hue that filled his cheeks if she hadn't been standing so close.

Is he blushing?

He cleared his throat and mumbled, "Ocean-eyes. Because, you know, the color of your eyes looks like the sea."

She frowned at him. No one had ever made that comparison, and she wasn't sure it fit. Her eyes were green. She didn't know what ocean he was used to, but the Pacific didn't match her eye color.

Shaking off the useless thought, she focused on what he'd said about the police. "You're right. I can't let Mr. Dao know I'm alive until we find Yumi."

"We?" His thumbs brushed the inside of her forearms as his low voice rumbled between them on the question. The heat from his large hands seared through the bunched hoodie fabric. If she'd had any blood left in her face, she would have blushed.

"Oh, I meant 'I'." Why was he still holding onto her? "I think I need to sit down."

Instead of releasing her like she'd thought he would, he guided her back to the chair. "Thanks."

His gaze thundered at the word, and he gave a sharp nod before returning to the stove.

Bo's changes in demeanor gave her whiplash. She wasn't sure if he was pissed that he'd helped her or if he wanted to. Blowing out a breath, she dropped her head in her hands, wincing when she made contact with the bandage on her left side. If she couldn't go to the police, who *could* help her?

CHAPTER 6

Bo

While the soup heated up, Bo set Selene's clothes to refresh since he'd left them in the dryer all day and were probably wrinkled as fuck. His sweats drowned her, but he remembered what the curves underneath looked like. He'd been trying *not* to think about them. The baggy clothing didn't stop him, though. Not that he particularly wanted her out of his clothes. Something about seeing her in them filled him with a sense of possession . . . like she was *his*.

But she's not.

And he didn't deserve her anyway.

With that fact cooling his blood, he glanced at her frustrated posture, slumped forward with her head in her hands. He leaned back against the cabinet by the stove and said, "I'm not the police, but I can help you. I work for a private security firm. Tactical Operations & Protection?"

He watched her for any sign of recognition, but she just gazed at him with those luminescent eyes.

Luminescent?

What the actual fuck? What was happening to him? He didn't use words like 'luminescent.' Maybe he'd finally snapped, and this was all some elaborate hallucination.

"Never heard of it. What, are you like bodyguards?" She spoke, and he mentally shook his head.

No. He couldn't conjure the melody of her words. That sirenic quality was too unique.

"Sometimes, but we also do other . . ." How could he put this? "Military-style operations."

The tiniest line formed between her brows when she squinted at him as if trying to understand.

He rubbed at the back of his neck and added, "Like hostage evac or, uh . . ."

Her eyes widened. "You kill people."

He met her shocked stare straight on. "Bad people."

He hoped the admission didn't send her running out the door. In this weather, he'd have no choice but to chase after her and hold her captive, even if it was against her will. Because the other option was death. And he didn't need any more of that on his conscience—at least not the innocent kind.

She blew out a breath and gave a tiny nod. "People like Mr. Dao."

Relieved that he hadn't repulsed her, Bo let out the breath he'd been holding. "To help you, I'm going to need more information about what happened."

Selene straightened, her gaze taking him in, assessing him before she leaned back in the chair. "Okay."

"Okay," he answered with the smallest twitch of his lips. Hell, he couldn't remember the last time he'd had a reason to smile, but she'd already made him want to more than once.

Before he got lost studying her face—she had the tiniest little mole next to her right eyebrow—he pushed off the counter and started working on the grilled cheese sandwiches.

She needed food. Then he'd grill her about her boss.

"Bo?"

He froze, unwilling to turn around and face those ocean eyes. With a grunt of acknowledgment, he went back to prepping the sandwiches.

"I can't pay you. I just lost my job." She followed her statement with a humorless laugh.

"Did I ask for payment?" he growled the question as he spun.

"No, but . . ." she trailed off at the fierce look he knew showed on his face.

Sure, Tactical Operations & Protection charged a hefty price for its services, but Selene was different. Fate had dropped her at his door. This wasn't about TOP. It was about . . . his chance at redemption or at least the opportunity to work toward it.

And maybe with her, it's about a little more than

that.

He shook that thought from his head before it could lead him into dangerous territory. Despite being a soldier-for-hire, he wasn't helping her for money. He'd offered without that ever crossing his mind. Acknowledging it, his chest tightened uncomfortably, and he had to look away.

He heard her soft sigh before she said, "Thank you."

Again, with that damn word! His hand tightened around the handle of the frying pan he'd just taken out for the grilled cheese. Setting it on the stove-top with more force than necessary, he ground out, "Don't mention it."

Ever again.

He didn't want her gratitude, but he did want the truth. If her boss wanted her dead, she knew more than she'd mentioned. Bo dropped a pat of butter in the frying pan and listened to it sizzle against the hot iron.

He needed to hear the whole story, call Victor and bring TOP into the equation. His team leader would have final say on their involvement . . . at least, officially. But Bo had every intention of seeing this through until he knew Selene would be safe.

He needed to save her to . . . his thoughts stuttered. He didn't know why he felt so strongly about this when he'd just met her. Hell, for all he knew, she could be a criminal. His gut clenched in protest, knowing that wasn't true. She was alone, scared, and running for her life. Whatever happened, she didn't deserve that. He knew on a soul-deep level. Enough to make him want to make things right for her.

A loud pop as the butter overheated pulled his thoughts back to the task at hand. Lowering the heat on the burner, he focused on grilling the sandwiches, not the intriguing woman waiting at his kitchen table.

His mouth watered as the meal cooked, sending the unctuous aroma of browning butter and fried cheese to his nose. He'd been eating civilian MREs for the last week, putting off his monthly supply run to Bozeman. Bo didn't mind the ready-made meals, but after so many days of lukewarm puree, he looked forward to what he typically saved as his last supper before restocking his pantry.

She remained quiet behind him as he finished preparing the food, divvying up the tomato soup into bowls and cutting each sandwich in half at a diagonal before plating them and carrying everything to the table.

As he set the meal in front of Selene, her pretty eyes warmed, and she opened her mouth to thank him.

Not wanting to hear it, Bo cut her off with a barked, "So what's the deal with your boss?"

A thoughtful frown tugged at her features while she studied him. He needed to look away, but her sea-swept gaze locked him in its eddy. The grays and the greens of her irises swirled together, like water lapping at his legs, threatening to pull him under. The world around him felt unsteady.

When she finally blinked, he swallowed and dropped his eyes to his plate. Gripping the spoon tighter than necessary, he dipped it in his soup.

She sighed softly, sipped her water, then spoke. "I work for Saber Tech as a translator. The company headquarters are in China, and I got stuck on second shift. Last nigh—"

"You speak Chinese?"

She made a face. "Mandarin. And, yes, among others."

Curious, he asked her a question in Pashto.

His mouth curved when she answered in the same language, "Not a chance, dude." Then she took a huge bite of the grilled cheese he'd asked for half of.

A chuckle surprised them both when it rumbled out of his throat. She recovered first, asking with a smile, "How do you know Pashto?"

Any mirth he'd felt evaporated under the screaming heat of his past. It burned, just like the scars on his leg. "I was a SEAL. My unit deployed to Afghanistan."

Her face clouded, something akin to sympathy flickering in her eyes. Ignoring it, he focused on his food and prodded, "What happened last night?"

He didn't miss the way her body shuddered, the hand holding the spoon rattling it against the soup bowl. "I found a piece of technology in one of my translation packages. I had no idea what it was, so I planned to ask my friend, Yumi. She's a programmer with the company. Right about then, the power went out, and I had to find my way to her desk in the dark."

When she audibly swallowed, he couldn't help it. He met her gaze. But her eyes looked through him, reliving what she relayed. "The CEO of the company, Mr. Dao, and another man he called Felix were at Yumi's station, asking about some technology model. They were looking for the microchip I'd found, so I turned it over. I thought that would be the end of it, but the next thing I know, I'm being knocked out and waking up in a car somewhere near here."

Her rush of words abruptly stopped, making him fight the urge to squeeze the hand she fisted on the table. As if he knew how to offer anyone comfort. Not only were his people skills rusty, but he was also the opposite of soothing. Internally shaking his head, Bo took another bite of his sandwich and waited for her to finish.

Her voice lowered in volume as if she still couldn't quite believe it. "Mr. Dao wanted to drug me and leave my unconscious body to succumb to the elements, so I ran. Felix shot me, and I fell."

Bo gripped his spoon so hard he thought he might bend it as he looked up to catch her dazed expression. The thought of anyone firing at her, trying to take her life, filled him with an uncomfortable fury. The force of it started building in his blood until it pounded out a tattoo on his temples.

"I remember the cold . . . and I was bleeding. They thought I was dead, so they left." Watching her fiddle with the crust of the sandwich she hadn't wanted to share, the rage slowly seeped out of Bo. He'd pay back this Felix and Mr. Dao, but for now, Selene needed to know he wouldn't let them get to her again.

Reaching for her restless hand, he stilled her fingers. When her gray-green eyes met his, he gave it a squeeze. "You're safe here, Selene."

She nodded slowly at his statement, staring down at his hand until he came to his senses and removed it. "Then, I started trekking through the snow until I saw your cabin." She forced a smile that didn't reach her eyes. "I think you can take it from there."

A heavy silence fell as she finished her story. If her boss had taken her anywhere else inside the national forest, she'd be dead. His property was the only one for miles, and she'd have either bled or frozen to death. Though he'd just met Selene, the thought of never seeing her ocean eyes smile at him felt like getting hit by a bomb again.

Something raw and wrenching threw his insides into chaos. His vision blurred while his lungs accelerated in his chest.

What the hell was that about?

He struggled to process his body's reaction when her head jerked up. "Did you hear that?"

The fear in her eyes cleared Bo's head. He strained to listen for what she might've heard. The fire crackled in his ears, followed by the hooting of a nearby owl, but there, a faint whir of a motor and the crunch of snow under something heavier than a foot.

Adrenaline spiked as he rose, heading for the pistol hidden under the couch. When he'd retrieved it, he shoved his feet into his boots and reached for the front door handle.

"Where are you going?" Anxiety strained her voice.

Meeting her gaze, he told her. "Stay here and bolt the door behind me. Don't open it unless I tell you to."

* * *

Bo

Bo didn't wait for Selene's response, but he also didn't step away from the cabin until he heard her throw the latch. Satisfied she'd listened to his order, he lifted his Glock 19 and descended the steps from his home.

A blast of icy wind cut right through his henley shirt, making him grit his teeth. It was stupid not to have thrown on another layer to combat the below-freezing temperature. He wouldn't do Selene any good if he froze to death before he found whoever had paid them a visit.

Because someone was here.

Having grown up in the mountains, he knew the sound of a snowmobile. It was one of the few methods to reach the valley where his cabin stood. He'd picked the site because it had no road in and out. Bo didn't do anything half-assed, and when he'd withdrawn from the world, he'd ensured it wouldn't intrude on him.

He hadn't had any problems with that . . . until now.

His boots sank into the snow as he crept toward the noise of the motor. Avoiding the openness of the valley, he climbed the west bank, heading into the tree cover. Pines and firs dropped snow as he pushed their branches out of the way. The snowmobile still sounded faint, but he felt it growing louder with each step.

When he topped the rise, he ducked behind a mature whitebark pine. Its scaly gray skin scratched against his shoulder as he leaned around the thick tree trunk, peeking at the figure he'd spotted fifty yards away.

It might be dark outside, but moonlight bounced off the frosty white powder covering everything from the trees to the ground. It made it bright enough to see a man climbing off a silver snowmobile. Bo almost smiled as he got a closer look. Whoever this guy was, he was tiny. It wouldn't take much to overpower his slight frame.

Unlike him, this stranger dressed for the conditions. White ski pants and a snow parka helped him blend with the environment as he glanced down at something he held in his hand.

A phone?

Stowing the device in a pocket, the man started in Bo's direction. A growl caught in his throat. Because the guy clearly headed to one place. Bo's cabin was the only building in this area. Getting off the snowmobile meant a better chance of reaching it undetected.

But whoever this asshole was, he wouldn't be finishing what Mr. Dao started.

Bo's hand tightened around the weapon at his side. He knew better than to shoot first and ask questions later. Still, it didn't mean he wasn't pissed off enough to consider it.

If this was how they operated, Saber Tech had to be more than just a technology company.

What did that model do if they're willing to kill Selene to keep it a secret?

Questions raced through his head as he waited for the hitman to reach his position. This fucker was going to give him some answers, no matter what he had to do to get them.

Thirty paces out.

Twenty.

Ten.

Fuck!

The man stopped, head swiveling as if he'd heard something. Bo hadn't moved a muscle, so whatever the guy sensed hadn't come from him. He cursed silently when the figure pulled out a nasty-looking knife. The blade looked sharp as fuck and was at least six inches long when it caught the moonlight. The way the man held it told Bo he knew how to use it.

Regretting not grabbing his SRK, he thought about shooting the asshole in the leg. He'd had his survival rescue knife since BUD/S—the Basic Underwater

Demolition/SEAL Training he'd endured to earn his SEAL pin. He'd taken it on every TOP mission, but now it sat useless in the loft of his cabin. Before he had a chance to decide about taking the shot, an eerie scream shattered the silence of the night, raising the hairs on the back of his neck.

Mountain lion.

The high-pitched sound seemed to echo, making it difficult to determine which direction the big cat was from his location. Bo didn't speak cougar, but he hoped that was a mating call, not an announcement that he'd found dinner.

Holding the knife at the ready, the man turned in a slow circle, clearly trying to find the threat. He was still too far away for Bo to reveal his position, so he waited, silently urging the guy to keep walking.

When quiet reigned again, the man picked up his pace, heading right for Bo's tree. Shifting to face forward, he held his breath and waited for the arm with the knife to come into view. As soon as it did, he used the butt of his gun to knock the weapon from the man's hand.

It fell with a jerk, landing blade down and spearing the snow. The hitman recovered quickly, spinning in Bo's direction with a kick aimed at his hand. But it would take more than that to disarm him. He parried the blow, then braced against a swing at his side. Pain stung as something cut into his skin. With a growl, he clutched the gash on his ribcage while the attacker backed out of his reach.

When did this fucker pull another knife?

They paced a few feet apart, assessing one another. He'd stopped the man's blade from piercing his chest. The cut was more annoying than painful now. But it pissed him off that he'd missed it in the first place.

As they circled each other, the short tanto-style blade gleamed with his blood, mocking his lack of situational awareness. Still, Bo had the advantage unless this guy had a gun hidden in his coat. Raising his weapon, Bo trained it on the man, "I could shoot you."

The man stilled but didn't lower his knife. "Who are you?" a decidedly feminine voice asked.

A woman?

Surprise rolled through him. Under the trees, he couldn't see her face clearly, but "he" was most definitely a "she." The idea of fighting a woman left a sour feeling in his stomach. It roiled in protest at the thought of striking her. The only thing that kept him from lowering his Glock was knowing she was here for Selene. "I'll ask the questions. But first, close the blade and toss it."

The woman hesitated, clearly unenthused about not having the upper hand.

Bo didn't take his eyes off her as he calmly stated, "You can still talk with a bullet in your leg. Don't tempt me."

To his relief, she complied, tossing the pocketknife at his feet. Crunching it into the snow under his boot, he asked, "Who sent you?"

"No one."

If she wanted to act dumb and do this the hard way, he could play along. "Fine. What are you doing on my property?"

"Your property? Who are you?"

The confusion in her voice nearly had him convinced she didn't know. It made him willing to throw her a bone and see how she reacted. Stepping closer to try and see her expression in the ambient light, he said, "Bo Larson. Who are you?"

"Yumi Nakano." A scowl crossed her face as she demanded, "Where's Selene?"

Despite her claim, Bo didn't lower his weapon. Instead, he wished for his tactical vest because a pair of zip ties for her wrists would've come in handy. She might claim to be Selene's friend, but he'd wait for her to verify that before letting down his guard.

Gesturing toward the cabin with his head, he said, "I think you know exactly where she is."

CHAPTER 7

Selene

Bo's floor had twenty-one, eight-inch boards. Selene knew because she'd been pacing and counting them for the last ten minutes as her feet traveled the distance from one wall to the other. Her heart drummed in her ears while her thoughts swam with fear and confusion.

Was someone here? What if it were Mr. Dao? They found her tracks and knew she was alive and—*No! Stop it, Selene.*

She was anxious enough without adding her worst fears to the list. But where was Bo? What if he didn't come back?

Something buzzed a loud warning tone, and she nearly jumped out of her skin.

Relax, it's just the dryer.

Startled out of her stride, she gulped down air and worked to get her pulse under control. If Bo didn't come back and someone else did . . . standing here petrified wouldn't help her. She'd gotten away before and could do it again, but she needed a weapon.

In case he had another one hidden there, she raced toward the couch, dropping to her knees to search underneath it.

No such luck.

Her gaze flitted around the tiny cabin. The small home didn't offer a lot of hiding places. She chewed her lip when her eyes fell on the loft. It seemed wrong to invade Bo's personal space, but her need for survival outweighed any sense of courtesy. Blowing out a breath, Selene climbed the ladder.

The low height of the loft ceiling meant she had to crawl on her hands and knees once she reached the top. Knowing Bo had several inches on her, she wondered how he managed to maneuver up there. She'd already almost bumped her head twice. On all fours, she stared at the cramped bedroom.

A king-size mattress took up nearly the entire space. The roof slanted, and Bo had the bed pushed all the way into the sloping corner. Piles of neatly folded clothes cluttered the wall at the foot of the bed. Nothing she could defend herself with there, but on the opposite side of the slant, a hard-sided case served as a nightstand.

That looked promising for holding a weapon. If she were lucky, he'd have another gun. She wasn't any kind of marksman, but her father had at least ensured she knew how to shoot.

Managing to scoot-crawl in between the bed and the low railing that kept her from falling fifteen feet to the floor, Selene paused in front of the sun-faded green box. It looked like an equipment case, though for what, she wasn't sure. Catching her lip, she undid the latch and lifted the lid.

A glance showed her it was full of personal items, but no weapons. On instinct, she reached in and lifted a photograph. The edges were worn and wrinkled, but it didn't seem that old. At least the Bo in the photo closely resembled the one she'd just met. He stood, smiling into the camera next to another man. A little younger and a touch shorter. Both wore military uniforms and held rifles. The background was hazy but looked like a dirt street with a mountain peak in the distance.

Afghanistan maybe?

He'd said he'd deployed there. She flinched when the dryer buzzed again as if warning her to stop snooping. Not wanting to invade his privacy any more than she already had, Selene closed the box and resecured the latch.

The only other place she hadn't checked for a weapon was under the bed. Sweeping her hands beneath the mattress, she felt the handle of a knife. A determined huff left her lips. With a grunt, she tugged it out, managing to lose her balance in the process and face-plant into Bo's sheets.

Sputtering as she got a mouthful of his scent, she pushed herself up fast enough to ram her injured head on the ceiling.

"Oww!"

Gasping at the shooting pain that followed, she closed her eyes and focused on breathing through it. Except that only brought the fresh smell of sea mist and minerals further into her nose. If stone had a scent, Bo embodied it. Dark and salty. She liked it, probably more than she should.

When the pain dulled, she sat back on her haunches and pulled the knife she'd found into her lap. It wasn't a pocket or a kitchen knife. The handle weighed down her palm. The blade was sheathed in a black leather cover but had to be at least six inches long. She left it encased as she tucked the weapon into the pocket of her hoodie. Backing until she felt the ladder with her foot, she started to climb down from the loft. She really hoped she didn't need to use the knife. It seemed like it could do a lot of damage.

Her feet had just touched the floor when there was a knock on the door. Her heart leapt into her throat, and she pulled the blade from her pocket. Unsheathing it, she crept toward the cabin's door.

"Selene, it's Bo. Open up."

Relief crashed into her at his voice, and she fumbled at the lock with unsteady fingers. He'd become her lifeline in the short time they'd spent together. She didn't know what she'd do without him. Not with the way things were going. Flinging the door wide, she stepped back even though she suddenly wanted to launch herself into his arms.

But it wasn't Bo who entered the cabin.

"Yumi!" The knife slipped from Selene's fingers to hit the floorboards with a thud as she launched herself at her friend. "You're okay!"

Despite nearly tackling the shorter woman, Yumi only laughed and squeezed back. "Of course, I'm okay! But what happened to you?"

About that . . .

Selene glanced at Bo, where he hovered by the door, his gaze trained on something behind her. Turning her head to see what he looked at, she hid a wince. "Um, sorry. I just . . . I, um—"

"It's okay." When his dark gaze met hers, she relaxed. The understanding she glimpsed washed the awkwardness from her tongue, as if he sensed her reason for needing the weapon now lying on his floor.

"Nice outfit," Yumi murmured with a smirk as she disengaged from Selene's crushing hug.

When heat tingled in her cheeks, she cleared her throat. "Oh, yeah, my clothes were drying."

Yumi arched a perfectly groomed brow, glancing between her and Bo, the look suggesting something more had happened between them than the reality.

The implication kept the color in Selene's cheeks as she tried to brush past the subject. "How did you find me?"

"I tracked the number you called from."

"Oh." She knew Yumi was way techier than she could ever hope to be, so the fact that she'd been able to track it didn't surprise Selene. "Well, I'm glad you did. But what happened with Mr. Dao? How did you get away?"

Her friend's bangs swished as she shook her head. "I was going to ask the same thing. What happened to you?"

Bo cleared his throat, grabbing their attention. "I have questions, too. Why don't we—" Cutting off, he waved a hand toward the couch.

Since they were still standing at the door and a knife lay in the walkway, moving their conversation to a more comfortable spot seemed like a good idea. She started in that direction, but Yumi wasn't so quick to follow.

She sized Bo up in an obvious way that almost made Selene snort. "Oh, I've got questions for you, too, big guy."

While she and Yumi settled on the sofa, Bo grabbed the knife from the floor with a grunt. They all stared at each other after he sat on the coffee table. For some reason, the tension crackling in the air made Selene laugh.

Shaking her head, she offered, "Okay, I'll start." Then, she filled Yumi in on what Mr. Dao had tried to do to her and how she ended up at Bo's cabin.

Her friend seemed paler than usual after Selene finished recounting yesterday's events. "God, Selene. I'm so sorry. I should've . . ." she trailed off instead of saying whatever she'd intended.

Worrying her lip, Selene asked the question nagging at her, "How did *you* get away?"

* * *

Bo

Bo stared at the petite Asian woman, wondering the same thing because all the pieces of this puzzle weren't adding up.

Yumi's voice dropped on her answer. "They let me go."

Confusion clouded Selene's sea-mist eyes. "But why? Why would they do that when they came after me?"

She wasn't going to like the answer to that question. If her friend even gave it to her. But Bo knew. The only reason Yumi would've walked away clear is—

"I offered him something he couldn't get if I were dead."

"What are you talking about?"

Yumi shrugged it off. "Just a program he wants that I have access to." She waved her hand. "That's not important. It's good he doesn't know you're still alive, but you need protection if we're going to keep it that way."

"'We're'?" Selene's question made it clear to him that she had no idea of her friend's background or her apparent ability to use a blade.

There was too much Yumi wasn't telling her for Bo to feel comfortable leaving Selene's safety in her friend's hands.

With a grunt, he spoke up, "That's my job. I work for a private security firm, and Selene is under my protection."

Yumi's gaze fell to his chest as if questioning his ability. Remembering the slice she'd given him, he glanced down with a scowl.

Dammit!

He'd forgotten the injury in his need to protect Selene. Though the cut was shallow, it had bled through his shirt, and he felt it dripping warm liquid down his stomach to the waistband of his sweats.

At Selene's gasp, his head popped up, senses on high alert, but her surprise was only because she'd finally noticed his blood. "You're hurt! What happened?"

He stared at Yumi, raising a brow in challenge. Would she tell her friend the truth?

Meeting his gaze, the woman smirked. "I cut him."

Selene's head swiveled toward her friend. "What?" she practically yelled. "Why would you do that? *How* did you do that?"

"I don't just work for Saber Tech, Selene."

"What do you mean?"

A frustrated sigh puffed from Yumi's lips. "I shouldn't tell you this, but since Dao . . ." she trailed off and shook her head. "I work for the Agency. We've been monitoring him for a long time."

CIA.

That explained how Yumi had tracked his phone

when it was supposed to be untraceable, but it didn't make Bo trust her any better. Especially, not after one of TOP's members, who'd been former CIA, just turned on the team. That fucker was the reason Crane wound up in the hospital with a gunshot wound.

Selene's gray-green eyes widened with shock. "You work for the C-I-A?" she emphasized each letter, disbelief clear in her voice.

Yumi only shrugged. "I'm sorry, Selene. You were safer not knowing. At least, until . . ."

Either she was an outstanding actress, or that was genuine concern in Yumi's expression. Bo wanted to believe it but wasn't ready to let down his guard.

Selene blinked. "Does he know?"

"No. He believes my cover, which is that I have connections to the Yakuza and can provide him with," she paused as if she'd almost revealed something she shouldn't, then finished with a vague, "things he finds useful."

Remembering the blades she'd carried and her skill in using them, Bo had a feeling her connection to the Japanese mob was more than just a cover.

"Yumi, what was on that microchip?"

His people skills might be rusty, but the hurt was evident in the tone of Selene's voice and the hand she'd fisted over her stomach. She felt betrayed. He was familiar with that feeling.

Damn Jordy for turning on TOP.

"Nothing. The one you found was empty, a fake copy I hoped I wouldn't need."

"A copy of what?"

When her friend hesitated, anger flashed in Selene's eyes. "Dammit, Yumi! I have a right to know. You almost got me killed."

The woman flinched, closing her eyes on an exhale. When she opened them, he read the apology before she said, "I'm so, so sorry, Selene. I never meant for you to get hurt."

When he sensed Selene softening, he spoke up before Yumi had another chance to evade the question. "What was on the real one?"

His gruff voice seemed to startle the women as if they'd forgotten he was there. Yumi recovered first, hands flexing before she forced them still in her lap. "Information, files, and an AI model."

Bo knew weapons, explosives, and several forms of hand-to-hand combat, but tech had never been his strong suit.

"Artificial Intelligence?"

Yumi nodded at Selene's request for clarification. "Not just any AI either. Saber Tech has weaponized it."

Well, fuck.

Bo had plenty of nightmares, but AI being turned into a weapon was one of those apocalyptic fuckers that scared anyone with half a brain shitless. How the hell did you fight that kind of thing?

"Weaponized how?" He wanted to know exactly what they were up against.

"Think of the model as a virtual brain. It's autonomous. It can search and engage targets without human intervention. And it's constantly learning and evolving. Any machine with a digital signal? It can hack into it."

Oh, so the worst possible scenario, then.

Bo could've groaned. If Dao had a weapon that could target anything, anywhere . . . it needed to be destroyed before he had a chance to use it.

"Oh my God," Selene breathed, ocean eyes swirling with a tempest of emotion.

"Where's the real chip?" He wondered if she'd already turned it over to the CIA and what they planned to do with it.

Her gaze darted to Selene before she answered, "Selene's apartment."

"What?" Her gasped question made Yumi wince.

"I needed a hiding place in case I was compromised."

Selene clutched her head and closed her eyes. "Was everything a lie?" she half whispered through the hurt in her tone, making Bo itch with the urge to comfort her.

What was it about her that triggered this need to protect her from anything, even emotional pain?

Yumi beat him to it, grabbing Selene's hands, she tugged until those gray-green eyes focused on her. "No. Your friendship wasn't part of the job. I care about you, and whatever it takes, I will make this right."

Refusing to acknowledge the answer his brain conjured, he said, "Let's start by retrieving that chip."

He didn't trust Yumi to get it and not disappear.

Despite what he didn't say, she understood his message, giving a slight nod in acknowledgment.

"We head over there now. The temps will continue to drop, and it's a half-hour trek to my outfit—on a sled."

At least she could drive her own. He kept his hidden under a tarp near the woodpile, and he'd rather not share it with someone he didn't fully trust. No need to make himself vulnerable to another knife attack. Because he'd bet she had more hidden on her person.

"Outfit?"

Selene's question had him blinking at her. *Oh, right. She hasn't been in Montana long.* "My truck," he explained.

"Oh." She gave a sharp nod. "I'm coming with you."

He and Yumi swiveled to look at Selene. Her friend shook her head, but he spoke first. "No. It's too risky. They could be watching the apartment. You'll be safer here."

"He's right. We don't want them to find out you're still alive."

Selene stood with a jerk. "No. They did this to *me*." She smacked her chest. "This is *my* life. I'm not going to just sit here and wait for them to find me. Either I go or none of us do."

He admired her ability to glare her demand at them but keeping her here would be laughably easy. And yet . . . he ached to give her what she wanted because he'd feel the same way in her shoes.

With a sigh, he stood. "Fine." He'd scout for any surveillance and ensure she stayed in the pickup truck.

"Fine." Yumi eyed him like she wasn't happy he'd given in.

Bo felt a headache brewing, right between his eyes. He needed to talk to Victor and bring TOP up to speed because this mission had morphed into a lot more than a simple protection op.

"Oh, but wait." The steel left Selene's voice. "Let me help you with that first." She pointed at his chest, and he cursed. He'd forgotten about the cut—again.

With a grunt, he headed for the bathroom. Hoping and dreading she'd follow him. He was only human, and the idea of Selene's hands on him . . .

Yeah, it didn't suck. He could clean the wound on his own, but letting her do it meant he could keep an eye on her, away from Yumi. Whom he still didn't trust. Maybe she was just cagey because of her job, or maybe she was hiding something. He intended to find out.

CHAPTER 8

Selene

As soon as Bo was out of earshot, Yumi pounced. "What's going on with you two?"

Selene glanced at her friend, then stared after Bo, who'd just disappeared into the bathroom. "What do you mean?"

Okay, she could admit she found him attractive and his wanting to protect her did something funny to her lady parts, but she was still trying to figure him out.

Yumi crossed her arms and cocked out a hip, before whispering, "He went all caveman over you."

"What? No, he didn't." She couldn't help shaking her head. "I don't think he even likes me. He just feels obligated to help for some reason."

Her friend smirked. "Oh, you sweet child."

Selene rolled her eyes, then tossed, "Shut up," over her shoulder on her way to help Bo.

Yumi liked to tease her, and Bo was just the latest target. Nothing he'd done gave her any indication he was into her. Yumi was reading into things that weren't there. Plus, she had bigger problems tha—

O-M-G.

Selene froze in the doorway, momentarily struck dumb at the sight of Bo in nothing but gray sweatpants tugged so low on his hips that she worried—*hoped?*—they'd slide down his legs.

The sparse patch of hair on his pecs matched his beard. The auburn fuzz tapered into a trail down the center of his chest over more ab muscles than she'd ever seen, leading to a bulge she needed to take her eyes off.

Right now, Selene!

Bo cleared his throat, making her face flame. Her eyes darted to his as he said, "Can you do the antiseptic?"

He'd already washed the dried blood from his skin, though a dark spot had stained the waistband of his pants.

"Uh-huh," she mumbled and stepped into the bathroom, letting her hair fall to cover her face.

Embarrassment made her clumsy, and she fumbled the bottle, sloshing isopropyl alcohol all over her hands. When the liquid found the cuts and scrapes she'd made shoving branches out of her way during her death-defying hike, she let out an involuntary hiss at the stinging burn.

She'd closed her eyes against the sensation, but

they flew open when Bo's hands landed on hers. He cupped her palms, lifting them toward his mouth. Meeting her wide eyes, he opened his lips and blew. The warm air soothed the sting, *or* she was just too shocked to notice it anymore.

Selene gulped. His umber eyes held her transfixed. Her legs felt wobbly, and she wondered how hard she'd hit her head in the loft earlier. Surely, the dizziness she felt was from that and not her reading more into a simple gesture than she should.

Stop staring and say something!

"Thanks."

The word transformed Bo. He dropped her hands and stepped away, giving her as much space as he could in the small bathroom. "Don't mention it."

He'd forced that out through clenched teeth, making her wonder why he had such an issue with gratitude. She'd noticed his discomfort with it before.

"Your turn," she told him softly, letting it go for now.

Blowing out a breath, she stepped closer. She wasn't squeamish, but the almost two-inch cut along his ribcage twisted her stomach. It looked painful. The skin on either side was raised and angry, mottled with pink and red. Despite that, the wound was shallow enough that it no longer bled.

Grabbing the washcloth he'd laid on the sink and the bottle of antiseptic, Selene met Bo's eyes and sent a silent apology because pouring antiseptic over the cut would feel way worse than what she'd experienced with the scratches on her hands.

"This is going to sting like crazy."

He nodded, the muscle flexing in his cheek as his jaw went taut.

Concentrating, she caught her lip with her teeth as she placed the washcloth against his abs, ready to catch any dripping liquid.

When her fingers touched his skin, he sucked in a sharp breath.

"Try to relax," she murmured, tipping the alcohol over the slice.

He tensed with a growl.

"I'm sorry."

She stood close enough to hear his teeth grinding together against the pain. Wanting to soothe the burn like he'd done for her, she bent her head and blew air across the wound.

When his palms gripped her head, she stopped, shuddering as excitement flushed through her at his touch. He lifted her with gentle hands until her gaze locked with his. The look in his eyes was anything but calm. They held a need so hot it seared her all the way to her core.

Maybe Yumi was right.

Maybe there *was* something here.

When his stare fell to her mouth, she leaned in. Something about him pulled at her, hypnotizing her into a trance. His mineral scent surrounded her. It had to be the soap he used, wafting from the shower, because Bo didn't seem the type to wear cologne. She breathed him in. Rich earth with a hint of citrus and salt, like an orange grove growing on a cliff by the sea.

His head lowered, and Selene closed her eyes, waiting for the tickle of his beard against her chin, then the feel of his lips moving against hers.

But it never came.

He cleared his throat, and her eyes popped open. Confusion raced through her body to pour over her face as he tilted her head to the side to examine her head wound.

In a gruff voice, he said, "The bandage is holding, but we'll need to change it tomorrow."

Selene didn't know what to say. She opened her mouth, but no words came out.

Hadn't he been going to kiss me, or did I only imagine it?

Now, he was talking about bandages.

Mentally, she tried to shake the mistake from her mind. She must be letting her attraction to him cloud her judgment if she couldn't see he wasn't interested in her that way.

Or this was Yumi's fault for putting ideas in her head.

Turning away to gather herself, she screwed the lid back on the antiseptic. "Okay."

Overheated with embarrassment, she needed to escape the bathroom. She was about to exit when he stopped her. His rough palm closed around her wrist. "Selene, wait."

She kept her head tucked, using her hair to hide

the mortification on her face.

A sigh lifted his chest before he pushed out, "I'm sorry."

The apology surprised her enough to meet his gaze. Guilt and something else she couldn't quite decipher warred in his eyes.

It made her brave enough to ask, "Why does it bother you when I try to thank you?"

He did a slow blink, then shook his head as if he didn't want to answer her question.

Fine. He could answer another one, then.

With a huff, she broke her arm free from his grasp. "Sorry about what?"

Remorse swam in his pupils. "I was going to . . ."—another head shake—"I shouldn't have."

She crossed her arms. "Tried to kiss me or *not* kissed me?"

A tortured sound left his throat. "I don't deserve it—your thanks." He glanced away as he rasped the rest, "And definitely not to taste you."

Oh, Bo. That broke her heart. "Why?" When she stepped into his space, he avoided meeting her gaze. Hesitant but determined to get an answer, she reached up and cupped his cheek, coaxing his eyes on her. "Why would you think that?"

She didn't understand how this man, who'd served his country, had probably saved countless lives before her own, who was even willing to help her when she had no one else, could be anything but deserving.

How could he not see his worth?

He caught her wrist, but she didn't release his gaze. "I'm not a hero," he ground out through a tight jaw.

Her voice turned fierce as she said, "You are to me. I could've died, but you didn't let that happen."

Angry lightning flashed in his stare, but he didn't jerk his head away. A growl rumbled from his chest like thunder before the storm brewing in his eyes broke, and he crushed her lips with his own. The kiss was rough, hungry, and fueled by a mix of guilt and anger. She knew he meant to scare her, to prove he wasn't what she thought, but it would take more than that to convince her.

Riding the onslaught of need crashing around her, she gave as good as she got, clinging to him and thrusting her tongue past his lips to take what she wanted. He tasted faintly of the grilled cheese sandwiches they'd eaten. It would've made her smile if they weren't battling each other.

Bo groaned at the intrusion, and his hands moved to her neck, pushing her until her back hit something solid.

The shower partition?

She was too lost in him to care. Sensations fluttered over her, lighting up her nerve endings until she was aroused enough to forget everything but him. Her heart raced to pump blood through her body, but it pooled in her core. Everywhere he touched, she tingled in anticipation.

When his fingers grazed the juncture between her

thighs, she moaned into his mouth.

Had anything ever felt as good as Bo owning her?

"Are you two read—"

They sprang apart at Yumi's interruption. Or tried to. The bathroom didn't have enough room for all three of them.

Her friend quickly stepped out, though Selene didn't miss the smirk in her voice when she murmured, "I guess not."

She waited for embarrassment to come, but instead she only found herself annoyed that they'd been interrupted. "Bo?"

He breathed heavily but refused to look at her. When he spoke, his voice was harsher than she'd yet heard it, "You need to go. Now."

Hurt weaseled into her chest, forming tears in her eyes that she refused to let fall. Gathering dignity like a coat, she wrapped it around herself, brushing past him without another word.

Something ate at him, and he was using it to push her away. The words he'd said about not being deserving . . . they made her heart ache.

She wanted to help him, but he had to let her.

* * *

Bo

What the fuck?

That's not how that kiss was supposed to go. Bo

leaned against the bathroom sink, gripping the edge hard enough to rip it from the wall. What had he done? He never should've kissed her because he couldn't stop wanting to do it again.

She deserves better.

He'd kissed her with no finesse, intent on scaring her away. He'd expected a slap, and instead she'd come awake in his arms. The sounds she'd made . . . *damn!* Just thinking about them made him hard.

Bo gritted his teeth and shook the memory from his head. He couldn't let it happen again. He didn't do relationships, and there was no chance of this being a one-night stand when she was under his protection.

Damn it all to hell!

He needed to get his head on straight. Her life was at fucking stake. With a growl, Bo pushed off the sink. He had to call Victor and let TOP know what was going on. If he were lucky, they'd be able to help.

He slapped a bandage over his cut, refusing to think about the tender way she'd blown on it, while he waited for the line to connect.

"Bo?" surprise colored Victor's voice when he answered.

Bo sighed. He'd never called his team lead. Usually, their conversations were a one-way street, with him getting a call from Victor whenever TOP had a job. Not the other way around. "Yeah."

"We missed you last night." Bo heard the smile in Victor's voice, but he didn't have time for pleasantries.

"I've got a situation."

That's all it took to transform Victor into the Delta Force troop leader he'd once been. He sounded all business as he said, "Report."

Bo broke it down, catching him up to speed on everything he'd learned about Selene's situation so far. Then he finished with, "Can TOP help, or am I on my own?"

"Fuck, frogman. You brought me a shit sandwich." Victor blew an audible breath. "I'll talk to HQ and let you know."

The five people who made up TOP's leadership were people Bo had only met once when he'd been hired. He was more than happy to leave reporting to them on Victor's shoulders.

"In the meantime, I'll send the team out," he tacked on.

"Copy. But leave the newlyweds alone." It was the least Bo could do for Crane and Rogue. Considering the rest of the team, he scratched at his beard. "It wouldn't hurt to have Duke on standby in case we need him." He was the team's pilot. He'd been in the Air Force and managed to be a pain in the ass most of the time. "I've got to move on the apartment now, though. We don't have time to wait for Romeo and Herc to get here." Romeo had been a SEAL like him, and Herc was a former Green Beret. He'd appreciate the backup, but time wasn't on his side. He lowered his voice. "This CIA chick's not going to want to hand over the chip."

Victor cursed. "If it contains what you said, it

needs to be destroyed."

"Agreed." An AI weapon with the capabilities Yumi claimed was too damn dangerous to exist. He didn't trust that even the CIA wouldn't abuse its power. As soon as Bo had the opportunity, he'd dispose of it.

By the time he ended the call with Victor and emerged from the bathroom, the women were dressed and ready to go.

He cleared his throat. "Let me grab a shirt and we'll get going."

They didn't say anything, so he headed for the loft. After he'd dressed appropriately for the conditions, they exited the cabin and he locked it behind them. The wind bit at his nose and the exposed skin of his cheeks. Riding on the sled was going to feel ten times worse. They needed to get moving before the temperature dropped anymore. He opened his mouth to tell Yumi the plan, but she spoke first.

"My car's not far from here. I'll meet you at the apartment."

Bo frowned. He bet she'd like that, but it wasn't going to happen. If they split up, she'd have the opportunity to reach the apartment first, get the chip, and disappear.

Not on my watch.

"We go together. Meet us at this location." He extended a hand, waiting for her to hand over her phone so he could share the pin he'd dropped. It was the spot where he kept his truck parked. With a huff, she complied. "We'll be there in half an hour. If you don't show by twenty hundred . . ." He didn't finish the statement, but she understood what he didn't say—they'd leave without her, and if she ended up at the apartment first, things wouldn't go smoothly.

"Fine," she quipped. After shooting a smirk at him, she hugged Selene. "Be safe."

"You, too," Selene told her with a squeeze.

For Selene's sake, he hoped Yumi showed up at the meeting point. With a grunt, he broke them up. Then, after a nod to Yumi, he told Selene, "Let's go."

She trailed him to the woodpile, where he dug around until he found the edge of the blue tarp that covered his snowmobile. Grunting at its weight, he tugged, pulling a couple of feet of snow off with the plastic.

The sled underneath was clear of the precipitation. Once he'd started the engine, he climbed on and offered a hand to Selene. When her bare hand landed in his, he cursed. "You need gloves."

"I don't have any with me."

And they were losing time. "Climb on," he growled over the noise of the engine.

When she settled behind him, he felt her hands fluttering for something to hang onto. Sighing, he told her, "Wrap your arms around me."

When she did, he backed away from the pile of logs for the fireplace, then came to a stop. "Good." The word rasped from his lips as he tried and failed not to think about her body molded around his. He had no right to think about cupping the curves pressed into his back. No right.

Dammit! This ride would be torture.

Gritting his teeth, he said, "Put your hands in my coat pockets. I've got spare gloves in the outfit you can use for the way back."

"Okay." Her response was a squeak, making him wonder . . .

"Have you ridden one of these before?"

"Once. When I was a teenager."

Fuck. They didn't have time for a real lesson. "Just do what I do, okay? If I lean, lean with me. If I stand up, do the same."

"All right." She sounded slightly less terrified.

After a grumble, he said, "You'll be fine. I won't let you fall off."

With that, he hit the gas. Old and fresh snow covered the path to his truck. The ride would be bumpy as hell, and the temperature made it feel like driving through an ice storm. She had to be miserable.

Well, that made two of them.

Liar.

Selene wrapped around him, leaning into him, and it felt too damned good. Most of the way there, he struggled to think about anything but finishing what they'd started in the bathroom. He wanted to make her come. Watch those ocean eyes fog over as she screamed his name.

Too bad that wasn't going to happen.

They'd been riding for twenty minutes when he felt her shivering. Though she wore his sweats, she wasn't used to this weather. Snow-covered trees whizzed by as he pushed the sled into the powerband. The engine squealed, but he yelled over it, "Almost there. Hold on, Selene."

She'd buried her face in his neck to protect it. With the wind chill, the temperature felt below zero, but her breath kept him warm. He only hoped his body blocked enough of the gusts that she didn't freeze before they made it to his pickup. He'd been driving hard, determined to arrive before Yumi.

When they reached the pull-off where his Super Duty stood, a flicker of surprise coursed through him. The suspicious part of him expected her to be a no-show, but Yumi waited in an SUV with snow tires.

She rolled down her window as he cut the sled's engine. "I've got a scraper. Crank the truck and I'll help you clear it off."

Bo heard Selene's teeth chattering behind him. She hadn't taken her hands from his pockets, and her shivers were violent enough to shake him, too.

Cursing under his breath, he stood, turning to help her off the snowmobile. "Thanks," he called over his shoulder to Yumi, "but leave yours running. She needs warmth."

"Selene?"

She blinked up at him. He wasn't sure if it was the moonlight or the cold, but her lips were a disturbingly light color. "I'm so-o-o cold," she chattered.

He placed a hand on her back, ready to guide her to the passenger side of Yumi's car. "Let's get you inside where it's warmer."

She stumbled on legs gone stiff from the freezing temperature. By the time they reached the SUV, he was half-carrying her. When he opened the door, a blast of heat swept over their faces.

Selene closed her eyes. "God, that feels heavenly."

"It'll feel even better when you're inside." He started to lift her into the vehicle, and her eyes flew open.

"Oh, I could've . . ." But he'd already set her on the seat.

"Alone" by Heart played through the speakers, taunting him. He started to lean away, but her pretty sea fog eyes pulled him closer until they were mere inches apart. Her gaze fell to his mouth in invitation. All the reasons he shouldn't kiss her again blared a warning in his head, and he blinked, jerking away.

Stepping back, he gripped the car door tight enough to turn his knuckles white as he told her, "Stay warm. Yumi and I'll handle the outfit."

He shut the door before she could respond or he could do something he'd regret. Slammed it was more like it.

Grumbling under his breath, he walked back to his pickup. Yumi had cleared half of it already. The thermostat would help do the rest. After cranking the engine, he grabbed his scraper and went to work on the remaining snow, sloughing off a foot of it with an angry swipe.

How the hell was he supposed to resist Selene

when she practically begged him to kiss her? She had to be confused. Her life had been turned upside down in the space of a day.

He hadn't saved her. Not really. She'd saved herself.

Maybe when Herc showed up, he'd turn over guard duty to him. Maybe it'd be better that way. He could trust Herc to leave her alone. Romeo, on the other hand, . . . that idiot hit on anything with boobs.

If he let Herc be her bodyguard, it'd prevent him from taking advantage of her. Because that's what it would be. Just like the kiss he'd stolen.

Thinking about what he'd done, he wanted to roar but settled for throwing snow a few yards with another swing of the scraper. Yumi didn't say anything, but he felt her gaze, sizing him up. He expected her to lash out at him. She probably thought he was an asshole for kissing her friend, considering the situation.

For fuck's sake, the woman had almost died yesterday.

The reminder burned through his gut, and his head turned to the SUV, searching for Selene.

What is it about her?

He wondered why she had him so churned up. No other woman had caused him this much grief. Her head turned, catching him staring, and he swallowed, his insides twisting. He felt lost. Like he floated on a rickety raft amid the rocking waves of the salty sea, one wrong move would send him toppling into its depths. And he was so damned thirsty—thirsty for another taste of her.

Aw, fuck.

Those ocean eyes might be the death of him.

CHAPTER 9

Bo

When Selene gave Bo her address, he plugged it into his truck's GPS. They'd follow Yumi to Selene's apartment, but he wanted it as backup just in case. He still didn't fully trust the agent and wouldn't put it past her to try to lose him.

Mulling that over, he asked Selene, "Do you trust her?"

When she didn't answer right away, he glanced over and noted the furrow in her brow.

Maybe she's not sure about Yumi either.

Waiting, he tapped his fingers on the wheel to the beat of the classic rock song on the radio. With the volume turned down, the lyrics were barely discernible over the crunch of snow under the tires. The county never treated this road. They probably wouldn't find any cleared ones until they got closer to Big Sky. It was a good thing his pickup was built for this type of weather.

"Yes," Selene finally answered. "She wasn't lying about our friendship. I think she wants to help fix this."

"Are you sure? What she did almost got you—" Bo cut himself off, cursing internally. He shouldn't have brought that back up. He doubted it remained far from her mind, and he didn't need to up her stress level.

Her voice came out soft, and he had to strain to hear when she responded, "She made a mistake." She shook her head. "But who hasn't? It doesn't mean you just give up on someone. Not when you care about them."

He didn't think he'd ever be so blindly trusting. Not when he'd seen what humanity was capable of. With a grunt that wasn't really a response, he focused on the treacherous road. He'd make up his own mind about Yumi. Let her actions prove her loyalty because words were too easy to betray.

Jordy had them all fooled. For years.

Thinking about his TOP teammate, Bo felt the need to explain. With a disgruntled sigh, he told Selene, "We had a former CIA agent on our team at TOP up until a few months ago when he turned on us."

She let out a small gasp.

"So my trust mechanism's a little rusty. I just want you to be sure about Yumi."

Her hand landed on his arm, and he nearly jumped before she squeezed it. She was trying to offer him comfort, but his dick saw it as a green light.

Fuckin' A.

Bo gritted his teeth.

"I'm sorry that happened." She dropped her palm back to her lap. "But Yumi's different."

For her sake, he hoped she was right.

Clearing his throat, he changed the subject. "Are you warm enough now?"

He'd removed his gloves but was starting to swelter with the heat cranked up.

"Oh, yes, you can turn it down."

Not wasting a second, he adjusted the temperature. He knew he was going to hell, but he didn't need to feel like he'd already landed there.

They rode the next few miles in silence, which typically wouldn't have bothered him, but he couldn't help wondering what she was thinking. He didn't do small talk, backstories, or hell, conversation, but he wanted to with her. He wanted to learn everything about Selene.

Because he couldn't help but look, he watched her from the corner of his eye. She lifted her arm and her hand fluttered, like she would touch her mouth, but she dropped it, looking away and shaking her head slightly. Caught up, he turned his head, watching her. Was she . . . . she couldn't be thinking about the kiss, could she?

His hands clenched around the wheel.

Nope. Doesn't fucking matter. It was *not* happening again.

"Bo! Look out!"

His gaze snapped forward to find Yumi stopped in front of them. He slammed on the brakes. The tires lost purchase, and they fishtailed.

"Oh my God!" Selene screamed when they came dangerously close to sliding into the guardrail blocking what would've been a steep drop-off down a snow-covered slope.

By the time he got the truck under control, his hands shook. He cursed himself for not paying better attention and being too wrapped up in thoughts of her that he had no right thinking. His job was to keep her safe, and he'd almost fucked that up.

This *is why kissing her is out of the question.*

"I'm sorry," he growled, angry at himself.

Her breathing was rapid enough he heard each expulsion. "I think that scared ten years off my life." She placed a hand over her breastbone, letting out a strained chuckle. "Did I mention I hate the snow?"

Bo let out a weighty sigh. He loved the snow, but he got it. She hadn't had any good experiences with it yet. Glancing out the windshield, he tried to see if anything blocked the road, but it seemed like the SUV had just stopped. Shaking his head at the situation, he told Selene, "I'm going to check on your friend. Do you want to stay here or . . .?"

"I'm coming," she supplied with a sharp nod.

"Fine." He'd leave the car running so she'd have the warmth to return to. "Here," he said, leaning over. He intended to open the jockey box for his spare pair of gloves, but she went rigid as soon as he was in her space.

Worried he'd scared her, he met her gaze and froze. Her gray-green eyes were hazy with desire. They fell to his mouth, then she licked her bottom lip.

Aw, fuck me.

He'd never wanted to kiss a woman so badly. But he couldn't. She was a job. Not some chick he'd picked up at a bar. His focus needed to be on keeping her safe, not wondering what she'd feel like with her legs wrapped around his waist as he—

Yumi's car door slammed, cutting off his thoughts. He glanced toward the SUV again and saw her assessing how buried the tires were. She must have gotten stuck. He'd have to pull her out.

Making sure to avoid Selene's ocean eyes this time, he reached between her legs for the jockey box. When she let out a strangled little moan, it was nearly his undoing. Clenching his jaw so tight it ached, he forced a deep breath in through his nose. But that was a mistake.

Because she wore his clothes, she smelled like him. Like she was his. He'd never let a woman stay in his space long enough for that to happen, and he realized now how fucking intoxicating it was. Which was another reason for putting some distance between them.

Grabbing the gloves, he shoved them into her lap. "Put these on."

He didn't wait for a response, couldn't stand to be in the cab with her a moment longer without taking what he wanted but didn't deserve.

Climbing down, he walked to her side and opened the door. "Still coming?"

A sadness lurked in the wells of her eyes as she laid a gloved hand in his. "Yes."

He helped her down and tried not to think about what put it there.

As they reached Yumi, Selene seemed to brighten. She laid a hand on her friend's arm. "Hey, what happened?"

Yumi turned with a scowl. "A freakin' mountain lion jumped in front of me. I feel like the stupid cat is taunting me."

"There are mountain lions here?" Selene shuddered as if thinking she could've run into one while tramping through the woods.

A sharp growl echoed from the trees, and she practically jumped into his arms. "Oh my God," Selene breathed as she clung to him, her head swiveling in all directions. "Everything here wants to kill me," she muttered.

Gritting his teeth against the desire to pull her closer, he grunted in what he hoped was a soothing manner.

Yumi ignored Selene's outburst. "When I slammed on the brakes, I got stuck."

She looked at him, and he answered before she could ask. "I've got a tow strap. I'll pull you out."

Selene's eyes were wide when she tore them away from the trees. "Maybe I'll wait in the truck, after all."

Bo released her and instantly missed her warmth. His heart squeezed in his chest as she walked back to his pickup. His hand twitched, wanting to massage the spot, but he clenched it into a fist and ignored the feeling. He didn't have time to worry about what it meant. Not when they were losing the race. Every second it took for them to retrieve the chip was a second Dao could use to find it first.

* * *

Selene

Selene drummed her fingers on the armrest as she stared out the windshield of Bo's truck. The night remained quiet enough that the soft tapping of her fingertips against the dark leather echoed in her head. They'd managed to make it the rest of the way to her apartment without incident, but the churning of her stomach left her with an unshakeable feeling of unease.

Bo had parked in the back corner of her apartment building's lot—away from any lampposts—then demanded she stay inside while he and Yumi retrieved the hidden microchip from her home. She'd wanted to argue, but she was scared. She didn't have the skills they did. Hiding in the truck provided a measure of safety, no matter how small.

But it also left her with too much time to think—to worry. About their kiss, about almost dying, about her best friend being in the freaking CIA. She was a planner, and not having one was upping her discomfort. She needed a way forward, but the situation she faced was one she'd never expected to encounter.

Bad people wanted her dead.

How do I plan for that?

Her thoughts revolved from one problem to the other and back again, until she'd worked herself into a pressure cooker of anxiety.

How do I fix this?

Having Bo's protection was comforting, but where did she go from there? She couldn't expect to have him as a bodyguard for the rest of her life. A pang reverberated through her chest, reminding her of the hurt he'd caused her.

That kiss had left her aching in more ways than one. It also left her with more questions than answers. What had Bo been through to think he was undeserving of her? If she asked him, would he even give her an answer?

Doubtful.

"Ugh," she huffed and shifted in the passenger seat. Now was the worst time to start falling for someone, especially someone who wasn't interested in her, but no matter how much she might wish it, the heart didn't abide by logic. No pro-con list would stop it from stuttering whenever he came near.

A frown tugged at her lips. Maybe she was just lonely. She'd been so busy helping her dad the last two years that she'd barely dated. And Bo was nothing like the men she was typically drawn to. She'd always gone for the light-hearted artsy type while Bo . . .

Bo was like a wounded bear—big and grumpy.

She had to tread carefully, or she'd spook him into charging away. And right now, she needed his help more than she needed him to kiss her.

Somehow, they had to get rid of Mr. Dao if she was ever going to be safe. When they recovered the information Yumi downloaded, they could turn it over to the authorities and put him behind bars. She hoped.

Headlights flashed in her direction, and she instinctively ducked below the dash. Her heartbeat sped up as she crouched, waiting for the lights to disappear. When they did, she took a deep breath and sat back up, searching for the car that had driven by. A black SUV pulled into a parking spot two rows in front of her.

Her body vibrated with nerves even as she told herself it was probably someone who lived in her complex. The building with her apartment held twelve units, six per side, with two on each floor spread over three floors connected across a breezeway with dual outside staircases. She hadn't met all her neighbors yet, with her weird hours and only living in the building for a few months. This vehicle could easily be someone she didn't know.

They're just your neighbors.

Despite trying to calm herself, she gasped when

the SUV's doors opened and four men in dark suits climbed out.

Those guys don't look like they live here.

She squinted as if that would help her see them better, where they huddled in front of the car. Even though she couldn't hear their conversation, the intent was clear. A short, stocky one seemed to be in charge as he signaled for them to split up. Two suits headed toward the left-side units, while the leader and the remaining guy headed for the building on the right.

Selene gulped. Her apartment was on the top floor of the right side. She had to warn Bo and Yumi. She feared for both their lives. The thought of either one getting hurt made her heart heavy with dread.

Without another thought, she exited Bo's pickup. Due to her intense focus, her body was oblivious to the cold. Her breaths puffed out in a frosty cloud as she headed toward the service elevator. As far as she knew, it was only used for moving furniture to the upper floors. She'd been given a code to use when she moved in.

Praying the manager hadn't changed it yet, she crept around the building to the side facing the woods. Tall trees surrounded the complex as if the developer had cleared only what he'd needed to build and left the rest wild.

Avoiding the light cast by the lampposts around the parking lot, she stuck to the shadows. She didn't know if that was necessary, but it seemed like something Bo would've told her to do. When she reached the elevator, she punched the code into the panel and begged it to work.

With a ding, the lift opened. She released her breath in relief and stepped inside.

Now what, Selene?

Her breathing accelerated as she thought about how crazy what she was doing was. What if those men worked for Mr. Dao? What if they saw her? What if she didn't make it to Bo and Yumi first?

She didn't have a weapon—again. Regretting not asking to keep Bo's knife, she flinched when the doors slid open onto her floor.

This is crazy, this is crazy, this is crazy.

The words sounded in her head in a staccato rhythm that matched her pulse as she exited the elevator, entering a short hallway connected to the breezeway. Footsteps on the metal stairs echoed off the concrete floor between the buildings, alerting her to the fact the men were still searching.

She turned the corner and dashed down the hall to her apartment with no time to lose. When no one shouted at her to stop, she turned her doorknob and slipped inside.

They hadn't turned the lights on.

Not seeing anyone in the moonlight streaming in from her living room window, she whispered, "Yumi? Bo?"

If they were lucky, the men would first check the apartment next door. But she couldn't count on that.

The four suits had separated, so she assumed they didn't know which unit was hers. With adrenaline tripping through her veins, she crept down the hallway, past her tiny kitchen, past the laundry room, calling out again in whispers, "Yumi? Bo?"

Where are they?

By the time she reached her bedroom, she'd begun to wonder if they'd already gotten the chip and left. Frowning at the slightly ajar door, she pushed it all the way open.

When she would've stepped inside, rough hands grabbed her from behind. One covered her mouth, muffling her shriek. Fear spiked, sending tremors through her limbs as someone jerked her backward.

She'd messed up by not staying in the car. Now those men had found her. If they worked for Mr. Dao, she was dead.

Regret choked her to the point she couldn't breathe. Her vision started to waver at the lack of air, then her thoughts fuzzed, leaving her with nothing but a plea.

Help me, Bo.

CHAPTER 10

Selene

"What are you doing?" demanded the enraged whisper in her ear.

Bo! Selene silently screamed, nearly collapsing with relief. She tried to explain, but he hadn't uncovered her mouth.

"Four men are coming. We have to go. Now!" she mumbled through his fingers.

The statement came out more as sounds than words, but he understood because he released her lips, spinning her around. He gripped her upper arms, and she tilted her head, struggling to see his face in the faint light filtering through her bedroom window.

"Explain."

Words rushed out of her as she told him about the black SUV and the men in suits.

His jaw worked, clenching and tightening before he growled in a low voice, "You should've stayed in the outfit."

He was probably right, but still . . . she was only trying to help. And they so didn't have time to debate this. "Where's Yumi?"

He huffed out a breath and dropped her arms. Though the look in his eyes promised he planned to revisit the topic of her disobeying his order. "I don't know. We both hid when we heard the front door."

"Do you have the tech?"

"Yes." Yumi stepped out of the shadows, making Selene jump.

Sweet baby Jesus!

She could do without any more scares today. Lowering the hand she'd lifted to cover her heart, she told them, "We can use the service elevator. I don't think they know about it."

Yumi glanced at Bo, a silent question passing between them, before he said, "I'll take her. Meet us back at the cabin."

Selene would've protested them not all sticking together, but she was too busy trying not to wince at the bite underlying his words. She didn't know if he was pissed at having to be the one to babysit her, separating from Yumi, and therefore the information on that microchip, or both.

Yumi opened her mouth to speak, but the sound of the front door opening froze her into silence. The stillness lasted all of a second before Bo pulled Selene into her bedroom, and Yumi disappeared down the hall.

Oh God, oh God, oh God.

Leaving the bedroom door cracked open, he tucked Selene behind it. Then, he stepped in front of her. Placing a finger to her lips, he signaled to stay silent. She nodded, but he frowned down at her rapidly rising chest. She was in total freak-out mode. Her breathing was way too loud, sounding like thunder in her ears.

Bo laid a palm over her heart and mimed taking a deep breath. His touch soothed her a fraction as she obediently filled her lungs. When she released her breath, the fear clawing at her melted into something else.

With his hand on her, his body was close enough that she could smell his citrus and salt scent, and warmth built low in her belly. No matter how inappropriate, she couldn't help it. With Bo hovering over her, blocking her from harm, she felt safe. And she desperately needed that right now.

She couldn't be sure in the dark, but it felt like he leaned closer. Tilting her head, she searched for his eyes among the blackness, then sighed. The door blocked the moonbeams, leaving her dissatisfied. She'd have to wait and hope her eyes adjusted enough to see him better.

Kiss me.

She didn't dare speak but wished he could hear her. She wanted him to kiss her and make her forget the danger waiting for them. Because if she thought about that, she'd panic.

Please let us make it out of here alive.

Her heart tripped, then jumped into overdrive with the thought. He must've felt it under his palm, because his forehead met hers. His even breathing fanned across her lips, infusing her with reassuring calmness. Unable to resist touching him, she gripped his waist, comforted by the solid feel of his obliques beneath her hands.

Just breathe, Selene.

She felt like Bo spoke the words inside her head. Focusing on the steady rise and fall of his chest, she fought to keep the fear at bay. She wasn't sure how long they stayed like that, forehead to forehead, breathing each other in. Until something thudded in the living room, dissipating the calm she'd gained.

Please let Yumi be okay!

Bo pressed a finger to her lips again in a sign to be quiet, then pulled away. One minute he surrounded her, and the next he'd disappeared. His absence spiked her fear, sending her heart pumping overtime. Her whole body trembled, then her legs tensed, desperate to flee. She tried to take another calming breath, knowing bolting anywhere right now would be a mistake. As she waited, she strained to hear anything over the pounding of her heart.

She stifled a scream when a dark shape appeared in front of her. Bo grabbed her hand, tugging her from behind the door.

"We need to move before the others come looking for him," he spoke, but not to her.

Glancing beyond his shoulder, she let out a breath

in relief. Yumi stood in the hallway. Surging forward, she hugged her friend.

"Be safe," Yumi whispered in her ear before Bo tugged her toward the front door.

She swallowed around the lump in her throat. They weren't out of danger yet. Bo cracked open her apartment door, then reached again for her hand. With his rough palm encasing hers, a sense of calm settled over her nerves like a weighted blanket. No matter what waited for them outside, she wasn't alone. Leading with the gun in his right hand, he cleared the door, and they stepped onto the landing.

The shorter man who seemed to be the leader was nowhere in sight, which meant he was probably searching the apartment next door. Hoping he stayed in there long enough for them to escape, Selene urged Bo toward the freight elevator.

They were almost to the passageway with the lift when the leader of the men in suits stepped out of it. He seemed startled at first until he noted Bo's weapon and reached for one of his own from inside his jacket.

The next few moments happened so quickly that Selene felt like she was slugging through mud.

Bo fired at the man who dove for cover behind the hallway wall. The sound of the gunshot bounced off the concrete of the open breezeway. She flinched, covering her ears, but Bo pushed her toward the stairs.

"Selene, run!"

She blinked at him, and then everything seemed to

move forward fast. Dropping her arms, she ran, nearly tumbling down the open stairwell as she took them two at a time. The sound of more gunshots kept her moving. When she heard feet pounding on the stairs behind her, she prayed it was Bo, but she didn't stop to check because if it wasn't . . . a dry sob caught in her throat.

Please let him be okay!

When her feet hit the bottom floor, she raced through the breezeway into the frigid night air. Her breath rasped white clouds in front of her as she pushed her legs. Fear clouded her brain so that she thought only of escape. Her body responded on instinct, keeping her moving without any heed to direction.

Away. She had to get away.

The trees surrounding the apartment cast menacing shadows, warning her not to enter the woods. Her mind replayed the screech of the mountain lion, and a shudder skittered down her back. The last thing she needed was to get lost or run into one of those animals.

She veered north where the land sloped into a retaining pond with a fountain. It graced the entrance to the community, but with the water feature broken, the pond had frozen over in this weather.

Minutes later, she whimpered at the stitch in her side sharp enough to double her over if she let it. Her lungs felt like they'd burst, forcing her to slow. Pain filtered through the fear, making her pay attention.

She'd stopped at the edge of the pond, but she'd run far enough that she'd nearly reached the road.

Where's Bo?

She turned around and started to shake. One of the suits had caught up to her. She hadn't even heard his pursuit.

"About time you stopped running." He stood ten feet away, his breathing coming out in harsh pants.

"Who are you?" Selene started backing away with the question. She didn't know where Bo was, but surely, he'd show up if she stalled.

Please God!

"I'm nobody but you . . . you're not supposed to be here."

Did they work for Mr. Dao? If not, what could he possibly mean by that? Instead of asking, she kept retreating as she said, "I live here. You're the one who's not supposed to be here."

He grinned at that, his teeth flashing white in the moonlight as he pulled a gun from inside his jacket. "That's far enough, Miss Coleman."

The man knew her name, which meant he likely worked for Mr. Dao. She ignored his order, but her stomach knotted at the news. If he was going to kill her, she'd at least die fighting. "What do you want?"

Another flash of teeth. "You know that already. So why don't you tell me where it is?"

He had to be talking about the microchip Yumi hid in her apartment. Mr. Dao had found out the one she'd given him was a fake and sent his men to find the real one. But she wasn't going to make this easy.

Scanning behind the suit for any sign of Bo, she told him, "I don't know what you're talking about."

"I said stop moving!" the man growled out the warning and lifted his gun toward her head.

She'd made him angry. Gulping against the sight of the weapon, she stopped backing up, or she would have if her heel hadn't caught in a hole and thrown her off balance.

She screeched, and a bullet whizzed over her head as she tumbled backward down the hill toward the retaining pond. The sides were too steep. She couldn't stop her fall. She felt like a bowling ball, picking up momentum as she somersaulted toward the frozen water. After one final flip, she squeezed her eyes shut. A breath later, her body smacked the ice.

A cry of pain burst from her lips as her head connected with the solid floor of frozen water. It stunned her into stillness. She stared up at the twinkling stars while the ache spread throughout her body. Everything hurt, but she couldn't stay here. The suit would come after her.

Get up, Selene!

Before she could make her body obey her frantic mind, an ominous cracking sound broke the stillness, then her head plunged into the freezing pond.

* * *

Bo

Bo's eyes searched the darkness for Selene, his actions desperate after hearing her cry out. He'd scoured the edge of the woods but didn't track any movement through its snowy branches. When he was about to plunge into the foliage, Nugg appeared. Bo sucked in a sharp breath.

I don't fucking have time for this!

Nugg stood at the edge of the tree line next to a pine, arms crossed over his tan desert fatigues. With a shake of his dark blonde head, he nodded in the opposite direction. "You're forgetting she's a civilian, man."

Bo spun around. Nugg was right. She wouldn't have gone into the woods.

Adrenaline flushed his veins as he took off running. He made it from one end of the complex to the other in record time. Tagging the suit standing on the ridge above the retaining pond, Bo barely stopped to lift his pistol, taking the guy out. The asshole hadn't even seen him coming.

"Selene!" he called down to her.

She came up gasping, struggling for a handhold on the cracking ice as he slid down the slope toward her. Instead of running for cover in the woods like a member of TOP would've, she'd headed for the road, which left her exposed. He cursed himself for not giving her more direction as he skidded to a stop at the edge of the frozen pond.

While he tested the ice, she climbed out of the

water, sliding onto her stomach, then collapsing. He took a step, and the ice creaked under his feet.

Shit!

It was too unstable to risk walking on. The last thing he needed was to plunge them both back into the freezing water.

"Selene! Can you roll toward me?" He needed to get her off the thin section so he could reach her without cracking more ice.

She didn't respond to his shout, and the sight of her body violently trembling pitched his stomach.

Fuck!

He needed a rope. He had one in his truck, but he hated to leave her. Hoping she heard him, he yelled, "Hang on, Selene! I'm getting a rope."

She didn't acknowledge him. Fear and anger started to claw at his focus. Shoving the emotions aside, he flew up the slope, through the parking lot, to his pickup. After snagging the length of black climbing rope from the bed, he raced back to the pond.

He tied a loop and tossed it to her. When the rope hit her back, she lifted her head. "Grab it and I'll pull you away from the edge."

She blinked at him, looking dazed.

"Come on, ocean-eyes, grab the rope for me." He tried to keep the worry from his voice, but considering how rough it sounded, he didn't think he'd succeeded.

He pulled the rope so it lay next to her face and silently begged her to take hold of it. If she didn't . . . he was going to have to risk crawling toward her.

With what looked like tremendous effort, she reached up and slipped an arm through the loop, hugging it to her chest.

"Good girl," he murmured, pulling her to safety.

When he'd tugged her onto the thicker ice, he crouched and rolled her over. She whimpered at the movement. Wanting to get them further from the broken edge before more ice decided to give way, he lifted under her arms and dragged her backward up the slope.

Reaching the top, he sprawled out and pulled her to his chest, happy to be against solid ground. Despite the cold, warmth fizzed around his heart at having her safe in his arms. "I've got you, ocean-eyes."

Sitting up, he pushed the hair from her face. Her eyes were closed, her lips blue, and her body shook with cold tremors. If he hadn't already dispatched the man who'd been after her, he'd have shot him again when he felt the goose egg forming on the back of her head.

Dammit! He'd nearly failed her. Letting her come with them had been a mistake. She was soaked through and holding her was wetting his own clothing.

With another curse, he lifted her limp body. Cradling her against his chest with an arm underneath her legs, he ran toward the truck. They needed dry clothes fast, but they couldn't stay here. Her apartment wasn't safe. Whoever those men were, he had no doubt more would be coming.

Acid burned through his gut. The black SUV was

gone when he made it to the parking lot, which meant one of those fuckers had gotten away.

Reaching his pickup, he tucked Selene inside and rounded the hood. As soon as he cranked the engine, he blasted the heat. Hoping it warmed up fast, he shut the door and palmed his gun. He'd do a quick circuit of the lot and building to make sure those fuckers were truly gone.

It didn't take long to find that Yumi had already taken out the trash. The men they'd dispatched were gone, and he saw no trace of more. But someone had gotten away with news that Selene still breathed. Bo was so pissed his hand wanted to shake.

By the time he returned to the truck, he had himself under control. But when he climbed in, Selene's slumped, shivering form made him fight a wave of panic. It would take too long to get her back to the cabin. He had to get her out of the wet clothes— now.

He tugged off his coat, the damp flannel underneath, and climbed into the backseat, pulling Selene with him, so he'd have more room to strip her down.

"Bo?" Her question was a whispered groan when he'd gotten her reclined on the bench seat.

"We've got to get your wet stuff off." He pulled her heavy coat down her shoulders, and her eyelids fluttered.

"I'm co-o-ld."

"I know. I'm sorry. This'll help," he soothed as he

tossed the coat in the foot of the truck, then tugged the sopping hoodie over her head. He noted with disappointment that she'd retrieved her underwear from the dryer, not that it wasn't pretty. A pale, lacy bra covered her breasts.

She shivered again, and he stopped ogling her to yank the drenched sweatpants down her legs. Next, he went to work on her waterlogged boots. He struggled with the laces—she'd double-knotted them. When he'd gotten them undone, he tugged the shoes off. Feeling water sloshing inside, he opened the door and upended them onto the snow-covered asphalt.

Selene whimpered when the cold air hit her bare skin. He'd left her with only her bra and panties. Cursing, he slammed the door. After tossing her boots down, he hugged her to his chest, letting his skin warm hers.

He flinched at the temperature of her body. It felt like hugging an ice cube. Her hair was damp, which didn't help. Feeling for the door's side pocket, his fingers connected with a blousing strap. The short elastic band with a tiny hook on each end was a leftover from his Navy days. Then, he'd used them to secure his trousers to the top of his boots, but now, it was all he had for a makeshift hair tie.

He hooked the end of it in his mouth. With Selene's weight lying against him, he used both hands to gather her short black hair into a knot. When he had it contained, he used the blousing strap to tie it up. At least now it wouldn't drip water onto her chilled skin.

He accidentally grazed the bump on the back of her head, and she whimpered. "I'm sorry, ocean-eyes," he mumbled.

Avoiding the bump, he gently brushed his lips over the scab on her left side where the bullet had grazed her. The bandage had come off in the pond, and he winced, knowing they'd have to clean it out again. If the cut on his chest were any indication, it would burn like a motherfucker.

A growl built in his throat. He'd fucked up and she'd almost died—again. Not only had he sent her into danger, but he'd let one of those men live. Yumi had taken out one in Selene's apartment. He'd put a bullet in two more, but they'd let the fourth slip away. If they worked for Dao, it was safe to assume he'd know Selene was alive by now.

Another way he'd messed up. Bo closed his eyes and leaned his head back against the seat. He hoped Yumi made it out and that she actually showed up at the cabin. Because losing the tech she'd downloaded would be the sewage-scented frosting on this shit cake he'd been served.

Selene's hand lifted to lie on his stomach, and she snuggled into him with a soft sigh. When his body flushed with warmth, he hugged her tighter and wished he could hold her like this when it wasn't a life-or-death situation. But that wasn't in the cards for him.

Despite knowing he didn't deserve her, he wanted her. And not only for sex, but this cuddling or whatever the fuck they were doing. He'd never just . . . *lain* with a woman before, and it was . . . nice.

Nice? It felt a whole hell of a lot better than nice. Like maybe his future wasn't as bleak as he thought. And wasn't that a frightening fucking possibility?

Bo gulped and noticed her trembling had finally stopped. He gently eased her back, cupping her cheek with his palm. Flickering shadows highlighted the contours of her face, making her eyes glow as she stared up at him.

He traced the tiny mole by her eyebrow. "We have to get out of here. I need you to be strong for me. Can you do that?"

"Yes."

"That's my girl," he murmured, surprising himself. She wasn't *his* anything. Clearing his throat, he pushed her away. "There's a blanket in the back." He opened the door and stepped into the frigid night before he did something stupid like kiss her again. The shock of the cold air was a slap to the face. One he deserved.

Grumbling under his breath, he snagged the blanket from the lockbox in the bed of his truck. Opening the door, he tossed it at Selene, then climbed into the driver's seat. "You can come up here for the vents if you want."

Without a word, she climbed into the passenger seat, holding the blanket tight around her shoulders. "Thank you."

That phrase was a knife cut, tearing through his

skin with a hiss of pain. He'd nearly gotten her killed. He deserved many things, but her gratitude wasn't one of them. It made him growl, "You don't have anything to thank me for."

Her reply calmed the angry beast beating out a tempo in his blood. "I'm too tired to argue with you."

Way to be an asshole, Bo.

He glanced over at her as he pulled out of the parking lot. She'd curled into a ball, leaning her head against the door. "Rest. I'll wake you when we get to the cabin."

Turning away, he frowned at the snowy landscape that filled the windshield. They still had to ride back to the cabin on the sled. How would he manage that without any clothes for her to wear?

CHAPTER 11

Bo

Yumi threw the door to Bo's cabin open, gasping at the blanket-covered lump in his arms. "What happened?"

So, the agent had gotten away without running into any more suits. *And* she'd actually come back to the cabin. But the real question was, did she have the chip?

Bo shook his head. He'd worry about that after he took care of Selene. "She fell into the pond."

And then rode half an hour on the sled with only a blanket for protection against the wind.

But he didn't say that part out loud. Yumi could come to her own conclusions. He'd driven the whole way with Selene in his lap after tying the blanket around both of their bodies, but it had still been damned cold.

"Blankets," he barked at the gaping woman. "Loft,"

he added when she glanced around with a bewildered expression.

As she scrambled up the ladder, Bo laid Selene on the couch. Her eyes were clenched shut above her chattering teeth. Wishing he could do more, he rubbed her shoulders over the blanket. "I'm going to crank up the fire for you."

Yumi returned, tossing a shirt at his head before dragging his bedding across the room to smother Selene in its downy comfort.

"Thanks," he added as an afterthought.

"Figured you might want it," she said with a smirk. "Your nipples could poke an eye out."

Ignoring her attempt at humor, he checked the cut on his rib cage. The bandage was dry, but he should douse it in isopropyl alcohol again in case any pond water made it into the wound.

Sighing at that inevitable ass-pain, he tugged on the black henley. Then he knelt in front of the fireplace. It had burned down to a few glowing embers, so he tossed more logs on as he told Yumi, "One of those fuckers got away. Assuming they work for Dao, he's going to know Selene's still alive and that she has help."

"Good."

His frustration level had already pegged the meter. Her response didn't help. "Good? Why the fuck is that good?" he practically snarled at her.

"Because, G.I. Joe—"

"I was a SEAL," Bo snapped, cutting her off.

"Well, excuse me." Yumi rolled her eyes and tucked the blankets around Selene. "What I was trying to explain is it gives us an in."

Not following, he raised a brow, waiting for her to elaborate.

"Dao has a security issue, which means he'll need to hire a security team."

"TOP," he interjected when her meaning became clear.

Yumi grinned. "Exactly."

Mulling that over, he realized Selene must've told Yumi who he worked for. But with the technology on that microchip recovered, his sole focus was protecting her. He didn't see a need to get cozy with the man trying to wipe her from existence.

Frowning, Bo shook his head. "We don't need an *in*. We need an out." An exit strategy because Selene couldn't remain on the run under TOP's protection forever. When the rest of his team got here, they needed to come up with a plan to take that bastard Dao out of the equation.

"Yeah, eventually, but you're jumping the gun, Captain America."

"Also Army," Bo told her, but without any anger this time. "How do you figure?"

"Weaponized AI, remember?" She shook her head. "Maybe you don't care about that, but it's kind of my job, so . . ."

The fire popped as a log shifted, making him jump. Sweat broke out on his neck. With a curse, he shoved to his feet. "I thought you had the chip?"

Yumi arched a brow at him but didn't comment on his jumpiness. Because his brain liked to torture him, the scars on his leg burned, and he made a conscious effort not to scratch at them. "I do. But it's only proof that the AI model exists. The amount of data that thing uses?" She sighed like she knew she'd have to give this explanation again. "It operates in the cloud. We want to get rid of it, we need to find the actual physical data sets."

"Fuck," Bo muttered and rubbed at the headache that sprang to life between his brows.

"Yeah. We have to find the servers they store it on."

"There's a server room in the Saber Tech building." They both stared at Selene. He'd thought she'd been asleep, but apparently, she'd been listening.

Before hope could sprout in his chest, Yumi said, "I checked it months ago. Unfortunately, it doesn't have what we're looking for."

Damn. Why is nothing ever easy?

Bo scratched at his beard as he thought about their probability of locating the servers.

Selene sat up, tugging the blankets around her upper body. "Um, can I have some dry clothes?"

Yumi smiled. "There's a duffel for you in the bathroom. I grabbed some essentials from your apartment."

"Thank you!" Selene leaned forward, pulling the smaller woman into a half-hug through the blanket she used as a shield.

Bo frowned at the covering. Her modesty was pointless. It's not like he hadn't already seen her in and *out* of her underwear. Fuck. That's the last thing he needed to think about at the moment. All that smooth olive skin. How soft it felt pressed against his own.

He avoided looking at her when she stood and headed for the bathroom. When the door shut, he let out a breath, corralling his thoughts before they got him in trouble.

Focusing on Yumi, he asked, "Where's the tech?"

He felt he was being picked apart under a microscope when her gaze fell on him. Fighting the urge to fidget, he demanded, "Do you have it?"

A slow smile started at the corner of her lips and spread across her face, lighting up her dark eyes. "Yes." Unzipping a pocket of her snow pants, she pulled out a tiny plastic bag. Through the clear material, the microchip caught the light.

He had an urge to snatch it from her hand, but that probably wouldn't go over well. With a grunt, he asked, "What do you plan to do with it?"

He'd wanted to destroy it when he thought it contained the AI weapon, but now . . . he wasn't sure that would make much of a difference. Not if the model was on a server somewhere, waiting to be used.

"Destroy it." Yumi frowned and glanced toward the bathroom. "I'm not heartless. This thing has done enough damage already."

She'd surprised him. The CIA had to want the

information on that chip, but she was willing to get rid of it for her friend's sake. Maybe she *could* be trusted.

Testing her, he crossed his arms over his chest. "Won't your people want what's on that?" He nodded his head toward the bag in her hand.

She shrugged. "They know what I found out, but this . . ." She glanced down, clutched her hand around the chip, and made a fist. "Hand me that poker."

Curious what she planned to do with it, he picked up the wrought iron fireplace tool and brought it over. She'd laid the chip on his coffee table.

When he approached, she reached for the poker. "Thanks."

Gripping the handle in her fist, she brought it down hard, smashing the microchip until it was unrecognizable.

He didn't see any wood splinters, but there was bound to be a dent in the table after that. Somehow, he didn't care. The table was nothing compared to Selene, and with that thing destroyed, she was one step safer.

The constriction that had settled around his chest since he'd heard the words 'weaponized AI' loosened a fraction. Knowing no one else would get their hands on the information about the weapon the chip had contained, he breathed a little easier.

Staring at the broken pieces, Yumi spoke softly, "It got damaged after retrieval. That's what I'll report."

With a grunt of acknowledgement, Bo returned the poker to its spot beside the fireplace. One problem down, but how many more to go? "So, how do we find the servers?"

Yumi tucked the ruined chip back into her pocket and sat on the edge of the couch. "I keep looking. I've been running covert searches at Saber Tech for nearly six months. My cover's intact. I'll return to work tomorrow as if nothing has changed."

Except so much had. Bo glanced toward the bathroom as he heard the shower cut off. In the span of two days, he'd gone from wishing for death to living with a purpose. All because of Selene.

The pit in his chest was still there, but maybe this mission—protecting her—was a bridge spreading across it. The dark hole lingered, but he wasn't drowning in it anymore. Something like hope swelled around his heart.

Wary of the feeling, he stomped toward the door. "I'm going to get more firewood."

* * *

Selene

Selene looked like crap. Staring at herself in the bathroom mirror, she sighed. Her complexion was off, her skin washed out, highlighting the dark circles around her eyes. If she had more energy, she would've used some of the cosmetics Yumi had grabbed for her. But every bone in her body ached. Despite the scalding shower she'd given herself, she still suppressed shivers. It felt like the cold had seeped into her very marrow, making her tired and sore.

Will I ever be warm again?

When she'd fallen into the pond . . .

Selene closed her eyes on the memory, shaking her head against the reminder. She could've died—again. Twice in as many days was just too much. This whole situation was getting old. She wanted the freedom to go back to her life. To stop looking over her shoulder.

God, when will I be able to do that?

Her eyes flooded with tears at the possibility she'd never be able to forget all this like a bad dream. She blinked furiously to keep them from falling. As she stared at her reflection, something harsh burned in her gut, the fumes poisoning her with a sickening mix of frustration and anger.

This is stupid.

Feeling sorry for herself wouldn't help.

Irritated without an outlet, she pushed away from the sink and stalked into the living room to confront Bo and Yumi. "So, what do we do now?"

Bo had been stacking firewood but jumped to his feet at her abrupt entrance. He looked ready to spring into action as if she had run from a threat. But the only threat on her heels now was the thought of forever being on the run.

She crossed her arms with a scowl and waited for one of them to answer her. "Well?"

"Are you all right?" At Bo's question, she glanced over at him. A line wrinkled his forehead as he studied her.

No. She was most definitely *not* all right. Didn't know if she ever would be again. But she needed answers if she wasn't going to let that send her into a spiral of self-pity. Ignoring the concern etched on his face, she said, "What's our next move?"

"Sleep," Yumi answered, but Selene didn't care for it.

She glared at her friend. "That's not what I meant, and you know it."

Bo cleared his throat, as if hoping to break the tension. "You two can have the loft. I'll sleep on the couch."

Yumi grinned but with a bite. "Or you two"—she pointed a finger at Bo, then Selene—"can sleep in the loft and I'll take the couch."

"Yumi!" She couldn't believe her friend had said that. She tried to give her the evil eye, but Bo's words broke through her pointed stare.

"That's not going to happen," he grumbled in response, and it felt like a sucker punch. Her stomach fell along with her ego.

Geez, tell me how you really feel.

She'd thought he'd almost kissed her again in the truck when he'd gone for the gloves. She could've closed the distance between them, but she'd hesitated, unsure he'd reciprocate it. Even though he'd been the one to kiss her to start with, she hadn't tried to make a move on him.

But it was good to know he found the idea of

sharing a bed with her that repulsive. Tears threatened again, and she swallowed hard. She turned away, determined to keep them at bay.

Yumi's voice softened, like she felt sorry for the shit she'd just stirred up. "Actually, I have to leave." She blew out a breath. "Gotta be back at Saber Tech in the morning. You two can figure out the sleeping arrangements on your own," she rushed to add.

With her vision still blurry, Selene jerked back to face Yumi. "What? That can't be safe! What about those men? There could be more."

Her friend approached, eyes turning kind as she squeezed Selene's shoulders. "Mr. Dao still believes my cover. I need to use that while I can. Look, if we want this to end, we have to find the servers where he stores the weaponized AI. Working at Saber Tech allows me to keep looking for them."

Her anger leeched away into worry. Walking to the door with Yumi, she grabbed her friend's arm. "Be careful."

Yumi's grin had an edge to it. "Always am." She turned to Bo, her face hardening. "Keep her safe, leatherneck."

Bo's eyes squinted, his lips pinching together as he shook his head. Selene wasn't sure, but she thought that was a term used for Marines. She frowned slightly, wondering if Yumi was aware or had intentionally said it to pick at Bo.

The tension left his face as he grunted and answered, "I will, spook. You find those damn servers."

She grinned at his rejoinder, clearly pleased he'd made a jab at her before slipping into the cold. Selene latched the door behind Yumi and took her time turning around.

When Bo didn't say anything, she sighed, then headed toward the fireplace to help him finish stacking the wood.

Of course, as soon as she knelt and reached for the log pile, he dropped beside her. "You don't have to do that."

She ignored the strain in his voice as he tried to beat her to the task. "I don't mind the couch. It's closer to the fire."

He shook his head. "No, you'll take the loft. It's more comfortable." He dropped the last log into place with a grunt and a mutter, "I sleep on the couch most nights anyway."

Despite crouching in front of the roaring fire, a shiver wracked her, and she hugged her arms over her chest. The sweater and jeans she'd put on that Yumi had grabbed from her apartment weren't as warm as his sweats had been.

Bo noticed, asking, "I don't, uh, have any hot tea, but if you want a nightcap . . .?"

She was willing to try anything that might send the aching cold from her bones. Sitting back on her heels, she faced him with a nod. His eyes were a warm mix of milk and dark chocolate, reflecting the blaze in sparks of fiery color that gleamed among his irises.

Despite his comment about not sharing a bed, his gaze fell to her lips. She found herself leaning toward him in invitation. A kiss would undoubtedly warm her up better than any shot of whiskey. She licked her lips.

His eyes drifted back to hers, his face pinching in pain before he cringed away from her and stood. "I'll get you that drink."

She nearly winced at his gruff voice. He was clearly determined not to touch her, and she . . . God, she wanted him to. Right now, she'd love to feel anything other than stressed out. And what he'd made her feel with one kiss . . . it was more than she'd experienced before. That much tightly controlled passion. How it exploded in a fury of emotion. She wanted more of it—more of him. Rough or not. She didn't care.

Shaking her head at herself, Selene made a comfortable seat on the floor, sitting as close to the fire as she dared. Because the only warmth she'd find tonight would come from the flames.

CHAPTER 12

Selene

The fire's crackling should have been white noise lulling Selene into peaceful dreams, but she could only toss and turn in Bo's bed. The whiskey had warmed her belly, and with his down comforter covering every inch of her below her chin, she'd stopped shivering. Yet sleep eluded her. She couldn't get comfortable. If she lay on her back, her head throbbed from where she'd smacked the ice, but she found no relief on her side either. Perhaps she'd gone past the point of tiredness to a place where she'd become too exhausted to rest.

After what felt like an hour of struggling, she believed it was possible. Her brain refused to settle as if some hypervigilance switch had been hit. Every little noise sent her pulse into overdrive. The wind howling against the cabin walls, animals calling into the night, it was all so unfamiliar. Then, there was her whole situation and her confusion surrounding Bo, which kept her awake.

She'd tried counting sheep and relaxing her muscles one by one, but nothing had put her any closer to a state of drowsiness. Huffing out a breath, she rolled over for the thousandth time. Through the cracks in the railing, she could see Bo passed out on the couch. The glow from the fire revealed his softly rising chest. She was freezing, and he slept without a shirt on, a single blanket tangled in his legs.

It must be a Montana thing. She didn't know if she'd ever get used to the cold or if it mattered now. Without her job at Saber Tech, she should head back to California. Except, the mere thought sent panic coursing through her veins. She loved her parents, but spending the rest of her life in Santa Barbara was out of the question.

I need more than that.

She needed . . . a frown tugged at the corners of her lips. Her instinct was to say adventure, but after the last two days, she wasn't so sure that was what she wanted. Safety was her main priority. Well, that and sleep.

She'd never been one to rely on sleeping pills, but Benadryl had always knocked her out. Maybe Bo had some. Wondering, she watched him. His rest seemed sound, and it was doubtless that he needed it after dealing with everything she'd brought to his doorstep. She didn't want to wake him to ask about the medicine, but she could check the bathroom. If she found some diphenhydramine hydrochloride, that would be great. If not, maybe she'd try another shot of whiskey.

Selene snorted to herself. Whatever Bo liked was strong. She didn't often drink hard liquor, but the stuff he'd given her had burned all the way down. If she had enough of that, she'd probably pass out. Set on her plan to find relief one way or the other, she slid out from under the covers and crawled to the ladder, careful not to bang her head. It had been through enough.

After the shot of whiskey, Bo had insisted on checking her bullet graze. Thankfully, it had scabbed over and washing it with her shampoo meant it was clean without needing more stinging antiseptic. She'd offered to tend to his cut in return, but he'd declined—adamantly. As if he were afraid they'd wind up in a liplock again. With a sigh, she took the last rung of the climb down.

As soon as she stepped onto the floorboards and turned, one of them creaked under her foot. Wincing, she glanced at Bo. He didn't stir. Releasing a breath in relief, she crept toward the bathroom. When she crossed the threshold, she shut the door before flipping the light switch to keep it from spilling into the living room.

It was cold in the room, making her shiver. Regretting not putting back on her pants, she tugged at the hem of her sweater. It barely covered her bottom and stretching it didn't make it any longer. Rubbing her legs together for warmth, she opened the under-sink cabinet, hoping to spot the pink package she needed. Her first glance provided no hope, so she squatted and rifled through bandages, peroxide, washcloths, and every medicine she didn't need.

About to give up, she found the first-aid kit and lifted it out. A box of condoms had been squashed underneath it, dragging a long sigh out of her.

Not going to need those.

Unless she somehow managed to crack through the wall Bo was determined to erect between them. Shaking off the thought, she opened the kit and found what she was after.

Palming the single dose of Benadryl, she zipped the bag and replaced the first-aid kit under the sink. Opening the wrapper, she pushed the little pink pill into her hand. She searched the bathroom for a cup before she popped it into her mouth. Not seeing one, she set the pill down and turned the cold water on. About to cup her hand beneath the faucet, she stopped when a strangled shout seemed to shake the cabin.

Turning off the water, she flew out of the bathroom. Bo thrashed in his sleep as if he fought against something or *someone.* She raced to his side, then froze, unsure how to help him. Was he having a normal dream, or was he caught in the throes of something else? She'd heard about people with PTSD and how you shouldn't wake them during a night terror.

Is that what this was? He hadn't mentioned having any post-traumatic stress, but if he'd been a SEAL in Afghanistan . . . she gulped. Surely, he'd seen things— disturbing things.

Another shout caused her to jump. He sounded like he was in so much pain, she couldn't let him keep dreaming.

Sitting on the coffee table, she leaned over him and spoke, "Bo, wake up. You're having a bad dream, okay? Wake up."

He showed no sign of having heard her. Worry mounted, but she kept her tone soothing as she tried again. "Bo, it's Selene. You're having a bad dream. Please, wake up."

His body jerked with a cry of agony, and she reared backward, barely avoiding a swinging arm. Her eyes welled with tears as garbled noises stuck in his throat. He was covered in sweat.

Since talking wasn't working, it was time to try something else. Reaching out a tentative hand, she placed it flat on his shoulder and gently shook. "Bo, wake up. Wake up!"

After several harder shakes, his eyes flew open, and he lurched into a sitting position. His chest rose with his quick breathing while he blinked rapidly at her. His head swiveled, taking in the cabin before returning to her face. "Selene?" he croaked.

She winced in sympathy, unsurprised that his throat was raw after the screams he'd made. "Yes. Let me get you some water."

He grabbed her hand, stopping her before she had a chance to stand. "No, wait. Please."

"Sure." When he didn't say anything, just gripped her hand tightly, she felt compelled to ask, "Are you okay? That was . . . intense."

Major understatement.

As if he knew how bad it had been, his shoulders drooped. "I'm sorry. I can't . . ." He cleared his throat. "That happens sometimes. I didn't mean to wake you."

"How often?"

He frowned, and she figured it had to be more than he was willing to admit.

"Nevermind. It's none of my business." But she couldn't help wondering if it was part of why he thought he didn't deserve gratitude.

What did you go through, Bo?

She wanted to pry so badly, to know what drove him, that she pressed her lips tightly together to keep from asking.

But he surprised her. "I don't sleep much. It's why I usually end up on the couch."

He hadn't let go, so she brushed her thumb across the back of his hand. "Can you tell me? Maybe talking about it will help."

His breathing had returned to normal, but he still looked lost. She gave his hand a squeeze, urging him to answer.

"I left Afghanistan after a suicide bombing. It was a woman." He closed his eyes, and a pang of sympathy bowled over her at the strain on his face. "I could've stopped her, but I hesitated. The bomb went off, killing dozens, including my—" His voice broke, making her want to gather him in a hug. Instead, she tracked the movement of his Adam's apple as he swallowed hard. After a shake of his head, he opened his eyes. "A SEAL from my team, Nugg."

Something in his voice told her he and Nugg had been close. "I'm sorry," she whispered. It seemed like a lame offering, but he didn't try to shrug it off.

"Me too."

The guilt she read on his face forced her to speak, "What happened is not your fault."

The weight of his sigh pulled his shoulders even lower. "Yes, it is."

Oh, Bo.

Her heart sank as she realized why he tortured himself. Guilt and blame were nasty emotions. They had the power to eat away at you if you let them.

"How long ago was it?"

"A little over four years."

And he'd been letting it fester all that time. No wonder he thought he didn't deserve something as simple as her thanks. A deep sadness rolled through her chest followed by the opening of a tiny bud of relief at knowing his pushing her away wasn't about her.

He was punishing himself, but it wouldn't bring his friend back.

Stifling a sigh, she patted his leg. "Let me get you that water."

* * *

Bo

Bo released Selene's hand and immediately missed its warmth. But then she stood up, and his focus shifted entirely. She wasn't wearing any pants. Her long legs were bare, the swell of her curvy hips and the edge of her light blue underwear peeked beneath the length of the dark sweater she'd slept in.

Before she could step away, he caught her thighs, holding her in place. "Wait."

He heard her sharp intake of breath at the contact, but his gaze didn't leave her mound. His thumb was so close. All he had to do was move it a half-inch, and he could touch her there. Or he could slide it under that thin blue barrier, run it through her dark curls, and part her folds.

The image made him instantly hard. In answer, alarm bells sounded in his head. He couldn't do this. The nightmare about his past always left him raw, but the only comfort he deserved came from a glass of whiskey.

Closing his eyes, he shook his head slightly, releasing his hold on her. "Sorry." His voice sounded like he'd chewed on gravel then swallowed. Maybe he *could* use that glass of water.

"Don't apologize. I want . . ." When her quiet voice trailed off, he met her eyes. Her lids half-shielded the haze swirling among those sea-green irises.

His stomach quivered, but he wasn't sure if it was from dread or anticipation.

"You." She took a deep breath, stepping closer. "I want you, Bo."

A part of him shattered, splintering off in sharp shards. He shuddered from the pain as it tore its way through his body. "No." The word sounded as broken as he felt. "I'm damaged goods, Selene. The best thing you can do is keep your distance."

"I don't care." Her eyes stayed on him as she gripped the bottom of her sweater and lifted it over her head. Her scent drifted to his nose. It was different. Something bright and floral but no less enticing.

Like wildflowers.

Yumi must have retrieved her soap with her clothes. The thought fled on a groan. The sight of Selene naked but for her underwear tortured him. He couldn't look away. When she picked up his palm, placing it over her breast, the air backed up in his lungs. Despite the warning he gave himself, he didn't take his hand away.

"Make me forget, Bo. Please." Her plea made him weak. "I want to feel something other than fear." Her eyes glistened with unshed tears, and he knew he'd lost the battle. He didn't have much to offer her, but he could at least give her that.

With the hand cupping her breast, he dragged his thumb across the peaked point. She shivered, closing her eyes. He repeated the motion and marveled at the moan she let out.

It filled him with an excitement he hadn't felt in a long time. One that meant he might enjoy this. Hell, he couldn't remember the last time he'd been gentle with a woman. His usual method ended up being a quick fuck in a bathroom stall or the backseat of a car. He didn't do dates or stayovers.

Guilt stewed in his gut, but he buried it deeper. None of that mattered because this wasn't about him. Using his other hand, he tugged Selene closer. Then, he replaced his thumb on her nipple with his tongue. She gasped as he tasted her flesh, teasing that tight little nub until she squirmed in his arms. "You like that, ocean-eyes?"

Her answer was a throaty moan that made his dick jump.

Yeah, you're not getting any relief, pal.

Ignoring his body's reaction, he focused on hers. Her skin warmed under his mouth, but he was far from finished. He moved to her other breast, while using a hand to do what he'd imagined earlier. Slipping a thumb under the edge of her panties, he tested her wetness. When his finger came away slick, he grunted against her skin.

She was so damn damp, and he'd barely touched her. He wanted—no, needed—to put his mouth there. He stopped suckling her breast to slide the underwear down her legs. As soon as the cool air hit her wet skin, those gorgeous golden buds perked up, and she shivered.

"Lift your leg, beautiful," he prompted when he had

her underwear down to her ankles.

She placed one hand on his shoulder for balance and lifted her opposite leg. He tugged the cloth off her foot, then trailed his lips up her inseam from her calf to her thigh.

"So smooth," he murmured as her olive skin glowed in the firelight.

Her pulse fluttered under his mouth, tightening the pressure in his sack. He was in for an epic case of blue balls. Pulling her closer, he grabbed her hips and plunged his tongue between her folds. She tasted like salvation.

She squirmed, the gasp she made driving his hunger. With a grunt in satisfaction, he dove deeper with his tongue, thrilling at the feel of her nails digging into his bare shoulders.

"Bo, I need—" Her words cut off on a groan when he nibbled on the tight bundle of nerves at the apex of her thighs. Her legs trembled as he continued to work her with his mouth. "Mmm, more," she panted.

Since she'd asked for it, he teased her bud while he thrust a finger into her slippery heat.

"Unh, God. Yes!" she mumbled and gasped. A slew of words, some incoherent, tumbled out as he added a second finger, stretching her open.

God, she was sweet. Her response was a huge turn-on, and his cock strained to take the place of his fingers. Her arousal filled his senses, drowning him in pleasure until he never wanted to smell, taste, feel, hear, or touch anyone else.

Whoa. Where the hell did that thought come from?

Before he had a chance to worry about it, her inner walls started to clench. She was close. "That's it, ocean-eyes. Come for me," he growled the demand against her sex, and she exploded.

Watching her liquefy with the orgasm made his erection throb, but he didn't care. She was resplendent in her ecstasy.

Resplendent? What the fuck, Bo?

He cradled her in his arms as tremors shook her limbs. When his heart did a belly flop, he squeezed her tighter. Selene had a way of opening him up. Frankly, it shocked the hell out of him. He'd spent so many years closed off, wishing for the end, and now . . . maybe if he saved her, he could find a way to forgive himself.

Like hell. He laid her on the couch and frowned at where his mind led. Her eyes closed, then she settled into the material with a contented sigh.

Or maybe he'd just bring his shit into her life.

Because no matter how much he wanted her, he couldn't have her. He was too damaged. She didn't need the clouds blackening his soul to cast their gloom over her. After what she'd been through, she deserved sunshine and rainbows.

All he knew was the storm.

A great calm seemed to suffuse her as she curled onto her side. "Thank you," she murmured.

For once, her gratitude didn't send that burning anger blazing through him. He watched her until she fell asleep. It didn't take long. Grabbing the blanket he'd shoved to the floor, he tucked it around her body, covering up her glorious curves.

Even so, they flashed in his head on a continual loop. She was soft in all the right places. Distinctly feminine. Like a drunk, he stumbled to the bathroom to relieve his aching dick. Whatever just happened . . . there couldn't be a repeat.

If he was going to protect her, that included protecting her from himself.

So, he'd keep his distance and hope he didn't lose his resolve. He wasn't religious, but he was desperate enough to pray. Remembering the little sounds she'd made as he'd tasted her, he knew he'd need it.

God help him.

CHAPTER 13

Selene

Selene woke to the sound of voices. Disoriented, she waited for her mind to clear. When it did, images from the night before filtered in. Remembering what Bo had done for her, she flushed. Especially as she found she was still naked on his couch. At least she had a blanket covering her.

Last night had surprised her. She wasn't sure what had come over her to beg him like that. Or what had made him give in to her request. But, boy, was she glad he did.

She'd never dated a bearded guy before, and she'd been missing out. The scrape of his beard against her was . . . *electrifying.* She'd never come so quickly or easily. The hair had tickled and teased her as it rubbed against her sensitive skin. It was simply another layer of his incursion—one she'd welcomed with absolutely no regrets.

He can storm my castle any day.

With a soft chuckle, she stretched like a contented cat. Then a thought intruded. She hadn't meant to drift off without taking care of him, but the sleep eluding her had drifted over her like a fog. She'd welcomed its dampening blanket, closing her eyes as she'd slipped into its embrace.

Where is he?

Lifting her head, Selene saw Bo gatekeeping at the cabin door. He spoke to someone—*no, more than one person*—as two sets of unfamiliar voices met her ears.

Who would be here?

Her heart started to beat faster when her brain jumped to the likely answer to that question. It had to be Mr. Dao. Or someone he'd sent after her. She told herself to get up and hide in the bathroom, but her legs refused to move. What if they saw her when she passed by the door?

Worrying about that possibility, she curled into a ball and pulled the covers over her head.

Please go away. Please. Please.

She wasn't sure how long she'd been cowering when Bo's deep voice broke through her invocation. "Selene? Some of my team's here. You probably want to get dressed."

Her breath rushed out in a massive gust of relief.

Not Mr. Dao.

As the tension left her body, she sat up, pulling the blanket together to hide her nakedness. Although why she bothered when he'd seen her bare on more than one occasion, she wasn't sure. But a sudden shyness swept over her, heating her skin. "Hi," she breathed like an idiot.

His eyes took her in, lingering on the fists she'd made around the blanket clutched to her chest. Something flickered in his gaze, and she prayed it wasn't regret before he backed away from her. "Morning." She thought she saw heat flare in his eyes before he looked away. Then, he cleared his throat and said roughly, "You should get dressed."

Selene chewed her lip. Was he mad she'd fallen asleep on him? Ready to apologize, she opened her mouth.

"Last night can't happen again."

Deflated at his statement, tears sprang to her eyes. She blinked furiously to keep them from falling. She wanted to ask why not, but she gathered what remained of her pride and stood up. "Fine. If you'll excuse me?" Brushing past him, she hurried to the bathroom.

When she made it inside, she collapsed against the door. Losing her battle with the tears, they streamed down her face. Dropping the blanket, she hugged her arms around her middle. His rejection made her sick to her stomach with humiliation. He had no right to make her feel this way.

Damn him!

And damn her! As anger surged, she swiped the tears from her cheeks and took a deep breath. She was a mess because she cared about him. He deserved so much more than he gave himself credit for. But with his past haunting him, how could they ever have a future? Falling for Bo would be hopeless.

Despair weighed her down, nearly pulling her to the floor. She stumbled to the sink and leaned against it. Physically, Bo wanted her, but emotionally . . . his trauma was a third wheel, preventing their relationship from going anywhere. Lifting her eyes to the mirror, she cursed. Crying had made her skin all splotchy. She let the water warm up, then cupped her hands and splashed it onto her face.

Pull it together, Selene.

If he wanted to push her away, perhaps she should let him because having her heart crushed as the alternative wasn't the least bit appealing. If she were to weigh the pros and cons, that one tipped the scales.

Hearing male voices, she quickly brushed her teeth, then put on another of the outfits Yumi had packed for her, more jeans, a sweater, and a pair of hiking boots.

Oh God, Yumi.

She hoped her friend didn't run into trouble when she returned to Saber Tech today. Combing her fingers through her shoulder-length hair, Selene tried to ignore the worry stewing in her gut. Yumi would be fine. She was a freaking CIA agent.

Unreal.

She shook her head. Her life was unrecognizable. It was as if she'd fallen into a Tom Clancy novel. But there was no going back.

Determined to appear calm and utterly unaffected by Bo's brush off, she squared her shoulders and placed her hand on the doorknob.

You got this.

Right. Because she was so cool under pressure. She blew out a breath and dropped her hand. Her stomach surged with nausea. He was her bodyguard now, which meant there'd be no escaping him.

Shit, shit, shit.

She closed her eyes and leaned her head against the door. Her world had fallen apart, and she'd latched onto him like a safe harbor in a storm. Whatever she felt, it wasn't real . . . it was just the situation.

Ignoring her inner voice's call of "Bullshit," she nodded and pushed off the door. After another deep breath, she forced herself to open it. When she stepped into the room, three sets of eyes trained on her, and their conversation came to a halt. It was so quiet, the scuff of her boots across the floor as she walked to the kitchen sounded like a bullhorn announcing her presence.

Bo was frozen at the stove. If the ingredients strewn across the counter were any indication, he'd been prepping breakfast. Two men, one tall and blond, the other trim and dark, sat at the kitchen table.

Well, this is awkward.

She stopped in the middle of the room, lifting a hand in a small wave. "Hi."

Her voice broke the pall, and both men jumped up from the table so fast that she almost stumbled backward. They came at her with palms outstretched as Bo said, "Selene, this is Hercules and Romeo."

Those can't be their real names.

The tall blond reached her first. "I'm Herc," he said, gripping her palm in a handshake.

She tensed at the power she felt in his grip, but he released her immediately. The guy looked like a bodybuilder. His shoulders were twice as broad as hers, and his arms in the tight-fitting ski shirt looked as big as her thighs. And she knew she had some extra weight there. He smiled and managed to seem completely nonthreatening despite his size.

She couldn't help but return it. "Nice to meet you."

When he stepped back, the shorter man slid smoothly in front of him. He had brown hair down to his shoulders and was only a couple of inches taller than her. Still, the way he moved told her he wasn't any less dangerous than the big guy. A slow grin spread across his lips as his eyes assessed her. When he spoke, his voice was like simmering chocolate, warm and dark as his eyes. "I'm Romeo. Bo didn't mention how beautiful you were."

She arched a brow at his charm and placed her hand in his. When Romeo clasped her palm and lifted it toward his lips, she noticed Bo stiffen out of the corner of her eye. Before the man could kiss her hand, she tugged against his fingers, and he released her.

As handsome as he was, she wasn't interested. "You're trouble, aren't you?"

Herc barked out a laugh. Clapping Romeo on the

shoulder, he dragged him away. "She's too smart for you, Casanova."

As they settled back at the table, she walked over to Bo, who'd started beating eggs with enthusiasm in a large plastic bowl. "Can I help?"

He tensed, his shoulders flexing into a tight line. With a grunt and a mumbled, "Sure," he handed her the bowl.

Setting it on the counter, she kept whisking the frothy yellow liquid inside. "What are we making?"

"Nothing fancy. Just scrambled eggs, bacon, and toast." He wouldn't look at her, which made her frown. With a shrug, he added, "Better than an MRE anyway."

Her mouth watered. Last night's dinner had long since evaporated into fumes. Breakfast might not be fancy, but it sounded like heaven. "Where did this all come from?" Yesterday, his fridge was empty.

Stretching slices of bacon across a skillet, he told her, "I asked the guys to bring it. My resupply's past due."

"Oh," she answered even though she wasn't quite sure what he meant. How exactly did he get food out here? She doubted anywhere delivered, and the trek into Big Sky or Bozeman was a multi-hour affair. Did he stock up, like, what? A month at a time?

She preferred her produce as fresh as she could get it, which meant she ended up at the grocery store multiple times a week. Cooking with ingredients that didn't come out of a can only once a month seemed particularly sad to her. In fact, some fresh fruit would be delicious with what he was making.

Almost finished with the eggs, she asked softly, "Is there any fruit?"

Bo scrubbed at his beard, then shook his head. "Um, no. Sorry."

He still refused to look at her. Her stomach dipped, shallowing out into an unpleasant plateau as she turned away. If he kept this up, she was going to wind up with a complex.

"So, Bo," Herc called from his seat. "We need a base, man. This place isn't big enough for the five of us."

Five?

Selene wondered who the fifth person was. Someone else on Bo's team?

He grunted but didn't turn around. He just kept flipping bacon. "Yeah, I know."

She poured the eggs into a hot pan as Romeo said, "We could put Duke on it. He should be landing at Bozeman any minute."

"Who's Duke?" She directed her question to Bo, but it was Herc who answered.

"Our pilot." He snorted. "And also, the cockiest bastard you'll ever meet."

"Can't wait," she muttered.

Stirring the eggs, she watched them turn into puffy yellow pillows. Was she going to have a whole team of bodyguards now? While that idea should've made her feel safe, it weighed her heart down with sadness.

She wanted more time with Bo—alone.

* * *

Bo

Bo stood at the counter holding his plate. Despite the opportunity for real food, he had to force himself to eat. His appetite for chow was nonexistent compared to the need he had for Selene, which was a big fucking problem. He felt as juiced up as if he held onto an electric fence. He never should've let things go that far. Making her come . . . all he could think about was doing it again. In multiple ways.

He avoided glancing at her but was acutely aware of her sitting on the couch, eating at the coffee table. Romeo had offered her his seat in the kitchen, but she'd declined, retreating from all three of them.

Herc's voice broke into his thoughts. The guy spoke between bites of breakfast. His calorie intake was equivalent to that of a pro-football player. Yet somehow, he was always hungry. "Victor's working the brass, and he's got the techies doing a full workup on this Dao guy. Once he sends the brief, we figure out our next move."

A scowl twisted Bo's face, and he clenched his fist around his fork.

"What's with the look, frogman? I thought that news would've been welcome." Herc stopped shoveling eggs into his mouth and studied Bo closer than he wanted.

Forcing himself to relax, he shrugged. "It is." The sooner they got rid of Dao, the sooner Selene could go back to her life.

And be out of his.

It should've relieved him, but instead, the thought was like an uppercut to the face. Painful and jarring.

Herc lowered his voice, "Hey, does she have family?"

Bo blinked. He'd never asked. "I don't know. Fuck."

"Yeah." Herc glanced in Selene's direction, his face grim.

What they didn't say, in case she could hear their conversation, hung clearly in the air. Dao could use her family to get to her. Bo should've thought of that.

"I'll find out," Romeo volunteered with a grin that made Bo want to strangle his fellow SEAL. He'd almost flipped his lid when the asshole had tried to kiss Selene's hand earlier.

"No, you won't," Bo growled.

Herc tried and failed to hide a smile while Romeo opened his mouth to protest. "Why the hell not?"

"You got a death wish, Casanova," Herc murmured.

Bo set his plate down before he cracked the thing in two. "Keep it in your pants around her or I'll slice your fucking balls off."

Romeo's eyes widened before he cursed, "Hijo de puta." He shook his head before spearing Bo with a sharp look. "You're into her."

"No shit, Sherlock." Herc's comment was meant for Romeo, but Bo heard it.

He changed the subject, refusing to acknowledge their suspicions. "I'll ask her about her family, then see if Victor can have Crane and Rogue check on them."

Turning away, he wished for some space. His cabin had never felt too small before, but now the walls seemed to be closing in. They had to move this op to a bigger base. Soon.

Romeo appeared at his shoulder with a whine. "You don't have a dishwasher."

"Nope." Bo grunted and set his empty plate in the sink. "And you just volunteered to be dish bitch."

Instead of protesting, he lowered his voice. "Hey, you don't have anything to worry about with me. I'll leave her alone." Romeo started running water in the sink. "We cool?" he asked.

Bo stared while the liquid started to climb up the sides of the stainless-steel tub. Why did it feel like he was drowning? Pulling air in through a constricted throat, he managed, "Yeah. We're cool."

He stepped away from the counter, eyes bouncing around everyone in his space. Suddenly hit with sensory overload, he had a desperate need to get the hell out of the cabin. "I've got to . . ." He made it to the living room on shaky legs. "Outside," he grunted to no one in particular.

None of them said anything as the door shut behind him. When the cold air hit his face, he breathed in deeply. Half stumbling down the steps, he made it to the woodpile before he hit his knees. His stomach roiled, threatening to bring up the breakfast he'd choked down. With a hard swallow, he shoved his hands into the icy snow, letting the cold center him because, fuck, he needed some grounding.

Closing his eyes, he tilted his face toward the early morning sunshine and focused on everything he could hear. The whistling call of a chickadee as it flew into the woods on his right. The slow drip of ice melting under the sun's rays from the logs not far from his head. The crunch of snow under a set of boots as someone approached from the cabin.

With a sigh, Bo opened his eyes, pulling his numb hands from the snow as he shifted onto his heels. At least his stomach had settled down, and he didn't feel like the walls were closing in anymore. Turning his head, he waited to see who'd come after him.

Selene. The fact that it was her made him feel both better and worse. There were so many things he'd like to say to her . . . to *do* with her, but he couldn't. This was an op, and if he wanted to do it well, he had to stay focused on the mission—protecting her.

She stopped a yard away. Her voice sounded unsure as she asked, "Are you okay?"

Her caring enough to inquire twisted his insides. He'd fucked up with her already. If she had feelings . . . that would be bad, right? Did he have feelings for her? Is that why he'd gone batshit over the idea of her with Romeo? Because he was jealous?

"I'm . . ."—*a fucking shitshow*—"good," he managed while his thoughts were in an uproar.

"What are you doing?"

He still hadn't stood up. She crouched in front of him, worry pinching her features.

He shrugged. "Just needed some air."

A soft smile flitted across her lips. "It's freezing out here."

She'd bundled up from head to toe, and he had on only his jeans and a flannel. It was pretty damn cold, especially as he felt the snow starting to melt and wet through the denim covering his knees and shins.

He stood up, brushing off the material, trying to avoid her gaze. If he kept looking into her eyes, he was liable to do something stupid like kiss her again. "Yeah. Why don't you head in? I'll be there in a minute."

Or ten. Or however the fuck long it took for him to get his head on straight.

She'd gotten to her feet, but her boots didn't start their retreat. While he watched the ground, they came closer. "Can I stay with you?"

Don't look at her. Don't look at her. Don't look—her palm landed on his arm. He lifted his head and met those gray-green whirlpools. Sadness, hope, attraction. It all swirled in her eyes, making him dizzy.

"Can I kiss you?" Fuck, did he just say that aloud? When she was this close, it was harder to hold everything inside. Things he couldn't contain anymore sloshed around in his head like a ship in a storm, spilling over the deck.

"Yes," she answered with zero hesitation, stepping into his space and gripping his other forearm.

He never should've opened his mouth. If she knew half the things he wanted from her, she'd probably run screaming. He told himself to step back, but his legs wouldn't move. He'd frozen to the spot. All he could do was stare.

Her eyes questioned him before she leaned closer. Then, she tilted her face up and murmured, "Kiss me, Bo."

Aw, fuck.

The way she looked at him made his blood heat until he no longer felt the cold. There was zero chance he'd deny her. Not that he wanted to. No, he wanted to strip her of her coat, use it as a blanket, and get to work melting the snow underneath it.

As if he needed more encouragement, she hooked her arms around his neck and rocked her hips in a way that had his cock standing at attention. His breath shuddered out as he bent his head and placed his lips on hers.

So soft, and that sound she made in the back of her throat? So fucking sweet. He licked along the seam of her lips, and she opened that tempting mouth. Cupping her head in his palm, he pulled her closer, wanting to feel her curves, only to grunt in disappointment at the bulkiness of her coat. It hid too much. Still, he had her lips.

With his other arm, he pulled her flush against his

arousal as he deepened the kiss. She tasted like the maple syrup she'd put on her eggs. The sweetness mixed with her floral shampoo until the heady bouquet drenched his senses. He felt no cold. Only Selene and her warmth. Warmth that made him forget about why he shouldn't be kissing her.

With their tongues stroking each other, he felt like he'd been made to kiss her. The idea that he wouldn't or couldn't do that was as far away as the city. The world might be in chaos around them, but she was his calm in the storm. With her in his arms, the past didn't matter.

A phone rang as if from a distance, the sound distorted. It was there but not fully in his reality. Until Selene pulled away, taking that ability she had to dampen everything but her. The noise grew louder.

With a soft curse, she pulled a burner phone from her pocket. Herc had brought new ones for all of them to use for this op. "Oh! It's Yumi."

She looked up at him, and he nodded. "Answer. Maybe she has news."

He leaned on the woodpile and only half listened to the one-sided conversation. Everything he'd forgotten a moment ago came roaring back. If that kiss was any indication, they were both in trouble. Because despite the warning sensors they'd tripped in his brain, he knew they would finish what they started.

Sooner or later, the pin they had their fingers wrapped around would come out. And the grenade would go off.

CHAPTER 14

Selene

"Okay, I'll tell him." Selene hung up with Yumi and tried not to fidget with the phone.

Would Bo regret kissing her?

She glanced at his face, but, of course, he avoided looking at her. He'd crossed his arms over his chest, making the ridges of his muscles stand out in sharp relief under his flannel shirt. While she admired the view, she worried whether he'd crossed them because of the cold or because he was pulling away again.

Whenever hope sprouted in her chest, a storm cloud appeared, ready to drown any chance of it growing into more. With a sigh, she tucked the phone in her coat pocket and shoved her hands in its folds for warmth. She hadn't felt the freezing temperature in Bo's arms, but now? It sliced into her like razors of ice.

"So," she waited for him to acknowledge her before

continuing. When his gaze finally met hers, it was stoically blank. Swallowing her disappointment, she told him, "Yumi has news on Mr. Dao, but she didn't want to give it over the phone. She said to send her our new location, and she'd meet us there as soon as she could."

Bo didn't say anything, but she could see the wheels turning in his head. He pushed off the woodpile, uncrossing his arms. "Do you have family?"

Doesn't everyone? Confused, she frowned at him. "What do you mean?"

"Close relatives? Parents, siblings?"

"Yes, I mean, my parents. Why?"

"Where are they located?"

She wasn't sure where this was going, but she figured he'd explain eventually. "Santa Barbara."

He nodded. "I'll have someone check on them."

She was still waiting for the lightbulb to go off. "Why would that be necessary?"

"If Dao can't get to you, he might tr—

"Oh my God!" she shrieked as what he meant landed hard. Fear stole her breath, and she wheezed in gasps of air. "He can't! We have to warn them!"

She was an only child. Her parents were her best friends. If Mr. Dao went after them, she'd, she'd . . . the fear slowly turned into something else.

She would hurt him. Badly.

The rage boiling her blood should've surprised her, but it simply drove her determination. "If he goes after them, he's dead."

The muscle in Bo's neck strained and twitched. "Dao's already a dead man walking."

The promise in his deep voice didn't scare her. Strange or not, it gave her comfort. To know he'd take care of her that way. "Good."

When he lifted a hand toward her, she waited to see what he would do. His palm cupped her face, and his thumb smoothed the frown line by her mouth. "He'll get what he deserves, ocean-eyes. Don't you worry about that."

Before he could drop his hand, she grabbed onto it. "Bo," she paused, afraid to say the words bouncing around in her chest. *Don't pull away again. Stay with me. Kiss me. Love me.*

Love me?

Shit. She tried to backpedal in her head, but the word refused to be forgotten. How many seconds had passed? She still held Bo's palm hostage, staring at him like an idiot. His eyes looked russet in the sunshine, glowing with gentle warmth. Almost as if . . . he'd heard the words, even if she couldn't say them.

"Hey," at Herc's shout, she broke their stare-off, dropping her grip on Bo. "Duke called. He found us a place in Bozeman. I don't know about you crazy kids, but I'm ready to reenter civilization."

A shiver raced down her spine. Normally, she'd agree, but leaving the safety of Bo's cabin put her on edge. She still felt like she had a giant target painted on her back.

"Yeah," he answered Herc. "We should get moving."

Without a word, she trudged back to the house. Once inside, she headed for the bathroom to pack her bag of the few meager belongings she had with her.

With her shampoo and clothes shoved in the duffel, she was about to call it good, but stopped. On impulse, she opened the cabinet and snatched the box of condoms. If she and Bo got to finish what they'd started . . . she wanted to be prepared.

Hope springs eternal.

With a roll of her eyes, she stashed them in her bag. The guys were waiting for her when she entered the main living area.

"Ready?" Bo asked.

"Yes." Despite her answer, she gave the cabin a last fond once-over. The thought of never coming back left her with an ache in her chest. Like a fissure had opened in her heart.

Rubbing at the spot, she followed them out the door. Weird that she'd become so attached to it in such a short time. But then, she'd done the same with Bo. The cabin was a little like him—isolated, but it was warm and comforting once you made your way inside.

Smiling a little at the thought, she followed Bo to his snowmobile. Now more familiar with the machine, she climbed on while he checked the gas.

Herc and Romeo had split off. Shielding her eyes from sun's glare on the snow, she saw the other snowmobile parked across the stream, cutting down the valley. She hadn't noticed the machine before now. "Is that how they got here?"

Bo glanced up, and she pointed toward the other sled. He shook his head. "They parachuted in and dropped that from the helo."

Seriously? Wow. She knew her eyes widened as she looked at Bo. She must've been tired if she'd managed to sleep through all that.

"I'm driving," Herc's statement floated across the frozen creek to her.

She heard Romeo snicker and turned to see him going toe-to-toe with Herc. Their size difference was almost comical as he sneered up at the blond. "Sorry, gordo, but I'm driving."

Herc propped his hands on his hips. "The hell you are."

"Oye, you pinche gordo cabrón—

"Insulting me in Spanish isn't any less cruel, Casanova." Herc clasped a hand over his chest as if wounded. The feigned hurt on his face nearly made her chuckle.

"Are they always like this?" she asked Bo.

"Yep."

Romeo climbed on the sled, staking his claim. "Well, if you weren't so damn heavy, we could've brought two."

Herc scoffed. "Not my fault muscle weighs more."

Romeo grinned and started the engine. "Either way, you need to suck it up, perra, because this baby's mine."

She was thoroughly entertained, but Bo had apparently had enough. Sighing, he scrubbed at his beard and called, "Can you assholes stop arguing like old women and get a move on?"

"Oh great, now you've made Dad mad." Though Herc spoke to Romeo, he glanced in their direction.

Selene couldn't help but laugh, especially when Bo's response was a scowl and a grunt of disapproval.

"Come on, Herc, get on the damn sled or I'm leaving your ass."

"Geez, everyone's so pissy this morning."

"Yeah, well, I'm not looking forward to riding butt to nut with you. The sooner we get there the better."

Herc grinned. "Afraid you might like it?"

She didn't get to hear Romeo's response because Bo shook his head and started their sled. After revving the engine, he hit the gas. He was clearly not in the mood for their goofing off. Although knowing Bo, she wasn't sure that was ever his thing. The one time she'd heard him laugh, he'd seemed surprised by the sound. As if he rarely did it.

Her heart squeezed a little. He needed some fun in his life. As far as she could tell, he'd spent far too long separating himself from anything remotely resembling joy.

Wrapping her arms around his chest, she clung to him and to the hope she could change that.

* * *

Bo

Bo glanced around the inside of the "cabin" Duke procured for them as a safehouse. It was near an airport and far enough outside Bozeman for privacy, but calling it a cabin was like calling a diamond a rock—a gross understatement. This house put his actual cabin to shame. There was nothing rustic or small about it.

He blinked and shook his head. A twenty-foot wall of windows let in natural light while giving you panoramic views of the snowy landscape and mountains in the distance. They must've been tinted, otherwise it'd be blinding as the rays bounced off the fallen snow.

A state-of-the-art kitchen branched off the main living space with a counter large enough to seat ten people. Not to mention the house had six bedrooms, four bathrooms, and an attached three-car garage. The place had to cost a fortune to rent, but with Tactical Operations & Protection footing the bill, Duke never shied away from lapping up the luxury.

"Wow, airman. You don't go for subtle, do you?" Herc's comment was punctuated with a grin when he opened the stainless-steel refrigerator. "Thanks for stocking up." He pulled out a chocolate protein shake and started glugging it.

Duke answered with his ever-present cocky smirk. "Go big or go home, my man."

Selene chuckled, and the sound sent ripples over his skin. He was as far away from her as possible. She perched on a stool at the kitchen counter, listening to his team with a soft smile on her face. Like she'd lucked out and gotten a ticket to her own personal comedy show.

Bo hoped the physical distance would diminish the emotional shit he couldn't stop. Like jealousy, protectiveness, and hunger. He was so damn hungry for her.

She wore a turtleneck for fuck's sake, leaving zero skin exposed. Still, the material molded perfectly to the curves he'd had his hands and mouth on mere hours before. He cursed internally when the thought made him half hard. His sex drive hadn't been this bad since he'd hit puberty.

Which is why he couldn't stand to look at her. Bo grumbled softly so no one could hear and turned away. Not as if he weren't acutely aware of her presence.

Romeo entered the kitchen and started arguing over bedrooms. Bo let his team's bickering drown out in the background as he stared through the windows.

He engaged with the guys as little as possible. It's a wonder they put up with him. He was always there but separate . . . like he was afraid of getting close to people again.

Makes it harder when you lose 'em.

Bo rubbed absently at the tightness in his chest. He was no stranger to loss—first, his parents in an avalanche when he was a kid. Then the grandmother who'd raised him succumbed to old age right before he joined the Navy. And most recently . . . Nugg. His brother from another mother. That one haunted him because he could've prevented it.

"Hey, Bo!"

He turned, realizing they'd called his name several times. "What?"

"Which room you want, man?" Duke asked, adding, "Herc took the one closest to the kitchen, Romeo's got the one all the way in the back, I'm taking the loft upstairs, which leaves the one off the den and the two in the center of the hall."

Which one was Selene in? Because that was the one he wanted. Of course, he couldn't fucking say that.

With a grunt, he told them, "Doesn't matter."

Duke dragged a hand through the brown waves on top of his head as if unsure he should push the issue. "You sure?"

"Is Victor coming?"

"Yeah."

"Leave the one off the den for him." Bo shrugged, mainly for their benefit. "I'll take whatever's left." He couldn't care less. He'd yet to even peek into the bedrooms. And with his record . . . yeah, he likely wouldn't sleep anyway.

"Okay, now that that's settled, let's talk security." Romeo set a slim laptop on the kitchen island, explaining, "We've got eyes on each entry and exit point thanks to this casa being wired like a smart home."

Duke cut in, "You're welcome."

Romeo ignored him. "I've set up an alert to ping our burners whenever there's activity."

"Great." Herc clapped Romeo on the back, nearly sending him folding over the counter.

"Shit, ham hands! Keep those mitts to yourself." Romeo glared at Herc, who only smiled back at him.

"Now all we need is our intel."

Bo ground his teeth together at Herc's statement, tired of waiting. TOP wasn't large, but it employed a small cadre of analysts. The "techies" dug up intel for his team—TOP's operational arm. Anything involving a computer wasn't his thing. Still, he needed to *do* something because having too much time to think was *not* helping. He had no solution for what he was starting to feel for Selene. Telling himself to steer clear of her only went so far. He needed a distraction.

And fucking soon.

Lucky for him, Romeo's laptop began beeping.

"What the fuck is that?" he growled.

"Video call." Romeo glanced at each of them. "It's Victor."

When they all crowded behind Romeo, Selene half-stood from her perch across the island. "Should I . . ." She made a shooing motion with her hand, asking if she should leave.

Bo shook his head, and she sat back down on her stool while Romeo clicked something that had Victor appearing on the screen.

"Victor," Bo addressed their commander.

He nodded in response. "Great, the gang's all

here."

"Except the newlyweds," Herc commented.

"You sent them to California?" Bo asked, checking to ensure Victor had followed up on his request to look in on Selene's parents.

"Affirmative, frogman." Victor's terse response didn't surprise Bo. His team leader was used to being followed and not questioned, but Bo had to be sure in this case.

"Good." From the way Selene had reacted, he knew she was close to her parents. It made him feel better knowing they weren't left to fend for themselves. Crane and Rogue would get eyes on but keep their distance unless something suggested that Dao targeted her parents. Then they'd step in and keep them safe.

"So, our inquiry into Dao set off alarms. TOP is bankrolling the op because they've been trying to get this guy for a long time."

Interesting.

"Why?"

"Is that Selene?" Victor asked, hearing the sound of her voice but not seeing her.

She blushed and put a hand over her mouth in an "oops" gesture. It was damned adorable. Choking back a smile, Bo grabbed the laptop and turned it in her direction. "Yeah. Selene, this is Victor, our team lead. Victor, this is Selene."

They exchanged greetings, then she came over to stand with them, so Bo turned the laptop back where

Victor could see everyone.

"There's not a single reason. This fucker's name is tied to multiple terrorist attacks and black-market dealings. Last year, he allegedly took out a high-profile competitor, and Interpol almost had him. The guy is greasy as shit, though, and always seems to slide his way out of trouble."

"So, how do we get to him?"

"I think I can help with that." Everyone jumped, spinning in the direction of the hallway. Yumi stepped into the kitchen with a smirk.

Shouts of "who the hell are you" bounced off Bo's ears along with Selene's excited voice. He'd let the agent do her own explaining, but he gave Romeo a sharp look. They'd had zero warning of her arrival.

How the fuck did she get past our security?

CHAPTER 15

Bo

After Selene introduced Yumi to the guys and everyone settled down, Victor reminded them he was still on the call. They all turned to the computer screen at the sound of him clearing his throat.

"Can we get back to business, people?"

Message received.

Before he could say another word, Yumi wedged herself in front of the camera. "Those attacks your firm wants Dao for? They were demonstrations."

Victor frowned, dark eyes narrowing. "What kind of demonstrations?" The guy's buzzed head and no-nonsense jaw were usually enough of a warning that he didn't put up with bullshit. Everyone on their team had learned that if you had a point, you got to it fast.

Yumi was about to get that lesson. She rubbed her right temple as if tension lingered there. "A proof of concept, if you will, for Sentient Shadow."

Romeo got the question everyone was thinking out first, "What the fuck is that?"

Something in Yumi's stare sent a chill through the room as her gaze trailed over them. "What he's calling the weaponized AI."

"Well, fuck," Herc muttered.

"How do you know this? Can you track it down?" Bo wanted answers. Not more questions.

Her face said she was annoyed her skills were being questioned. "Already have, G.I. Joe. The first trial was four years ago in Afghanistan."

Great, he'd made her testy. "Where?"

"Kandahar."

Little warning tones chimed in Bo's head. He was in Kandahar four years ago.

Yumi continued, oblivious to his inner struggle. "They used it to remotely detonate a female suicide bomber. Apparently, she was the wife of someone who betrayed Dao."

"So the fucker got his test, and he sent a message about the dangers of double-crossing him." Duke sounded almost impressed, which would've pissed Bo off if he wasn't too busy suffocating.

"Was it—" Fuck, his throat was dry as bone. He swallowed and choked out, "Was it in Martyr's Square?"

Yumi arched a brow. "Yes. Why?"

"I was there." His statement sucked all the oxygen from the room as if everyone were afraid to breathe. It was understandable. He was having trouble pulling in

 Blye Donovan

air at the moment himself.

Selene moved, breaking the tension. "There's nothing you could've done, Bo. That bomb was going to go off whether you killed the woman or not." She squeezed his forearm and whispered, "It wasn't your fault."

For the first time since he'd woken up in the hospital and his commanding officer told him Nugg was gone, Bo truly believed those words.

The detonation *wasn't* his fault.

With his acceptance, the darkness constantly stewing in his gut receded a fraction. Enough that he didn't feel in danger of drowning in it, at least. Maybe he couldn't have changed the outcome of the bombing, but now that he knew the fucker responsible, he had every intention of rendering justice for Nugg.

Dao was going down. And Bo wouldn't be gentle about it.

"There's going to be another one soon."

"Where?" Victor demanded.

"Taipei. The plan is to show the weapon off, then start the bidding. He's auctioning it to a group that makes even the Yakuza pucker."

And she'd know that how?

Bo wasn't the only one wondering as everyone gave her a hard stare. Of course, it didn't faze Yumi. She chose not to bother elaborating, simply stating, "The auction is your in."

"Why auction it now if it was operational four years ago?" Herc bit into an apple after his question, and the sound of his chewing filled the silence.

Yumi shot him a look. "He was developing Sentient Shadow for Beijing. The government wants it incorporated into all aspects of the military."

"But Dao wants to profit from it himself?" Duke cut in.

She shrugged. "The black market does pay more."

While this information was interesting, it wasn't helpful. Bo shifted on his feet, scrubbing a hand through his beard. "What's the demonstration—exactly?" He wanted to know so they could stop it. If the weapon failed, then no one would want to bid on it.

"Chaos." Yumi shook her head. "He's going to show it can stop a train, create a fuel leak, and blow up several city blocks that happen to be the spot of a popular night market."

Selene's gasp of horror made Bo's stomach roil. Her face blanched, and he took a comforting step toward her as she whispered in horror. "That'll kill thousands."

"We won't let it," Bo growled.

"Yeah, well, how do you plan to stop it?" Yumi's voice wasn't unkind, but she didn't sound hopeful either.

When no one had a good answer, she sighed. "We have to destroy it at the source—the servers."

"Have we found them?" Victor directed the question to Yumi, which meant TOP hadn't had any luck locating them yet.

"*I* haven't," Yumi said, answering Victor with a challenge in her voice.

His frown was hard enough to make your gut quiver. "Okay. Until then, we take precautions. We can shut down the station and cancel the market. Clear the area of civilians." Victor's confidence shifted the team into action mode until Yumi took the wind out of their sails.

"He'll just choose another location."

"Dammit," the former Delta Force leader cursed. "We have to do something."

"If we don't know where the weapon is, what about its handler?" Bo's question had all eyes on him. He was as frustrated as the rest but kept his expression stoic. "Can we find Dao? Take him out before he gets a chance to use it again?"

"Now, that's not a bad idea," Romeo's grin held a sinister glint.

"It's worth a shot," Victor weighed in.

Yumi looked skeptical. "He's not stupid. You'd need something to draw him out."

"Or *someone*," Duke smirked and nodded toward Selene. "Use her as bait."

Before he realized what he was doing, Bo's hands fisted, and he was about to pummel the cocky bastard into the dark colored cabinets until Herc gripped his shoulder, forcefully holding him in place. "Think, Bo, Dao's the kind of guy who doesn't like loose ends, and she's a big one."

Always the voice of reason, Victor said, "Herc is

right. But anything like that would be up to her. Selene?"

Herc might be right, but that didn't make Bo more comfortable with the idea. He needed to protect her. Putting her in harm's way again was completely counter to that objective. He begged her with his eyes to say no as everyone waited for her answer.

She'd caught her bottom lip between her teeth as she thought about it. It made him want to kiss her. Taste the spot with his tongue. Distract her so she wouldn't have to consider placing herself in danger. But while he wished for a different outcome, her eyes fired with a steely determination. Letting go of her lip, she spoke with a confidence he certainly didn't feel. "I'll do it."

Fucking fuck!

He broke free from Herc's hold with an angry grunt and shove. Not caring that Victor hadn't dismissed him, Bo stomped through the house, heading for the door and some air that didn't smell like bad fucking ideas.

He didn't like this. He might have a death wish, but taking Selene down with him wasn't part of the plan.

* * *

Selene

"What are you doing here?" Bo grunted at her in surprise, stopping halfway through the doorway.

Selene blinked him into focus, looking up from her seat on his bed. She'd almost fallen asleep after waiting hours for him to come back. Two big European-style pillows had been too comfortable as a prop. "You disappeared, and I wanted to talk to you."

After he'd stormed off, her stomach had clenched into disappointed knots. As the team discussed the plan, she couldn't help but wish Bo would support her choice. Yumi hadn't been thrilled either, but she'd agreed.

Because they had no other options.

Not unless they found the servers and could shut down Sentient Shadow before Mr. Dao's demonstration, which was planned for three days from now. With the time crunch . . . Selene wanted to be prepared for Plan B.

B as in bait.

She shook that thought from her head and watched Bo. When the surprise cleared from his face, he shut the door, but instead of coming closer, he leaned back against it, crossing his arms. "I needed some air."

Despite the calm timber of his voice, he didn't seem any less angry than when he'd stormed out of the kitchen this afternoon. His gaze darted around the room, taking in the double nightstands, the tall armoire, the low leather chair in the corner as if he refused to look at her.

Miffed by it, she asked, "Why are you upset?"

"Why'd you agree to be bait?" he countered her

question with a question.

She stood up with a jerk, her bare feet sinking into the plush oriental rug. "Because I can't hide forever!" Frustration made her raise her voice. "If I want my life to return to normal, Mr. Dao has to be stopped."

"Dammit, Selene! He's already almost killed you twice!" Bo advanced on her in two long strides, gripping her shoulders. "Why the fuck would you want to give him another shot at it?"

She was scared and wanted him to tell her that everything would work out. Not yell at her for her choices.

Oh God, don't cry. Tears welled up in her eyes, clogging her throat.

His grip on her shifted, his hands sliding up to cup her face. "Aw fuck. Don't cry, ocean-eyes."

She was trying really hard not to. Biting the inside of her lip, she blinked rapidly to keep them from falling.

"I'm an asshole." He kissed her forehead gently. "It's not like you don't know what you've been through. Sorry I threw it in your face."

She tried to laugh it off and only managed a choked warble. "I'm scared."

He pulled her in, hugging her to his chest. "You don't have to do this. We'll find another way."

Selene shook her head, dragging it across the muscles in his pecs. "If I don't, and we wait, innocent people are going to die."

His arms tightened around her. "You don't have to

be a hero."

She sighed, clinging to him and the comfort he offered. "I couldn't live with that on my conscience."

His grunt of acceptance rumbled through her as it climbed up his throat. "Yeah, I get that."

"Will you be with me?" Selene hated the desperate, clingy need that colored her question. But there was no denying it. She needed him there when things went down with Mr. Dao.

He tried to pull back, but she wrapped her arms around him and held on. "Look at me, ocean-eyes." With the demand, he fisted a hand in her hair and tugged lightly.

He hadn't answered her question. Embarrassment flushed her system, pinkening her skin. He was going to say no. Reluctantly, she lifted her face, tilting it up. "It's fine. You don'—"

"I'll be there," he growled, cutting her off.

"Oh." A powerful wave of relief crashed over her, loosening her knees. "Thank you," she whispered, caught in his stare. His eyes looked darker, the low light from a bedside lamp casting shadows over the brown.

The way he stared at her. It was almost . . . romantic.

She swallowed reflexively as he brushed the hair off her cheek. "I'd die before I let anything happen to you."

That's what I'm afraid of.

As much as she needed Bo with her, she couldn't

stand the thought of him getting hurt. Frowning, she gripped his shirt in her fists and stood on her toes. "No dying."

Before he could tell her no, she pressed their mouths together. Though the possibility of death hung over her head in an angry cloud, she clung to the last rays of hope. Hope they'd both make it through this unscathed.

His hands hovered by her sides, and his mouth didn't yield to her lips. Sensing his restraint, she wondered what it would take to break it. She licked across the seam of his lips, then caught the lower one in her teeth and gently sucked on it. He met her assault with a sound that was half a pleased growl, half a fervent plea. The kiss heated quickly after that.

Bo's hands pulled her flush against him while his head tilted, changing the angle of the kiss. He swept his tongue over hers, and his dark citrus and stone scent encompassed her. Her arms stayed trapped between them as he claimed her mouth.

He was all hot demand, and she gave in—willingly. If there was one thing she was sure of, it was that a night with Bo would be one she'd never regret.

He lowered his hands, trailing them over her hips before squeezing her bottom. A noise she was sure she'd never made before worked its way up her throat when his erection met her center. Now she was the one making pleas. In answer, cold air suddenly washed across her swollen lips.

Bo gripped the fists she still had in his shirt and

rasped, "We can't. Not here. With the team right next door." He sounded more like he was trying to convince himself than her.

But she wanted something else from him tonight. "Can you just . . . hold me?" She cringed as the words left her mouth.

How pathetic am I?

His eyes softened, and he lifted a hand to brush a thumb slowly across the beard burn she felt on her chin. "I marked you like you're mine, but I don't deserve to have you."

She reached up and gripped either side of his face to ensure he saw what was in her eyes as she said, "Yes, you do. You deserve to have fun, to be happy, to laugh, to—" She stopped herself, afraid of pushing him too much, but then she shook her head and took a deep breath. If she dared to face Mr. Dao, she could be brave enough to say it. "To love."

His expression darkened like a storm cloud at the feelings she knew swam in her gaze. "I don't do *love*." He put distance between them, scrubbing at the back of his neck. "I don't do relationships." His eyes traced her lips before meeting her stare. "Never have, ocean-eyes."

That sick feeling of disappointment knotted her stomach again. She didn't have the best dating history either, but at least she'd had a few relationships. Short-lived though they were. Her job as a translator had made it hard to build anything real when she planned to leave every six months. But she'd had a long-term boyfriend in college.

Jared had been great. By graduation, they'd decided to part as friends. He wanted to settle down, and she wanted to see the world. They realized their paths were taking them in different directions and didn't try to hold on to something that would've just broken miles down the road.

But what she felt for Bo was new. Different than anything she'd experienced before. It was so much deeper and therefore scarier. Especially when he didn't seem to feel it, or if he did, he shut it down instead of allowing them to see where it might lead.

Without question, she wanted more than he was willing to give. He'd shown her that.

With a sigh that did little to ease the constriction around her lungs, she asked softly, "Do you want me to leave?"

"No," his answer came out in a husky whisper that lit a spark of hope in her chest.

He moved toward the bed. Watching her, he kicked off his boots, then sat down, scooting until his back hit the mound of pillows against the headboard. Lifting his arms, he said, "Come here."

Warmth spread around the ember, lighting her insides. At least he hadn't pushed her away. At least he was giving her what she'd asked for.

With a small smile, she climbed onto the bed and settled into his embrace. She rested her head on his pectorals while his arms wrapped around her. When one of his hands played with her hair, she smiled.

"That feels nice."

He grunted in response, and she wondered why she found that charming. Maybe because he seemed almost . . . bashful? Like he'd never played with a woman's hair before.

Maybe he hasn't.

He probably didn't spend much time cuddling with women if he'd never had a relationship. Not that she wanted to think about him cuddling with other women. A sour expression twisted Selene's lips. She was jealous, even though she had no claim on him.

"Bo?"

She waited for him to acknowledge her. "Yeah?"

"If you ever change your mind . . . about relationships. You'd be really good at it."

His hand stilled its stroking motion in her hair. Before things could get more awkward, she changed the subject. "So, what's your favorite color?"

When his hand stroked down her back, she relaxed into him. Tonight, she would take what he offered— his company and the comfort of being held. For a few hours, she'd be safe and able to think of something other than the danger they were in.

"Your eyes."

CHAPTER 16

Bo

Bo woke up slowly from the deepest sleep he'd had in years. The birds chirping outside the window told him he'd managed to sleep through the night. With no nightmares.

Huh.

Felt like the last time that happened, he'd been in his teens. But judging by the enticing scent in his nose and the softness molded against him, he had a pretty clear idea of why. He was spooning Selene, his face buried in her neck. His left arm wrapped her waist, and there were precisely zero inches of space between his dick and the round globes of her ass. Before coming to his room last night, she'd changed into a loose t-shirt and leggings that molded to her like a second skin.

Do NOT get hard.

Of course, thinking that meant he instantly did.

Cracking an eye open, he peered at her, hoping she stayed asleep. Her back moved in a peaceful rhythm with her breathing. She was out.

Thank fuck.

She didn't stir when he shifted, trying to put some distance between her curves and his disobedient body. Either she wasn't a light sleeper, or the last few days had left her exhausted. He didn't want to move his arm, though. Didn't want to stop holding her.

Passing the night with her, even without having sex, was the best time he'd ever spent. They'd talked about anything other than her situation. He now knew her favorite color was red, she liked obscure European bands he'd never heard of, and she'd lived all over the globe, falling in love with paella in Spain. She'd even made him laugh—once.

They'd kept things light, and it had brought him . . . *peace?* A measure of it, at least. Is this what falling for someone felt like? Wanting to spend time with them doing nothing at all? Just listening to Selene's melodic cadence put him at ease. If he were a different man, a *better* man, he might've considered what she'd said about deserving to love.

But he wasn't. And he hadn't been lying when he told her he didn't do relationships. A frown tightened the lines of Bo's face. Still, it didn't change the fact that he cared for her. In a way he'd never cared for a woman. He could admit it. To himself.

But those feelings? He wasn't going to do anything with them. His feelings wouldn't matter in a few days, a week, or however long it took to complete this mission, and she walked out of his life forever.

Even if he hadn't been broken, Selene deserved better. What did he have to offer her? He lived in a cabin barely big enough for one, his job was unpredictable, not to mention dangerous, and his baggage was heavy enough to weigh down the strongest of shoulders.

She *should* walk away from him or *run.*

If the ache around his heart were any indication, when she did, that shit would hurt. But he was no stranger to pain. Closing his eyes against that inevitability, he breathed in deep. He didn't know much about flowers, but whatever her perfume was, it smelled exotic, like a plant that only bloomed at night when the moon danced over its petals.

About to curse at himself for thinking something that sounded like poetry, his eyes flew open as Duke burst into the room.

"Hey, Bo-man, Vic—" A cocky-ass smirk lit Duke's face. He'd woken Selene, and she'd shot into a sitting position. "Well, hello, sunshine."

Her hair was a sexy tousle, her eyelids heavy as she tried to get her bearings. Bo wished he could ignore Duke, pull her back into his arms, and finish what they'd started the night before. But he couldn't.

Aiming his scowl at the smug bastard, Bo barked. "Give me five. And shut the damn door on your way out."

When Duke left, Selene met his gaze. Her cheeks

had colored, and she shot him a tentative smile. "Hi."

Fuck, she was gorgeous. He cleared his throat and smiled—naturally, his lips turning up with ease. "Morning."

Her eyes lit, and with the sunlight streaming in, they were more gray than green. "I should probably go. Before . . ."

I jump you.

Her blush deepened as if she could read his thoughts. But he felt sure she'd only meant to imply before someone else came looking for him.

He stopped her when she moved to climb off the bed. Trailing his hand up her arm, he let it rest at the base of her throat. Her skin was warm against his. Her pulse fluttered under his palm. "How did you sleep?"

Trying to smooth her wild hair, she let out a nervous snort. "Like the dead." Her face fell immediately, realizing what she'd said.

And if that wasn't a total mood killer . . .

Playing bait meant there was a real possibility she might die. Being reminded of that made his blood run cold.

"Yeah." He dropped his arm and stood up. "I've got to—" He waved toward the Jack-and-Jill bathroom that connected his and Herc's rooms.

"Bo, I . . ."

He ducked inside without giving her a chance to respond, then he turned the water on and leaned against the sink with his palms gripping the edge of the counter. He wanted to break something, but it wouldn't take away this sickening fear. Bile burned in his gut, knowing he could lose her.

Putting his hands in the flow of water, he cupped it and splashed some on his face. Dripping onto the counter, he opened his eyes searching for a towel, only to get stuck on his reflection in the mirror over the sink. He might've slept well, but his expression held no refreshment. No, the look he sported was that of a haunted man.

Shaking his head, he snatched up a towel and buried his face in it. He wanted to yell for all the good it would do him. Clamping down on the rage, he grabbed his toothbrush and made himself ready. It'd already been five minutes, and he didn't need Duke coming back.

With minty breath, a fresh layer of deodorant, and a clean shirt, he wandered into the kitchen, searching for coffee. The whole damned team was there.

Duke, being Duke, had to poke the bear. "Nice of you to join us," he offered with his signature smirk. Bo was sorely tempted to knock it off his face.

"Shut it, unless you'd like to lose a few of those pearly whites?"

Of course, Mr. Trust Fund only chuckled.

"Where's the coffee?" The wall to his right had a row of upper and lower cabinets, broken in the center by a deep copper sink. The dark cabinets and white counter continued in an "L" on the far wall where the refrigerator stood. A mounted oven and microwave took up the area on his immediate left.

Where the hell was the coffee machine?

The kitchen wasn't tiny, but with five big men in it, the damned thing felt claustrophobic. Bo's skin stretched too tight. He needed caffeine and space.

"Here, man." Herc shoved a mug in his hand, and he took it gratefully.

Retreating to the opposite side of the island so he had the open living room at his back, he asked, "What did I miss?"

Victor leaned back against the sink and crossed his arms. His expression said Bo owed him an explanation, but he wouldn't reprimand him in front of everyone. The guy was a seriously solid leader, which is why a stab of guilt made Bo nod, acknowledging what Victor hadn't said. "She's going back into Saber Tech. We'll have eyes and ears on her, and the CIA friend will be onsite protection."

The coffee he'd sipped turned into lead sludge in his gut. He got that this was just the first step of the plan, but his entire being screamed at him not to leave her so exposed. Still, he grunted his understanding. "We wait for Dao to make contact."

Romeo lifted his head from his laptop. "Once he does, she'll set up an in-person meet."

Herc stopped shoveling a muffin into his mouth to butt in. "She'll offer to swap the *real*"—he made air quotes like Bo wasn't very aware Yumi destroyed the real one—"microchip. When Dao shows up to retrieve it, we take him out."

Victor's stare assessed Bo. "You think she's up for

that, frogman?"

Selene? Yes. Him? Fuck no.

He rubbed a hand over his mouth and beard. "Yeah. She can handle it."

But how the hell will I?

* * *

Selene

Selene never expected to step foot inside Saber Tech's building again. She waved to Henry and felt sweat break out on her forehead. He gave her a strange look when she nearly fumbled her badge.

"You okay, Ms. Selene?"

God, his genuine concern drowned her in guilt. Him, all these people working for this company, did they know who Mr. Dao really was? What he'd done?

She blinked. *Don't think about that right now!*

When she was about to lose it and blow the whole thing, Bo's voice reassured her. "We can see and hear you, Selene. As soon as Dao makes contact, we're pulling you out."

Thank you, baby Jesus.

"I'm fine, Henry." She forced a smile. "Just a little under the weather still." She swiped her badge and passed through the turnstile. Giving the security guard a small wave, she headed for the stairs.

Miraculously, she made it to her desk without passing out. As if the office were stuck in a time warp, she found Stuart hunched over the keyboard, squinting at the computer screen. She tapped him on the shoulder, and he jumped.

"Selene?" His eyes bugged out behind his glasses. "I thought you quit."

"Oh, huh. Nope, I've just been sick the last few days." She coughed for good measure. "Feeling mostly over it now," she croaked like her throat might still be scratchy.

Stu gave her a wide berth, clearly afraid she'd infect him. "Okay, well, I'll move out of your way. 'Night."

She sat down slowly and blew out a breath.

"Great job, ocean-eyes. Now open your email and go about your work like everything's normal."

She smiled a little at Bo's soothing tone in her ear, trying to convince herself everything *was* normal. If only her heart rate would get the hint. She caught a familiar laugh and murmured, "Yumi's incoming."

"You know I can hear you, right?" The smirk in her friend's comment nearly made Selene roll her eyes.

Her system was in overdrive. The wire connecting her brain to her mouth had come loose. She was so nervous she was going to screw something up, she'd forgotten Yumi had a comms device as well. The CIA agent acted as her bodyguard since she was the only one who could be in the office without arousing suspicion, but she'd given TOP access to the building's security cameras.

When Yumi appeared at her desk with a cup of

coffee, as if nothing had occurred to interrupt their usual routine, Selene told herself to relax. So far, it wasn't working.

"Here you go, champ."

Selene made a face as she accepted the mug Yumi held out for her. "Champ?"

Her friend's nose scrunched. "Yeah, that wasn't my best." She leaned closer and whispered, "Yours is decaf by the way."

Because she was jittery enough without more stimulants. All she could do was nod.

Yumi smiled and asked, "Are you feeling better? You still look a little green."

Her teasing had the desired effect. Selene scowled. "You know, I'm not one hundred percent. You might want to keep your distance."

"Nah, I've been vaccinated." The crazy woman winked at her.

Selene couldn't help the laugh that burst from her lips. Or maybe it was just a nervous puff of air. This was absurd. She didn't want Yumi to leave, but if this was going to look normal, she had to let her go.

She leaned away from her friend and shook her head. "No, you should probably go. I'd hate it if I got you sick, too."

"Okay, drippy, but text me later."

Self-conscious, Selene swiped at her nose. "My nose isn't dripping!" she called after Yumi, who chuckled. The sound faded too soon.

She was alone now. But not really. She had Bo in

her ear, and she took comfort in that. Especially after her monumental screwup this morning. Now she rolled her eyes—at herself.

She was an idiot, but in her defense, she hadn't been firing on all cylinders getting woken up like that *and* before coffee. She'd gotten nervous and blurted out that stupid comment about sleeping like the dead. Now he'd pulled away from her again. Last night had been special, and instead of building on it, she'd ruined it.

Gah!

"You're an idiot, Selene," she muttered to herself.

"You okay, ocean-eyes?" Bo's voice in her ear made her jump.

Shit! She shouldn't have said that aloud.

"Yep, fine. Super," she managed while internally yelling at herself, *Shut up!* Her shaky voice wasn't going to convince anyone she had things under control.

"What's wrong?" The urgency in his words, as if he were ready to storm the building, made her hands shake. This was not going well.

She cleared her throat and tried to keep it from trembling with nerves. "Uh, nothing. I just, um, forgot my password for a second. All's good."

"You sure?" He sounded less than convinced. If they hadn't been able to see her, she would've face-palmed.

"Yep." The fewer words she let loose from her mouth the better. Please, please let him believe her.

"It's not too late to back out. If you don't want to do this, say the word."

His comment made Yumi chime in from her seat down the hall, "What's going on, Selene?"

Okay, now she felt smothered. She would've groaned if they couldn't hear that, too. Because she was doing this, no matter what. Hoping for steel, she laced her voice with determination. "Nothing. I'm fine. Can everyone relax, please?"

Yumi chuckled. "Yes, ma'am."

Bo's only response was, "Roger," before she had what she needed—radio silence.

She blew out a breath, then opened her email. *Yikes.* She tried not to wince at the number of unread messages in her inbox.

Waiting for Dao to call could take ten minutes or ten hours. They had no clue, so she may as well pass the time with work. At least then she wouldn't seem suspicious when she felt like a giant sign was flashing over her head, with the words, "You're not supposed to be here," on it.

Later, after she'd exhausted her unread emails, the phone at her desk rang. Her hand squeezed around the receiver as soon as she put it to her ear.

"Bold move coming back here, Selene. I underestimated you." Mr. Dao's accented voice sent a shiver of fear down her back.

She swallowed and forced herself to play the part. "Are you checking on my well-being, Mr. Dao? That's so thoughtful of you," she paused for effect, "after you tried to kill me."

"Yes, about that. How *did* you survive?"

Like she'd give him the satisfaction of telling him. "Is that what you really want to know?"

She could feel his deranged smile through the phone line. It made her skin crawl, and she had to forcibly stop herself from glancing over her shoulder. "Now that you mention it, no. You gave me an empty file. Where's the real one?"

She pushed her shoulders back to shake off the sensation. "You can have it on one condition."

His breath huffed out. "Let me guess? I let you live."

"Yes. I want my life back." She wound her fingers in the phone cord, wishing she could strangle him with it. "I give you the tech and you leave me alone."

"I'm afraid I can't do that, Selene. I require . . . how can I put this?" He paused in thought before saying, "A clean house. And you, my dear, are a streak of dirt on the floor."

"What are you saying?" She hated the tremble that crept into her voice. Closing her eyes, she searched for strength. *What would Yumi do?*

"I'll agree to let you live, but only if you continue to work for me. That way, I can assure the floor remains spotless."

He wanted her to keep her job? "As a translator?"

The creepy smile was back when he said, "Yes, and no. You won't be at the Montana office. I want to keep your skillset closer at hand than that."

God. That didn't sound good. "Fine. I'll do it." She gulped and hoped he didn't hear it over the line.

"Good. Bring me the microchip, and we have a deal, Miss Coleman."

"Where?"

"Montreal. Tomorrow."

"Montreal?" She didn't have to feign the surprise in her voice. She thought he would've suggested something closer or Taipei, considering what he planned to do there.

"Why don't you visit, Ms. Nakano? She has something for you." Selene barely suppressed a gasp. "Have a safe journey," he added in Mandarin before hanging up on her.

"Selene? You should come to my desk." She heard Yumi first, then her ears buzzed with words.

"It's over, Selene. We're pulling you out."

"Wait!" Yumi interjected. "She needs to see me first."

"Negative. We are getting her out of there."

"We have what we need." Was that Romeo? Too many people spoke in her ear.

"Ocean-eyes, talk to me." Bo's plea broke through the fog.

"I'm going to Yumi." Selene rose on shaky legs and tried to take a deep breath. She'd done what they needed to. It was over . . . for now. Until she had to be bait—in person.

Do not panic! She scolded herself as her breathing hiccupped.

They were all still talking in her ear, but she couldn't make anything out. Instead, she focused on putting one foot in front of the other on her way to Yumi's desk.

The hallway seemed twice as long today. When she finally turned into the right room, someone gripped her arm from behind.

She flinched, then froze. Terror shot through her system like a stun gun, seizing her body until she couldn't move.

Please, no.

CHAPTER 17

Selene

The scream she'd been about to let loose lodged in Selene's throat when her eyes traveled up the arm of the person who'd grabbed her.

Bo.

Relief turned her legs to gelatin, and she wobbled, leaning into his chest. He wore a janitor's uniform, making her wonder where he'd gotten it.

"What are you doing?" she asked, shaken.

How did he even get in?

For a moment, his eyes were so warm with relief that her breath caught. Then she blinked, and he pulled her away from Yumi's office. "Time to go."

"But what about Yumi?" She glanced over her shoulder and froze. Bo dragged her a couple feet before she yelped, "Felix is here!"

"Shit. That meathead left a package for Selene on my desk. Does someone have her?" Yumi's question pierced Selene's ear, but she was too busy trying to breathe to answer her.

"She's with me." Bo sounded as calm as she was frantic.

She glanced over her shoulder again. "He's following us!" she hissed to Bo under her breath, even though Felix was too far away to hear.

"Going to need a little help here, guys." Bo kept steering her, but she wasn't paying attention to where they headed. He pushed open a door she'd never been through and started up a set of stairs.

Wait, why are we heading up?

Before she could ask, the door they'd entered through slammed open, and the dark-suited behemoth barged into the stairwell.

"Selene, run!"

She took off up the steps and prayed Bo was right behind her. Judging by the sound of stomping feet, he was, but so was Felix. She gripped the metal railing and used it to help pull herself up.

I'm so out of shape.

She panted even though she'd barely made it up one flight. Her gaze shot out, peeking past the overhang of steps. This building only had five levels, right? Were they going to the top? What if she couldn't make it?

Her breaths were wheezing out of her abused lungs by the second flight. Still, she didn't stop. Not until she heard a grunt of pain. Then, she spun around.

Bo and Felix grappled on the landing below her

position. She couldn't tell who had the upper hand, and all she could think about was Bo getting tossed down the stairs. He threw a punch, hitting Mr. Dao's henchman under the chin and knocking the bigger man's head back.

Glancing in her direction, Bo yelled, "Keep going! To the roof."

Felix recovered, charging at Bo, and she screamed. He managed to dodge at the last minute. She didn't want to leave Bo to deal with Felix alone, but he shouted, "Go, Selene. I'm right behind you. Go!"

He briefly met her gaze, and the look in his eyes— the calm calculation—told her he knew exactly what he was doing, and she didn't want to stick around for what was about to happen. Maybe that should've shocked her, but it gave her comfort instead. When Bo palmed the knife she'd found under his mattress, she turned and ran, breath sobbing as she pushed herself on the next flight. He would be fine, and Felix wouldn't be a threat anymore.

When she topped the last set of stairs, the huge "R" painted by the door made her groan, "Thank God!"

If she was going to be on the run, she seriously needed to think about doing regular cardio. Hot yoga three times a week did not prepare her for this. Pulling in huge gulps of air, she pushed the lever and stepped out onto the building's roof.

Now what?

As if in answer, a massive helicopter flew over her head. She stumbled in surprise as Duke landed on top of the building. When the skids set down, she gaped. The thing looked longer than a tractor-trailer. Its blades kept turning, throwing icy wind at her. She gritted her teeth and turned away to watch the door, waiting for Bo to exit the building.

Where is he?

When she'd started to worry that the fight with Felix had gone south, Bo burst onto the roof. "Let's go!" he shouted over the roaring rotor blades.

Her legs were wobbly with relief as he pulled her toward the helicopter. She'd never ridden in one before and didn't know what to expect. Bo helped her up, then hopped in after her. She plopped down on a forward-facing seat in what seemed like the cargo area, the muscles in her legs thanking her. She'd undoubtedly be sore tomorrow after the calf workout she just got from climbing the stairs.

When Bo shut the door, the machine's noise changed from a deafening whop to a loud hum. The vibrations intensified as they lifted off the ground. Letting out an involuntary gasp, she gripped Bo's hand. He caught her eyes, and the warmth she'd glimpsed earlier was back. It was dangerous, making her hope for things he likely wouldn't give. When he shifted, letting out a pained grunt, she trailed her eyes over his body, looking for injuries, but didn't see any.

Thank God.

Settling beside her, he squeezed her hand and spoke into a headset she hadn't seen him put on. Romeo and Herc sat in the two seats in front of their row. They swiveled to Bo at something he said, nodded, then turned around. She noted Victor's buzzed head in the copilot seat and realized the whole team was there.

Except Yumi.

Tugging Bo's hand to get his attention, Selene asked over the din when he met her gaze, "What about Yumi?"

He tapped the comms in his ear, then frowned. Hoping her friend could still hear her, Selene spoke, "Yumi? Are you okay? What was the package?"

But she got no response.

Bo must've seen the worry in her eyes, because he said, "She'll be okay, ocean-eyes. She knows the plan."

With a nod, Selene blew out a breath and tried to get more comfortable on the stiff seat. She had to trust that Yumi would be fine. She'd keep searching for the servers like they'd planned. Selene hadn't given up hope Yumi would find them before the meeting with Mr. Dao.

Bo's arm came around Selene's shoulders, pulling her into his side. When she leaned against him, she thought she felt his lips brush over her hair before he said, "This is almost over."

Was it? And what happened when it was? She ducked her head as her eyes welled with tears. She didn't want to say goodbye to Bo, but something told her he had no intention of sticking around when his job was finished.

The pain wrenching her heart made her desperate

enough to hope it never would be.

The thought terrified her. Did love make you stupid? Because that was the dumbest thing she could possibly want. To remain on the run for her life. Where had her control gone? Her organized and well-thought-out lists? She knew which side was heavier here, and yet . . . she was willing to ignore all the cons to be with Bo.

Would he ever feel the same way? Or acknowledge it if he did?

Her head supplied an answer she didn't want to hear. Staring at their joined hands, she ignored the single tear that tracked down her cheek. Even though her brain said pull away, her heart wouldn't let her. When the time came, she wouldn't allow him to leave without a fight.

* * *

Bo

The flight from Saber Tech to the airport near their rented cabin was too short. Bo could've spent another hour with Selene tucked against him, and it still wouldn't have been enough, not after being on the sidelines while she'd been thrust into danger. Hugging her closer as the aircraft landed, he squeezed his eyes shut at the fear that had coursed through him.

He'd known Dao would use any chance he had to get rid of Selene. It was why Bo had snagged the security badge of someone on a smoke break and snuck into the building.

The man who shot her showing up proved he'd been right. Dao had never planned to play nice. But the fucker who came after Selene wouldn't be a problem anymore.

Bo's right hand gripped the handle of the SRK strapped to his thigh as the remembered rage pulsed through him. That lowlife deserved worse than he got. Still, Bo made sure he'd drawn his last breath.

After dispatching Felix, he'd spoken to Yumi, telling her about the body and the need for a cleanup. She'd handed him the package the man left for Selene. It was a phone. He figured it was Dao's way of saying he'd be in touch. The sociopath would likely use it to contact Selene with the final details of their meetup.

None of them trusted the phone not to have some sort of tracking device, though. Yumi scanned it and said it was clean, but her reassurance didn't make him any less worried about carrying it on his person.

When the rotor blades slowed, Bo opened his eyes. The team, apart from Duke, had already exited the helicopter. Had Selene fallen asleep, or was she just as reluctant as he was to let go?

He didn't know how he would cope with just standing by while she was put in danger again. The mere thought of anyone trying to hurt her sent his pulse through the roof as his vision hazed in blood.

Sighing in frustration at what he couldn't control, he released her, then took off the aircraft's headset.

She sat up slowly and stared out the windscreen. "Is Felix . . .?"

She wanted to know if he'd killed the man, and Bo wouldn't lie to her. In a gruff voice, he said, "Yeah."

She turned to look at him. "Good."

Her face was both hard and sad. He cupped her cheek, brushing his thumb across the pinched line beside her mouth. "He can't hurt you anymore."

She nodded at his murmured assurance. "Thank you."

When her words didn't fill him with the usual guilt, he leaned forward and kissed her forehead. "It's my job to protect you. I won't let anyone hurt you. Especially not Dao." He couldn't help the growl that leapt into his voice. He wanted to kill that fucker something fierce. For Nugg. For Selene. And the multitude of people Dao would harm if he were allowed to keep breathing.

For some reason, she seemed sad at his outburst. Her eyes glossed with tears she immediately blinked back.

Before he could ask what was wrong, Duke's voice sliced through their bubble. "Okay, love birds. Time for the next leg of the journey." He cut all power to the helicopter and hopped out.

Ignoring his team member's cheeky-ass comment, Bo exited, then turned to help Selene.

She groaned when she stepped onto the tarmac. "My legs are already sore."

His gaze fell to her jean-clad thighs, and he

couldn't help thinking he'd love to massage them for her, soothe her tired muscles until he could mix it with another kind of release.

Shoving those thoughts away, he took her hand, ostensibly to hurry her along, but truthfully because he wanted the connection. Touching her soothed something in his soul.

Seeing the team had already boarded the Learjet, he broke into a jog, pulling a groan out of Selene as he forced her to keep up. "Sorry, beautiful, but you can rest soon."

The flight to Montreal would take three to four hours, depending on Duke and the weather. She could nap while he spoke to Victor because he still needed to apologize for blowing out of the briefing yesterday.

When they reached the jet, Selene paused at the boarding stairs with a whine. Panting, she said, "Oh God. Not *more* stairs."

Swooping her into his arms, Bo started to climb the steps. Her wide-eyed expression told him he'd surprised her, but then she broke out into a laugh. It made him smile as he carried her to the top. Once they were inside the plane, he set her down.

She leaned in and kissed his cheek. With a smile, she murmured, "Thank you."

The word didn't bring him an adverse reaction, and the lack of guilt made him return her smile. "You're welcome."

Her breath stuttered, and her gaze fell to his mouth. Damn, he wanted to kiss her, but not when they had an audience. Victor, Herc, and Romeo could see them from their seats. The plane only had room for eight passengers, albeit in cushy tan leather chairs with dark-wood tray tables.

Bo steered Selene to the back row since the guys took the front three places. It could hold three people across a set of bench seats. After they hit cruising altitude, she'd be able to lie down if she wanted. Telling her this, he settled opposite her in a rear-facing seat.

Her eyes shifted away, alerting him that Duke had poked his head around the cockpit partition. "Wheels up in five."

Selene blinked, taking in her surroundings. "I've never been on a private plane before. It's . . . smaller than I was expecting." She nibbled her lip in a nervous gesture.

Leaning forward, he squeezed her hand. "As much of a pain in the ass as he is, Duke's the best pilot I've ever flown with. You've got nothing to worry about."

She nodded, then startled as the passenger door closed. He gave her hand another reassuring squeeze, and she shook her head at herself.

"This is ridiculous. I fly all the time. Or I used to." Sadness flickered in her eyes, and she shifted, pulling her hand free. She closed her lids, asking, "Wake me when we get there?"

He grunted a yes but couldn't help watching her, wondering what she'd been thinking when the sadness clouded her gaze. Was she missing her life before all this? Or was she—like him—sad for the op to end if it meant never seeing each other again?

Mulling it over, he stared out the window while Duke got the plane off the ground. Thirty minutes into the flight, her breathing evened out, her head slumping over. Careful not to wake her, he shifted her body into a reclined position so she wouldn't end up with a neck ache.

Staring down at her, a part of him wanted to pull her head into his lap and run his fingers through her dark hair. How much more time together did they have? Depending on how things went tomorrow, tonight might be it.

He frowned, worry cramping his stomach. It wasn't enough. He wanted . . . more.

"Bo!" Hearing Victor call his name, Bo shook himself. This was an op, and he needed to focus on that. Not on whatever might or might not be happening with Selene.

Shoving to his feet, he moved to the front passenger area. Victor gestured to the seat across the tray table from him. When Bo took it, Herc and Romeo moved into the back, rear-facing seats.

Glad he wouldn't have an audience, Bo cleared his throat. "I was out of line yesterday. I'm sorry."

The scratch of stubble filled the space between them as Victor scrubbed at his chin. "That was unlike you, frogman." Bo met Victor's eyes. They studied him, working on an assessment. "Want to tell me what's going on between you and Selene?"

He fought a wince that would only make things worse. "I don't . . ." Bo rubbed the back of his neck. He was sweating. *Great.* "I can't stand the thought of her getting hurt."

Victor's hazel gaze narrowed. "You going to be able to handle her being bait tomorrow?"

Bo's hands clenched into fists. "I'm going to be there no matter what." Reckless as it was, the statement was a promise as much as a threat. He wasn't standing down even if Victor took him off the op. Not when Selene would be vulnerable. To make that point clear, he didn't drop his leader's gaze.

"I'd expect nothing less, Bo." Victor leaned back in his seat, breaking the tension between them. His stare shifted out the window before he said, "If you get a chance at happiness, take it. We both know how short life can be. It's better to take what good you can *while* you can. Or else"—his mouth thinned, the corners of his eyes pinching—"you'll end up living with regrets."

He knew jack squat about Victor's personal history, but the man sounded like he spoke from experience. Bo only grunted in response, ready to exit this uncomfortable conversation. He didn't talk about his personal life to any of his team, least of all his leader.

Even if Victor might have a point, it still didn't change the fact that Bo didn't deserve Selene. He had no doubt she would make him happy, but in the long run? He didn't think *she'd* be happy saddled with *him.*

I sure as hell wouldn't be.

Feeling morose, he slumped in his chair and glowered out the window. If he were going to make it through the next twenty-four hours, he couldn't think about that because what happened after Selene was safe . . . wouldn't include him.

Victor broke into his thoughts. "Now, tell me what happened inside the stairwell."

Bo knew why he was asking. There were no cameras inside it. Even though TOP had been able to hear him, they hadn't seen what went down with Felix or Yumi afterward.

Happy to move the conversation to something that didn't give him the cold sweats, he laid it out as concisely as possible.

CHAPTER 18

Selene

The first thing Selene noticed when she walked into the hotel room she'd be sharing with Bo was that it only had one bed. The second thing that struck her as she edged further inside was the huge glass-walled shower mere steps from the bed. The bathroom wasn't a separate room so much as part of the same cozy space. That was going to be . . . interesting.

Crossing her arms, she leaned out a hip and asked, "Did Duke pick this hotel?"

Bo stepped in behind her, shuffling with their duffels through the narrow hallway that opened into the bedroom where she'd stopped. "Yeah, why'd you as—" She turned in time to see his eyes widen at the setup. His throat sounded hoarse when he said, "There's supposed to be two queen beds."

"Uh-huh." She couldn't help but smirk at the expression on his face as he stared at the shower. The walls were tinted pink in an ombre fashion, starting at the bottom. If the hue were meant for privacy, it would do little to hide anything, judging by the silhouettes of the brass faucet she could see clearly through the colored glass.

"What the hell?" he muttered.

A chuckle tickled her throat. "Maybe it's French?"

That or the hotel had leaned heavily into the artsy vibe this part of the city had going on. The Honeyrose's lobby had proved to be a mix of vintage and modern with heavy art deco influences. Lots of mirrors, jewel tones, and gold accents. Their room kept the theme going.

In front of the bed, a deep pink tufted stool with gold spindly legs looked like it had never been sat on. The same pink continued in the floor-to-ceiling drapes that framed a window extending the length of the wall past the bed.

Night had fallen on the flight over, and the curtains were open enough to showcase the twinkling lights of the *Quartier des spectacles*. Even in winter, downtown Montreal's popular arts and entertainment district drew locals and visitors alike for its array of cultural events and festivals. Not that they'd be partaking in any of those.

Bo shook his head, drawing her attention. He dropped their duffels on the narrow white worktable across from the bed. It could be a simple mistake, *or* Duke was trying to play matchmaker. Either way, the bed was a king-size with plenty of room for both of them to sleep comfortably. They'd shared one before. Though if it were up to her, she wanted to do more than just sleep in it.

How would Bo feel about that?

Afraid she already knew the answer, she took off her boots and moved to the bed, her gaze trained on the wooden floors. They were a warm brown, topped by a distressed area rug underneath the platform bed. With a sigh, she stretched out on it, testing its feel. The mattress was both soft and firm, the perfect blend for comfort. She could've easily curled up on it if she hadn't napped for three hours.

Instead, she rolled to her side, propping up her head with her hand. "So, what do we do now?"

Leaning his butt against the worktable, Bo crossed his arms over his chest. "We wait for Dao to send you the meetup location. Before that,"—he scowled at the shower—"we need food."

He wanted to clean up before they went for dinner, but the look on his face said he wasn't enthused about putting on a show. Imagining watching him in there, washing the muscles that rippled over his chest and back, then lower, a cloth tracing the outline she'd admired in his sweatpants . . .

Moisture pooled between her legs. Squeezing her thighs together, she met Bo's gaze. "Do you want to shower first or should I?" The turn of her thoughts made her voice come out unsteady and laden with desire.

His pupils dilated, and his dark eyes took her in.

The look in them was so hungry that her breath caught. Holding his gaze, she sat up slowly. "Or we could shower together." As soon as the words left her lips, her face flushed with heat.

Did I really just say that?

Though it was what she wanted, she was terrified he'd reject her again. The possibility lodged her heart in her throat while her stomach went on a roller-coaster ride. Sucking in a steadying lungful of air, she told herself to be bold. Go after what she wanted.

When she stood up, his breath rushed out in a strained expulsion. He scrubbed his hands over either side of his beard. "Selene . . ."

Her name was a choked rasp that gave her the courage to move closer. Watching him, she gripped the edge of her turtleneck and dragged it slowly up her body.

When she lifted it off her head, his hands had gripped the edge of the worktable hard enough to turn his knuckles white. His eyes were on her breasts, so she traced a finger across the top of her bra, down her side, across her stomach until she found the button of her jeans. By the time she shimmied them down her legs and kicked them off, his pupils had nearly swallowed the umber of his eyes.

His chest rose and fell with his strangled breathing, but he didn't release his grip on the worktable. She wished he'd let go of whatever justification he used to stay away from her. Because she knew he wanted her. And she wanted him.

Enough to offer him the out he seemed to need.

Unhooking her bra, she let it slip from her arms. His Adam's apple bobbed on a swallow as it hit the floor. Baring herself, physically and emotionally, she slid her underwear down her legs. Naked, she closed the distance between them and whispered, "I'm not asking for forever, Bo."

He flinched, barely, but she watched him close enough to notice. It surprised her. Did the mere word 'forever' scare him so much, or was it something else?

Anger flared in his eyes, and he opened his mouth only to close it again with a grunt. The muscle in his jaw flexed and released with whatever internal debate he was having. All of a sudden, his expression softened. She blinked at the abrupt change.

Staring down at her, he lifted a hand that shook and traced a finger over her lips. "If I could give anyone forever, it would be you, ocean-eyes."

She shuddered at the intimate contact and the force of his words. They weren't enough, but it wasn't a 'no' either. If she couldn't have forever, she'd settle for tonight. Reaching for him, she gripped the hem of his henley. "Shower with me?"

Stuck in viscous anticipation, she waited for his answer. Instead of words, he used actions. He moved her hands from his shirt to place them on his belt buckle, then in one quick motion, he reached behind his head and pulled the henley off. She licked her lips at the sight of his chest.

Forgetting his belt, she rubbed her hands across

the auburn fuzz on his pectorals, the texture rough against her palms, before tracing her fingertips down the ridges of his abs. His skin was warm but firm. When her thumb brushed beneath his waistband, he sucked in a sharp breath.

His response made her heart pound harder. She wanted more. Was hungry for all of him. He'd removed his weapons before they entered the hotel, but he still wore his tactical belt.

Instead of trying to figure that thing out, she said, "Take them off. Please."

He undid his belt and kicked off his boots simultaneously. He hesitated when he unzipped his jeans, so she dropped to her knees to help tug them down.

Bo stopped her before she could reveal his calves. "I have scars."

Looking up at him, she tried to convey that it didn't bother her as she waited for him to release his hold. With a sigh, he let go, and she pulled his jeans to the floor. "It's not pretty."

Burn scars mottled his lower left leg, but they weren't gruesome to her. They were a badge of honor, proof of his courage and strength. She lifted her hand to trail her fingers over the leathery skin, but he shifted away before she could. Patient, she met his gaze. "Does it hurt?"

He shook his head, then grimaced. "Phantom pains. Sometimes."

She moved toward him again and caught sight of

a tattoo on the back of his calf. He'd had it done over the scarring. She nearly gasped, thinking about how painful that would've been.

Lifting her hand, she met his gaze for permission. When he nodded, she traced the black ink. "What is it?"

He scrubbed his hands over his face before saying, "A bone frog."

"For Nugg," she murmured. He didn't have to tell her what it meant. She understood it was his way of commemorating the brother he'd lost. Leaning forward, she placed a gentle kiss over the markings.

"Selene, you should know I—"

She rocked back on her heels, staring up at his tortured expression. His eyes swam with emotion while the muscle in his jaw worked. "You can tell me, Bo," she encouraged in a soft voice.

He puffed out a breath. When he spoke, his voice was a low rumble filled with pain. "I still see him—Nugg." He scrubbed his hands over his face and muttered, "Fuckin' A." When he met her gaze, he added, "I hallucinate."

For a moment, she remained quiet, taking in what he'd said. Knowing he battled this as well as nightmares, it clenched her heart. To ease the ache, she thought only of ways to help him. "Have you talked to someone about it? A counselor, I mean?"

He winced and shook his head. "Not since I got out."

Tracing her hand over the tattoo again, she coaxed,

"Maybe you could?"

He'd pulled a stoic mask over his features when she looked at him. She would've sighed, but wasn't ready to give up on him. This was just another reason he needed her—the understanding she could offer—to help him heal from his past. "You have to start somewhere, Bo."

In response, he cleared his throat. "Look, you can shower first." He rubbed the back of his neck as his gaze flitted around the room. "I'll . . . hide in the fucking closet or something," he grumbled.

"I don't want to stop." If anything, his vulnerability only made her want to comfort him more.

"You . . . don't?" he asked the question like he wasn't sure he'd heard her correctly.

"No." To prove her point, she lifted a hand to the bulge in his boxer briefs, stroking him through the material.

Pupils blown, he cursed under his breath, "Fuck."

Dipping her fingers under the waistband, she reveled at the quiver in his muscles. A small smile tugged at her lips as she pulled the material down, freeing his length. He was hot, hard, and ready. Sliding a hand up his thigh, she braced herself and leaned forward to lick the moisture at the tip of his erection.

The sound he made was so guttural it shook his whole body. Before she knew what was happening, he swooped her up, hiking her legs around his waist as his mouth descended on hers.

His onslaught took her off guard. Recovering, Selene wrapped her arms around his neck and held on as his tongue pierced, pleasured, and possessed her. He tasted dark and salty with that hint of citrus that made her think of orange groves. All she could do was cling to him as sensations pummeled her. She was a piece of driftwood tossed in a storm.

His hands brushed the sides of her breasts, lowered to squeeze her hips, then her bottom. His feet moved them, but she barely registered it until her back hit something cold and solid, making her hiss out a breath as it came in contact with her overheated skin.

When Bo lifted his head, their breaths mingled in heavy pants. "Shower," burst from his lips.

Selene blinked, turning her head slightly to find it was what she'd been pressed against. "Inside," she panted.

Their mouths reconnected. If she'd been hungry before, now she felt starved. The seconds apart had felt like hours, and she needed . . . just *more*. More of what he did to her, what he made her feel. It was blissful agony.

Somehow, Bo found the door and opened it. He pressed her back against the inside wall, still kissing her while he felt around for the taps. By some miracle, warm water poured down on them from the rainfall shower head.

His mouth finally released her to trail kisses down her neck. When he started to suck at the base of her throat, she moaned, letting her head loll to the side. The spot was sensitive, and the mix of his tongue, teeth, and beard sent bolts of electricity spiking through her, shooting straight for her core. "God, Bo!"

That felt way too good.

He shook his head as if to clear the fog of desire they were caught in. "Selene, I don't think I can wait."

Confusion passed over her like a cloud. Her mind was too lost in pleasure to understand what he meant. "I want you inside me."

His eyes closed, his breath shuddering as he lowered his forehead to hers. About to ask him what was wrong, words dried up as the hand not holding her in place slid between her legs. She arched against his touch and the lick of pleasure it brought her.

"You're so wet," he moaned. Leaning back, he lifted his finger to his mouth and licked her taste from his skin.

Her eyes widened. It was the hottest thing she'd ever experienced. She would've melted into the tile flooring if she'd been standing. Gripping the hair at the base of his skull, she pulled his mouth back to hers. This time, she was the one devouring him. With her legs locked around his waist, she rocked her hips, desperate for friction to ease the throbbing between her thighs.

Bo understood what she needed because she felt him at her entrance. Anticipation shallowed her breathing, but he didn't push inside. She made a sound of protest in her throat and tried to lower onto his shaft. She'd almost succeeded when his hands gripped her hips, stopping her slide. At the last minute, her eyes flew open.

"Wait," he pleaded on a choked breath. "Condom," he croaked.

Selene thought about the box she'd taken from the cabin. But she had a birth control implant and no desire to stop long enough to retrieve them. "You can come inside me."

Another guttural sound ripped from his chest. "I'm clean, but are you sure?"

She nodded. "I want you to, Bo."

"Damn, ocean-eyes." His lids lowered briefly. "You make me weak."

Not sure what he meant, she was going to ask, but any coherent thoughts fled when he entered her. Pleasure made her arch against him as he filled her. With her head thrown back, enjoying every tingle of her body while he stretched her, she gasped, "God, you feel amazing."

His forehead met hers, his lips pressing hers firmly before he started moving his hips. "So. Do. You." He punctuated each word with a thrust that had her chasing the release burning low in her belly.

She leaned her shoulders against the glass and rode each pump. He started slow, allowing her to watch what looked like wonder cross his features.

But it didn't last long. Her inner walls pulsed with each slide in and out.

Bo's gaze locked on hers, and something sharp

pierced the brown like thunder shaking a tree. His jaw clenched and unclenched before he groaned. "This is going to be fast."

He pressed his thumb against the bundle of nerves at the apex of her thighs, making a wave of ecstasy wash over her. She closed her eyes as he murmured, "But I'll make up for it the second time."

What happened next was pure mating. The animal in him calling to the one in her. Riding on instinct, her nails dug tracks across his back as he slammed into her over and over. The shower partition shook with each meeting of their bodies while the water rained down, feeding the storm that raged between them.

Pleasure built like a roll of thunder each time he hit the perfect spot. Selene couldn't catch her breath enough to speak, but she was so close to finding the bolt of lightning that flashed like her release.

As soon as the sky broke, that lightning speared toward the earth, and she bowed into a curve on a scream of intense gratification. Convulsing with ripples of delight, she lost her grip on Bo as he plunged into her again. He thrust one more time before he bellowed like the animals they'd become and emptied his release in her.

After the storm had cleared from her brain, she became aware of water dripping onto her face. Opening her eyes, she saw Bo hunched over her, his head pressed into the wall, blocking the spray from the shower. Droplets ran down his hair and onto her. His eyes were shut, and his breaths came quick, puffing across her cheeks. Their bodies were still joined, making her smile.

She pressed her mouth to his, and his eyes slowly opened. When she would've dropped her legs, so he didn't have to hold her weight, he shook his head. "Don't move yet."

"Okay." Happy and content to have him inside her as long as he wanted, she tightened her legs around his waist. Lifting her arms around his neck, she pulled herself up and kissed his lips again. "Thank you," she murmured around a smile she couldn't seem to stop her face from forming.

He barked out a laugh. "If anyone should be saying thank you, it's me."

When she chuckled at his response, the mirth on his face disappeared into a groan, and his eyes slid shut. "Don't. Laugh. Too sensitive."

Of course, his struggle made her want to do exactly that. She felt her muscles clench around him with each chuckle she couldn't contain. "Sorry," she squeaked.

With a low growl, he nipped the sensitive peak of one of her nipples and pulled out. She gasped then laughed, lowering her legs. When she stood, wetness trickled down the inside of her thigh.

Bo cupped her face, brushing off the hair that had fallen into her eyes with the spray of water. "Let me wash you."

His soft demand made heat bloom in her chest. She could only nod in response. Every second she spent with this man only made her want him more. She was falling for him whether she wanted to or not.

How was she going to cope when he walked away from her?

* * *

Bo

Bo's nightmare of the suicide bombing four years ago played out in its usual fashion with one notable exception. When he spotted the Tango in Martyr's Square, it wasn't the Afghan woman he faced across the roadway. No, this bomber had Selene's face.

Tears trailed down her cheeks as she begged, "Help me!"

The noise of the busy square faded until the single sound he heard was a ringing in his ears. Desperate to change the outcome of the dream, he charged forward only to be thrown backwards as the bomb went off and Selene disappeared.

"Nooooooo!" Bo's yell ripped his mind from sleep as he shot upright in the hotel bed.

His heart raced with adrenaline, sweat slicked his skin, and he couldn't catch his breath. Pain mixed with panic. His leg was on fire, but that's not what concerned him.

Where's Selene?

His eyes blurred. He could see nothing in the blackness of their room.

"Bo!" Selene's hands cupped his face.

He gripped her wrists and croaked, "Turn on the light." He needed to see her. To verify she was unharmed and prove the nightmare wasn't real.

Light from the bathroom flooded the room, washing over the bed. He'd scooted to the edge, and when she turned on the lamp beside it, she knelt in front of him. "Are you okay?"

He couldn't speak. He raked his gaze over her body. She was still naked. They'd ordered room service, then fallen asleep after he'd taken his time making love to her in the bed.

He'd never done that before—made love. But it was exactly what they did. It was so much more than fucking, than chasing mutual release. Not that he didn't enjoy the hell out of making her come, but his getting off was secondary. She stirred something in him that made him want to give her everything she needed and more. How the fuck was he supposed to let her walk into danger and even worse, walk away?

As if the emotional pain connected to the physical torture from his nightmare, the burning moved into his gut and then his chest.

Unhurt.

When his mind registered that Selene was in one piece, he wrapped his arms around her and pulled her close. Holding her, his whole body shuddered with relief, and the burning subsided.

She returned his hug, her hands caressing his back in slow, soothing circles. "What was it?"

He didn't want to think about his nightmare. Couldn't entertain the idea that he wouldn't be able to save her. If he did . . .

Fresh sweat broke out on his skin, and he swallowed hard.

I can't lose her.

If anything happened to her, he didn't think he'd come back from that. The pit in his chest would swallow him whole. Before Selene, he'd been merely existing, not even surviving. Each day had been a struggle to keep his head from sinking into the cloying pool of guilt and misery. But she'd given him a reason to live. If Dao took that away . . .

"You won't lose me."

Fuck, had he said that aloud? Hoping she'd let it go, he closed his eyes.

Selene reached up and tilted his face to hers. "Look at me, Bo."

She wasn't supposed to know how he felt because it didn't change things. He would still walk away as soon as she was safe from Dao.

Because he was broken, his nightmare proved that.

Nugg's death might not have been his fault, but it didn't change the fact that he'd lived, and his friend hadn't. Wincing at the stab of pain that truth brought him, he obeyed her, lifting his lids to gaze into her gray-green depths.

The swirl of colors was a mesmerizing blend of warmth and resolve as she said, "We're making it through this, okay?"

She would. Even if he had to die to make it happen. He nodded. "I'll make sure you're safe."

A tiny frown clouded her gaze as if she understood that he hadn't agreed he'd survive—only her. When she opened her mouth to protest, he kissed her.

It was gentle. Meant to soothe as much as distract. Her lips against his never failed to make his heart beat faster as if he knew in touching her, he was taking a risk. Like handling a grenade. She was just as fragile and just as deadly. At least when it came to his heart, because that thing had been under siege since the moment she crashed into his cabin.

Cupping her face, he deepened the kiss. She answered with a soft, throaty sound, making his blood flow south. Lying back on the bed, he pulled her with him, or he would have if she hadn't resisted with a gentle tug against his hands.

Worried, he sat up. "What is it, ocean-eyes?"

Though her gaze remained serious, a soft smile warmed her lips. "It's my turn to make you forget."

He wasn't sure what she meant until she knelt between his legs.

Oh, fuck.

Excitement flushed through his veins. If she wanted to give him a blowjob, he wouldn't deny her. Not when he'd imagined his dick in her mouth too many times to count. Just thinking about it made him rock hard.

She made a hum of approval then traced his length

with a finger. When she ran it over the tip, he jerked with a curse. The teasing smile she shot him in response made him grip the bedcovers in his fists to keep from reaching for her.

"Can I tell you something, Bo?" she asked the question as her hand encircled the base of his cock and squeezed.

He bit back a groan and asked, "What?"

She bent her head and placed a wet kiss on the top of his shaft. "I like the way you smell."

Damn, she was a tease. He liked it—a lot.

"Yeah? Well, I like the way you taste."

She smiled at his reply and lowered her mouth.

This was it. She was going to—

A growl of pleasure tore from his throat as soon as she took him into her mouth. "That feels fucking amazing," he panted as she swirled her tongue over his throbbing flesh.

When her cheeks hollowed out as she sucked him to the back of her throat, his eyes wanted to roll back in his head. "Oh fuck."

She murmured in agreement around her hold on him, and the vibrations traveled through his body. His lids half lowered, but he didn't unlock his gaze from the sight of her pleasuring him. It was too fucking perfect. If he died in this moment, he'd die a happy man.

With her hand and mouth working him in tandem, he felt his release hovering close. As much as he wanted it, he wanted to come inside her more. To give her what she'd given him. A moment where he didn't have to think about the past or their uncertain future. Where they could exist in the pleasure of the here and now.

"Selene, wait," he rasped. Brushing a hand through her hair, he gripped her nape. "I want to come inside you."

She gave one last long pull, then released him with a pop that had him grunting with need. Tugging her into a standing position, he slowly slid his hands up her rounded hips, across her ribs, until he cupped her heavy breasts. He teased her with his thumbs until her breathing quickened. Thrilled at the arousal glowing on her olive skin, he captured one then the other, working the golden buds with his mouth.

When she was squirming, whimpering with need, he released her, then trailed a finger down her body until he met her folds. "Are you wet for me?"

"Yes!" she cried out with hungry desperation as he pierced her heat.

When she clenched around his finger, he growled, "Good girl."

"Bo, please," she whined, clutching at his shoulders.

He was more than ready to give her what she needed. Gripping her hips, he coaxed her onto his lap. "Take me in, beautiful."

When she did, he lowered his head to her shoulder and just breathed for a minute. It might be better if he died protecting her tomorrow. Because living and knowing he'd never feel this again . . . it'd be worse than torture.

Her soft palms touched either side of his head. "Bo, what's wrong?"

Fuck, he was ruining this. Shaking his head, he cleared any thoughts but her and bringing her to the peak from his mind. Lifting his head, he captured her mouth and urged her hips to move. The sounds she made as she rode him were nearly his undoing. Freeing her mouth, he twisted, pulling her underneath him.

Her hands roamed freely over his chest, arms, and back. Everywhere she touched left an imprint, searing into his memory. Gripping her leg, he placed it over his shoulder. She arched, her eyes closing on a groan of pleasure at the new angle. "Oh, God. I'm close."

He was, too. Reaching between them, he added pressure with his thumb while he drove into her. "Look at me, Selene."

She moaned but met his gaze. He wanted to fall into those sea-green depths and stay, trapped in a storm he never wished to escape.

"Come with me," he demanded, half begging, half already gone and hoping she'd follow.

When she screamed his name, his release rocked him like a squall, exploding over him in a powerful wave that sapped the strength from his arms. He collapsed onto her, his head nestled by her breasts as his lungs gasped for air.

He rolled when he'd caught his breath, pulling her

into his side. Her hair was a dark tangle over her face, her breaths shifting strands of it as she huffed in air. He pushed it from her eyes, tucking it behind her ear. Bending, he kissed the top of her head.

She sighed as he ran a hand up and down her back. "Sleep," he murmured.

When she placed her hand on his chest, he covered it with his own. His heart flopped around in its cavity, angry at his decisions. He closed his eyes, hoping sleep would come and shut it up.

Holding her, he wished the hours would slow, for the night to last so he wouldn't have to face tomorrow and his decision to walk away from her. A part of him knew it would be what was best for her, but he couldn't help wondering . . .

What would happen if I didn't?

CHAPTER 19

Selene

Something rattled and buzzed near Selene's head. Her first thought was to ignore whatever it was as she basked in the comforting warmth of the body wrapped around hers. When the sound didn't stop, she cracked an eye open, not fully awake. The black burner phone from Mr. Dao vibrated, the screen lighting up, as it moved across the white marble top of the circular nightstand next to the bed in her and Bo's hotel room.

Dread spiked in her stomach, and her head cleared. Judging by the soft orange light filtering through the sheer panels over the window, dawn was coming. Still, she wanted more time. More snuggling, more kissing, more *everything* with Bo before she had to face the reality of her situation. The danger they'd meet today.

Bo was big spoon to her little, and from the even rise and fall of his chest against her back, he slept deeply. Knowing she couldn't put it off, she reached for the phone, careful not to disturb him.

Mr. Dao hadn't called. He'd sent her text messages in standard written Chinese instead. As she read them, a skitter of fear traveled down her back, and she gulped, clutching the phone in her fist.

He knows about Bo.

Mr. Dao had told her to ensure she came alone. To leave her 'janitor friend' behind, or their deal would be off.

Selene forced herself to take a deep breath. It wasn't like she trusted Mr. Dao to keep their deal anyway. He wanted her dead, but he wanted the microchip more. Whether Bo went to the meetup with her or not wouldn't make much of a difference. That's why they had to use this opportunity to . . . she stuttered over the thought.

To kill him.

Closing her eyes, she shook it from her mind. She couldn't focus on that. Getting rid of Mr. Dao was the only way she'd get her life back, wasn't it? When doubts plagued her, she chewed her lip. If she were going to get through this, she had to remember her parents and her need to ensure they were safe.

Nerves caused her body to buzz with restless energy. There was no way she'd get back to sleep now. Setting the phone on the nightstand, she rolled, trying to get out from under Bo's arm, but her movement made him clutch her tighter.

"Nrhmm," he mumbled incoherently.

It would've made her chuckle if Mr. Dao's message hadn't set her on edge. She tried to sit up, and Bo's arm pulled her back down. With a sigh, she twisted to face him. His rugged features were relaxed, still half asleep. A soft smile tilted the corners of his lips up. His eyes remained closed.

She lifted a hand to his chest, laying it over his heart. "Bo, I have to get up," she whispered.

"Stay, ocean-eyes." He tried to nuzzle into her hair, but since she'd turned around, his forehead met her collarbone. A sound rumbled from his throat, then he started kissing and sucking at her skin, sending ripples of pleasure across her senses.

Which only made her feel worse. Because this night they'd stolen was a fantasy. Real life knocked at the door. When tears sprang to her eyes, she tried to blink them away. She wanted to stay in this bed with Bo more than anything, but it was time to confront the future. "Mr. Dao texted."

Bo's eyes shot open. With an angry growl, he asked, "When?"

He wanted to know how long they had left. It wasn't long enough. "Noon." Only a few short hours from now. Her heart squeezed, and she had to swallow before continuing, "He wants to meet at noon." Bo's arms tightened around her as if noon were too soon. She sighed as disappointed as he seemed. "He told me to come alone. To leave *you*. He must've seen you helping me at Saber Tech."

A deep frown line marred Bo's forehead. "Yeah, or

Felix told him before . . ." he trailed off with a wince as if sorry he'd reminded her. "Uh, because Yumi said she'd scrub the footage."

Worry for her friend stirred in her gut. "I need to see if she's called or texted."

Bo gave a slight nod. "And I need to tell Victor about Dao."

Despite their assertions, neither moved. Her limbs felt heavy, weighed down with sadness. It must've shown on her face because Bo's eyes lost their hard edge. He lifted a hand toward her and traced the mole by her right eyebrow. "Don't be sad, ocean-eyes. You'll have your life back."

She wasn't sure that's what she wanted if it meant he wouldn't be in it. But she'd told him she wouldn't ask for forever.

Stupid, Selene!

Because that was what she wanted. Forever with him. The tears she'd been fighting sprang free and spilled down her cheeks.

Alarm widened his eyes, and he swiped at the droplets with his thumbs. "Don't cry, beautiful. It'll all be over soon," he crooned in his gruff voice.

His statement made her feel worse. A noisy sob shook her chest and scratched up her throat. Bo rubbed her back, pulling her closer while murmuring soft words she was too full of anguish to comprehend.

"Don't leave me!" The words rushed from her throat on a keening gasp. She hadn't meant to say them, but they were out now, polluting the air with her desperation and fear. Not of Mr. Dao, but of Bo walking away from her for good.

He went stiff next to her, then she heard him draw in a ragged breath before he rolled away. She sat up when he stood from the bed. He croaked with his back to her, "I can't, Selene. I'm sorry."

The heart she hadn't meant to give him cracked down the middle like a tree struck by a powerful bolt of lightning. Scorched and broken, she whispered, "Yes, you can, but you won't."

His shoulders slumped, but all he said was, "We'll talk about it later. Right now, we need to get TOP together."

"Fine," she answered, though he didn't wait for her response. He disappeared into the bathroom, so she pulled herself from the bed. The tears had dried up. They were pointless anyway. Bo had made up his mind, and what she felt didn't matter. She got dressed in a fog of misery.

When he exited the bathroom, she sat on the bed, staring out the window. She didn't even turn as he said, "Meet me at Victor's room in ten."

"Okay."

Footsteps moved in her direction, then stopped. She waited, but they retreated. The sound of the room door closing behind Bo widened the crack in her heart a little more. With a sigh, she pushed to her feet and headed for the bathroom.

After making herself ready, she grabbed the phone from Mr. Dao and her TOP burner. Remembering her need to hear from Yumi, she checked for messages. There were none. Worrying her lip, she dialed her friend's number. It rang and rang until the voicemail recording came on. Instead of leaving a message, Selene hung up and texted Yumi.

Selene: Are you okay? Did you find what we were looking for?

She didn't get a response right away and realized that, as early as it was in Montana, her friend was probably still asleep. Hopefully, the agent would get back to her before the meeting with Mr. Dao.

A chill washed over Selene, stopping her stride from the room. She didn't know if it was worry over Yumi or herself. Trying to shake off the unease, she exited, tightly closing the door behind her.

No turning back now.

She drew in a deep breath and headed for Victor's room.

* * *

Bo

Victor answered the door after one knock. The man didn't look the least bit groggy. *Had he even slept?*

"Frogman," he greeted Bo with a head lift, stepping aside to let him in.

As team leader, Victor had a suite. The door

opened onto a living room with a deep blue velvet "L"-shaped couch. Behind it sat the king-size bed that had been meticulously remade—or never slept in. A four-person round dining table took up the corner of the room immediately behind the couch, with a chandelier resembling an exploding star hanging above it. A gilded mirror, the height of the wall, hung opposite the window along the right side of the room. It reflected the first rays of morning sunshine that pierced the panes, keeping the room from being too dark.

Bo walked into the sitting area and sat on the corner of the couch when Victor waved for him to take a seat.

"We have contact?"

Bo scrubbed his hands over his face, regretting not getting coffee before heading up here. "Yeah. Noon."

Victor crossed his arms and leaned against the wall opposite Bo's seat. "Where?"

Bo huffed out air in a derisive laugh. He didn't fucking know where Dao wanted to meet because he'd run out of the room like a coward. He hadn't thought of the details, only the need to escape, so he wouldn't have to see the hurt and disappointment on Selene's face. "Selene can tell us when she gets here."

Victor's voice broke through the nasty pot of emotions stewing in Bo's gut. "You fucked it up, didn't you?"

He blinked at his team lead. "What?"

"Things with Selene."

"Yeah." Bo had to look away from the disapproval

on Victor's face. "I was always going to."

"Maybe. Doesn't mean you can't try and fix it."

He didn't look up at Victor's comment. His hands clenched and unclenched as his skin stretched too tight. He started to feel trapped, but bolting out of there wasn't an option.

Clearing his throat, Bo changed the subject. "Can we focus on the op? The rest of the team needs to get here so we can nail down our plan."

"They're already on the way."

On cue, what could only be Herc's massive hand pounded on the door. Victor opened it, then Herc, Romeo, and Duke filed in. The room suddenly felt too small, but Bo dealt with it because the tantalizing scent of coffee wafted in with the guys. He surged to his feet, snagging a paper cup from the holder Romeo carried.

"Sure, Bo, help yourself," the former SEAL sniggered.

Bo downed a gulp that burned his tongue and cursed. "Thanks," he barked before taking another searing sip. He didn't care that he scalded his mouth. After what he'd done to Selene, he deserved the pain.

When everyone who wanted one had grabbed a coffee, Romeo set the last two cups on the rounded table in front of the couch. Then, he and Duke snagged seats at the dining table.

They'd taken a brown paper bag with them. The smell of baked dough wafted from it, but Bo's stomach roiled, too upset to eat.

Herc sat down, taking up the entire chaise portion of the couch. "Where's Selene?" he asked before shoving a muffin into his mouth, whole.

"She'll be here in a minute." And he wasn't looking forward to facing her.

"Oh." Herc didn't often frown, so when he aimed one at Bo, he knew whatever was coming next wouldn't be good. "You left her alone?"

Dammit all to hell!

He'd left Selene alone when he was supposed to be protecting her. Rage at himself exploded through his veins. Bo shoved to his feet and stormed out of the suite. On his way back to their room, he berated himself over and over. He should've waited outside their door at least. Then he could've had some space, but he'd have known she was safe.

By the time he made it back to their hall, his jaw ached from grinding his teeth. He swiped his card and barged into the room, yelling her name. It took him less than five seconds to see she'd already left. "Fuck!" he cursed himself and headed toward the elevators. Maybe he'd just missed her.

But no one waited in front of the double lifts. He pushed the button to go back up to Victor's floor and tried to think around the beat of his pulse pounding at his temple. How the fuck could he have left her like that? Not only was it his job to protect her, but he fucking loved her.

I'm in love with her.

His chest started to heave in panic as he

acknowledged how he felt.

Where is she? What if Dao has her? What if she left to meet him on her own?

Bo had to find her. If anything happened to Selene, it would be his fault.

When the elevator doors opened, he was ready to bolt inside, but by some miracle, Selene stepped out.

"Hey," she said. "Can you take me to Victor's? I got turned around. All these hallways look the same."

"Fuck me," he mumbled before pulling her into a crushing hug. He closed his eyes as relief crashed into him. Lying his cheek on her head, he breathed in her wildflower scent and stroked her hair. "You scared the shit out of me."

"What?" Her question was a pained squeak, making Bo realize she was stiff in his arms. She hadn't returned his embrace.

His heart withered, collapsing against his rib cage, but he only said, "Nevermind. Let's go."

When they'd stepped inside the elevator together, she moved as far away from him as possible. He knew the distance was his fault but couldn't help feeling slightly bitter at how quickly she'd changed her tune. Less than half an hour ago, she hadn't wanted him to leave, and now, she acted like she couldn't wait for that to happen.

"I texted Yumi, but she's probably asleep," Selene commented without looking at him, breaking the tense silence that hovered between them as thick as humid air.

He only grunted in response. *Is this how things would be now?* When a scowl followed the thought, he pushed everything he felt aside. What mattered was keeping her safe.

Trying not to growl, he said, "You didn't tell me where Dao wanted to meet."

"Oh," she spoke softly, her voice flat. "He gave me the location of a building, 1 Square Phillips."

Bo nodded. "Then our first order of business is scoping the place. Find the weak points in its security and all the modes in and out."

"Okay," was her only response.

The elevator stopped on Victor's floor. As the doors opened, he wanted to keep her from exiting. Pull her into his arms and tell her what his mind screamed at him.

I love you, dammit!

But it didn't matter because their future didn't involve being together. After the op was over, they'd go their separate ways. She could start somewhere new, be happy, and he would be . . . as fucked up as he'd always been.

CHAPTER 20

Selene

Is it physically possible for the heart to explode?

Selene's beat so quickly that she feared it would. On top of that, her hands shook uncontrollably. She balled them into fists and tucked them in her coat pockets to hide the nerves and fear turning her into a hyper-sensitive mess.

The worst part? They hadn't even entered the building yet.

How was she supposed to face Mr. Dao when she couldn't stop trembling enough to step out of the van Duke had "borrowed" from a local florist shop? It was the cover TOP would use to access 1 Square Phillips and stick close to her.

If my heart doesn't burst before I make it inside.

The residential building was the tallest in Montreal, with over sixty floors and seven hundred feet of height. They'd done some digging and found that Mr. Dao owned a penthouse on the sixty-first floor. Not that she had any intention of seeing it. Their meeting was happening in the lobby.

A tremor of fear shook her body, and she gulped in a breath. Maybe she could blame her shaking on the cold. The temperature was barely warmer here than it had been in Montana. Light snow dusted pavement, building tops, and cars everywhere she looked.

"Are you ready, Selene?" Victor's question jarred her focus as someone placed a communications device in her ear.

She was afraid of what would come out of her mouth, so she only nodded. She blinked when Herc's beefy arm filled her vision. He pinned a camera onto the fold of her wool beanie and advised her not to take it off or they'd lose visual.

"O-o-kay," she stuttered, internally cursing herself.

Bo stepped in front of her and leaned in close. Lowering his voice, he asked, "You sure?"

The concern shimmering in his eyes and the strain on his face only made her feel worse. How was she supposed to keep it together when he looked at her like that? After rejecting her, she needed him to be cold, angry, *something* that would make the inevitable separation easier.

If only she didn't love him so much.

Breaking his gaze, she swallowed hard, then managed not to stutter on her answer. "Yes."

Grateful when he didn't say anything else, she

blew out a breath and reminded herself this would be worth it. Soon, Mr. Dao wouldn't be an issue anymore. She'd no longer have a threat to her life hanging over her head. She'd be safe and so would her parents. As much as she didn't want to live in Santa Barbara, she was desperate to fly out there, see her mom and dad, and spend some time wallowing.

Until she got over Bo or figured out what to do with the rest of her life.

"It's go time, people."

Her breathing hitched at Victor's declaration. She blinked rapidly as her vision blurred, but she caught movement as the van's back doors swung open. Bright sunlight streamed in. Bo, Romeo, and Victor disappeared to take up their positions inside the building. Duke would be on aerial surveillance.

When her vision cleared, Herc waited on her. Dressed as a delivery driver and carrying an elaborate bouquet of multi-colored blooms, he would stick closest to her.

Her heart ached as she remembered how Bo argued over that, but Mr. Dao knew his face. Like it or not, he'd been forced to take a backseat. She preferred having Herc by her side because of the way things had fallen apart between her and Bo. She didn't need the messy mix of emotions attached to him, making her any less focused on what she had to do.

When she stepped out of the van, she took it back. The wind chill made Montreal feel even worse than Montana. As if it used the city like its own personal raceway, the wind whipped around corners, cut between towering structures, and whistled like a rocket through narrow alleyways. She gritted her teeth and slammed her eyes shut against the force of its assault.

"He loves you, you know."

"What?" Her eyes flew open wide to stare at Herc.

"Bo's in love with you." He shrugged. "Thought you should know, in case, uh, you know."

Oh, God.

Her eyes watered from the cold or his words, she wasn't sure. Blinking tears back, she shook her head. "It doesn't matter. He still doesn't want a future with me." And depending on how this went, one or both of them could die.

That thought made the shaking worse, and her stomach decided to join the party, roiling and twisting as violently as the rest of her.

Am I going to be sick?

"He thinks he doesn't deserve a future," Herc's soft statement was filled with sympathy, but he hadn't told her anything she wasn't already aware of.

"I know." It dragged a sigh from her lips. Was Herc stalling? How long before the rest of the team wondered where they were?

"So make him believe otherwise." He smiled, encouraging her.

Easier said than done. Hadn't she *been* trying?

Selene shook her head. "Let's get this over with before I throw up or pass out."

He gave her a nod. "You head in first. I'll follow close behind." Reaching up to his ear, he tapped the communication device, making her realize he'd turned it off for their conversation.

But hers hadn't been. She blew out a breath. If she lived through this, then she'd worry about that. Tugging the lapels of her puffer jacket closer together, she tucked her head down and practically ran across the street. The faster she made it out of the wind, the better.

Her feet hurried over the pavement, past two large landscape beds with snow-covered maple trees and half-dead ground cover. The main building towered far above the trees. Its glass construction made it seem like an icicle, reaching for the frosty clouds.

The wind stopped buffeting her as she passed beneath the overhang. Two sets of double glass doors marked the entrance. Pulling open the one on the right, she stepped into the lobby.

Her impression of the space was sleek and modern before two large men flanked her, cutting off her perusal. They wore dark suits as Felix had. The shorter one spoke without making eye contact. "Come with us, Miss Coleman."

"Where's Mr. Dao?" She crossed her arms with the demand, pointedly trying to see beyond the muscle for the man in question. She had no intention of following these dudes anywhere.

"He's waiting on you in the penthouse." The taller one spoke this time.

Shit. That wasn't part of the plan. She took a step backward in a deliberate move to drive home her point. "Well, you can tell him I'll be *waiting on him* right here."

In the silence that followed her demand, the noise of the busy lobby filled her ears. People hustled by them on their way in and out while others spoke loudly on their phones or lounged with computers in the communal spaces marked by unusually shaped chairs and indoor plants.

She recognized Romeo and quickly looked away. He had his laptop open in the lounge, watching the video feed from the camera on her hat. Down here was public—safe. If she went to Dao's private apartment, she'd likely be signing her death warrant.

She knew she was in trouble when the suits glanced at each other. Shorty opened his mouth with a sneer. "That's not how this works."

Sweat broke out on the back of her neck. Trying for nonchalance, she said, "If he wants the tech, he can come down here and get it himself."

This time, they communicated without even a glance. In tandem, they closed in on either side of her, each gripping an arm. The tall one growled, "Make a scene, and Mr. Dao's demonstration happens ahead of schedule."

Her stomach bottomed out, and she gulped. There was no way she'd risk the lives of thousands of people. TOP wasn't going to like this, but she saw no other choice. "No, please. I'll go with you."

With a terse, "Good," they started dragging her toward the bank of elevators.

Her heart went back to trying to hammer its way out of her chest. She gulped in air and prayed the guys had a backup plan. They'd melted into the background. Other than Romeo, she didn't see them, but she knew they were there, watching. One of them would be on Mr. Dao's floor before she made it up there, but still . . . she couldn't ignore the strong sense of foreboding that weighed down her legs.

When the suits shoved her into the elevator, she stumbled toward the back wall. Pushing off the mirrored surface, her eyes widened as the bright bouquet Herc carried filled her vision. She spun around as he squeezed inside.

"Man, glad I caught this. My delivery's already late." He stepped in next to her, his bodybuilder frame making it impossible for the suits to box her in. "Mind hitting 52 for me, ma'am?"

Before she could make her mouth work to respond, Shorty stabbed a finger into the floor Herc had asked for.

As if he had no clue what was going on, Herc kept talking, slowly edging closer until he was between her and the men. "This place is brand new, isn't it? It's my first delivery here. I hear there are penthouses starting on the fifty-fourth floor." Ostensibly, his vision slid to the wall of numbers, but she could tell he watched the suits carefully. "Sixty-one! Is that where you're going? Man, I'd love to see those. What's it like up there?"

When he got no answer, Herc's hand shifted, adjusting the flowers, then a couple of muffled thumps sounded in her ears. The next thing she knew, the two suits had crumpled to the floor.

"What just happened?"

She didn't realize she'd asked the question aloud until Herc said, "Suppresser."

She peeked around his side and swallowed. Each man had a bullet hole in his forehead. Dark red blood dripped from the wounds.

Her stomach roiled again, and she instinctively covered her face, backing away until she hit the wall of the lift. Her legs gave out, and she slumped to the floor.

A large hand squeezed her shoulder. "Deep breaths, Selene."

His comment made her realize how short her inhales were, but she couldn't seem to fill her lungs with enough air. Not when the rest of her was too busy freaking the hell out.

It's not as if she hadn't known TOP would be taking lives today. She just hadn't expected the front-row seat.

"Herc, report." Victor's command knocked the shock from her limbs, and she opened her eyes, pushing to her feet.

She only half heard him relaying what he'd just done because the comms had been quiet until now. Her ear started to buzz with commentary while she tried not to think about the two dead men she was sharing space with.

Duke's cocky tone confirmed, "Four more in the penthouse with Dao. Hey, did you guys know this thing has a private terrace?" He monitored the building through an aerial drone with thermal capabilities. Keeping an eye on things inside and out.

"Yes, because some of us actually looked at the floor plans," Herc spoke over Duke's response after moving the bodies of the two men so they wouldn't be visible when the elevator opened.

"I want one."

"Great, you can put an offer in after Dao's comes on the market." Romeo goaded.

"Lock it up, people," Victor's order made everyone go silent.

Still, Selene wished she'd heard Bo's voice.

Where is he?

The elevator opened on floor fifty-two. Herc cursed, leaping forward to slam the 'door close' button.

Things seemed to be moving in slow-motion for her, so she shook her head and focused on him. "What now?"

"You knock on Dao's door while Romeo takes out the cameras in his hallway. When they open it, we'll go inside together." He gave her a quick smile. "You won't be alone."

"How's that going to work, exactly? They won't let you just waltz in." Herc seemed comfortable making the plan up on the fly, while she was used to weighing and measuring outcomes before taking action.

"That's why you're bait, remember?" He grinned, nudging her with his elbow and almost knocking her over.

When she teetered, he caught her arm. "Sorry," he laughed.

Selene blinked up at Herc, completely dumbfounded at how he could find anything humorous right now. The fáct that he'd just taken two lives didn't seem as if it were even on his radar.

She opened her mouth to ask him how he did that when the elevator stopped, the doors opening with a ding.

"Shit, we have a problem." Duke's voice filled her ear before surprise fuzzed everything out.

"Flowers, Miss Coleman? You really shouldn't have." Mr. Dao stood right outside the elevator doors as if he'd been expecting her. He wore a light gray tunic suit with a Mandarin collar. He tugged at his left sleeve as two more beefy men in dark suits flanked him. One stuck his hand on the jamb, holding the doors open.

Mr. Dao's gaze zeroed in on Herc, but the sociopath seemed unperturbed by the gun in his hand or the dead men on the floor. "First a janitor, now a delivery man." He actually tsked at her. "I told you to come alone. Your inability to follow instructions is making me reconsider my job offer."

Anger heated her skin and left her mouth in a surge of words. "Are you serious? Not five minutes after you offered me the job *and* my life, you sent Felix to kill me!"

Instead of answering her, Dao spoke to his men, "Take that from him." He waved toward Herc's weapon, and her stomach twisted and knotted. Where was the rest of TOP?

To ensure Herc cooperated, the suit holding the door aimed his weapon at her. She noticed Herc glance at the elevator buttons and tense. If he wondered whether he could get the door to close before they got a shot off, he didn't take the chance. With the hardest look she'd yet seen him make, he handed over his weapon.

"Step out of the elevator, Miss Coleman."

"And if I don't?" Maybe if she stalled long enough, another member of TOP would show up to help them.

Mr. Dao actually smiled at that. The smile spoke of how unhinged he was. It said he was delighted by her obstinacy and imagined ways to make her obey.

She had to look away. Fear snaked around her spine, tightening every cell in her body. She gulped as bile rose up her throat.

Please, God, let TOP help us. Now!

A rough hand closed around her arm and dragged her out of the lift. As soon as she was out of the way, Herc lifted one of the bodies as a shield and slammed the close button. She let out a strangled wail as the two suits fired on him. Right before the doors closed, she heard a yelp of pain. Then, he was out of sight.

"One of you deal with that," snarled Mr. Dao.

Please let Herc be okay!

As if in answer to her plea, she heard him in her ear. "I lost Selene. Dao has her on the sixty-first floor."

A series of curses filled her ear as Dao's man, who hadn't gone after Herc, pushed her toward the penthouse.

Victor's clear voice penetrated the profanity. "Injuries, Herc?"

"Graze to the leg. Burns like a mother and messy as hell, but I'll live."

A small wave of relief made her dizzy, and she stumbled only to be jerked forward by the suit's rough hand. "Keep moving, lady."

Where is everyone? Because she could really use some help right now.

She followed Mr. Dao down a carpeted hallway before he turned a corner and stopped outside the door to what she assumed was his penthouse. Feeling his henchman come up behind her, she braced herself for more rough handling.

Thankful when it didn't come, she glanced at the man trailing her. A black bandana with white skulls printed on it covered his head while wraparound sunglasses covered his face. He kept it bent, almost like he didn't want to look at the camera. Her breath hitched when she realized why. He shifted closer, and she caught his familiar mineral and citrus scent.

It's Bo!

Somehow, he'd switched places with the other suit. Though relief flooded her veins to know he was alive and safe, they were hardly out of the woods yet. He gave a slight shake of his head, and she schooled her features to not give him away.

The door opened after Mr. Dao glanced up at the camera in the corner. Bo shoved her through the threshold, but not before giving her arm a solid, reassuring squeeze. The penthouse opened into a cavernous space. She stumbled to a stop, catching herself on a cushioned dining chair. No walls separated the rooms, making it feel larger than it was. Still, it had to be five times the size of Bo's cabin.

To the right, a long metal table demarcated the dining room. On the left, a wall of sleek wood cabinets and a quartz waterfall island marked off the kitchen. Beyond both, a large sectional, matching chairs, and a tan area rug designated the living room. Floor-to-ceiling windows wrapped the entire home in an "L," giving her a panoramic view of Montreal.

Before she was pushed again, she noted the hallway to her left. If she remembered the floor plans correctly, it led to the two bedrooms and bathrooms. By the time she reached the living room, Mr. Dao had sat in one of the chairs across from the half-wall that sported an electric fireplace. Narrow paneling wrapped around it while it flickered with color-changing lights, keeping to the modern vibe the place had going.

"Have a seat, Selene."

She would've remained standing to spite Mr. Dao, but Bo shoved her into the other chair, keeping his back to her former boss. When she was seated, she glared at Mr. Dao.

He leaned back in his chair with a sigh. "Before we discuss what you owe me, let me clarify something for you." He crossed an ankle over one knee. "I didn't send Felix to hurt you. He acted on his own. Well," he shook his head before amending, "not on my orders anyway. Felix was trying to retrieve information on Sentient Shadow for the Russians." The disgust that flared in his eyes had her shrinking back in her seat. "I would gladly have given them the weapon if they won the bid. But to try and steal it? That's bad business." He sighed, managing to sound very put-upon. "Now I have to make an example out of them."

Remembering the Afghan wife he'd used as a suicide bomber, Selene didn't want to ask how he planned to do that.

"Where's the file, Miss Coleman?"

She blinked at his abrupt change of subject. "I don't have it here, but I can show you where it is."

Mr. Dao uncrossed his legs and leaned forward. "I'm tired of being toyed with, Selene. If you don't have the microchip, then you can come with me. I have another appointment in the city this evening." He grinned at her with enough malice to make her blood run cold. "Maybe watching what Sentient Shadow can do will incentivize you to tell me where that file is."

She gasped. Was he planning a demonstration here? Had Yumi been wrong about Taipei?

Before she could ask, his guard—i.e., Bo—yanked her to her feet. Instead of shoving her away, this time he held her close. She tried to remain stiff when her body wanted to lean into him.

Mr. Dao had turned away, but he suddenly spun toward her. The quickness of the movement made her jerk against Bo's hold. "Perhaps there's another form of persuasion we might try."

Her heart skipped a beat, then hammered with the speed of a bullet train at the look on Mr. Dao's face. If she managed to live through this, it would haunt her nightmares for sure.

His eyes moved past her as he said, "I don't believe I've shown you the terrace."

CHAPTER 21

Selene

Considering the below-freezing temperature and that they were 700 feet in the air, Selene would rather *not* see Mr. Dao's terrace. She glanced up at Bo, wondering what the plan was, but she stood too close to read his expression. It made her swallow a groan. Now would be a great time to develop ESP because she had no idea what he wanted her to do.

Dao's voice broke into her thoughts. "If you didn't trust me to hold up my end of the deal, why did you risk coming?" She glanced at him and squirmed. He squinted as if he were trying to see inside her head. "What are you after, Miss Coleman?"

Getting rid of you.

Worried he'd somehow find the reason she couldn't voice, she started to fidget, twisting her hands together and rubbing them against her coat. Why was she sweaty all of a sudden?

When it was clear she wouldn't give him an answer, Mr. Dao scowled. "Take her," he barked the command at Bo with a wave toward the terrace door.

She turned in Bo's grip as he started walking her away. They'd almost reached the door when Mr. Dao yelled, "Stop! Guards!"

Shit! He must've noticed Bo wasn't one of his men for hire.

Selene froze, then stumbled because Bo tried to keep moving, leading her to the terrace.

At the sound of a gun cocking, he muttered under his breath, "Damn it."

"Bo," she whispered, clinging to his arm, terrified and wondering what they would do now.

He glanced at her, the grim expression on his face adding to the fear choking her. "Stay behind me."

Her eyes filled with tears, but she nodded. Then he turned, shielding her as he raised a gun and faced Mr. Dao. She peeked around Bo's arm. Three men had joined the CEO after his shout. All in dark suits and all with weapons trained on Bo. She gulped. Where the hell was TOP?

"Ah, the janitor, wasn't it?" Mr. Dao asked with a creepy smile. "Who are you?"

Romeo's voice filled her ear. "Dao's snakes are crawling all over this fucking building. I'm pinned down. Can someone get to Bo and Selene?"

Everyone on the team responded in the negative, all dealing with the same problem. Her stomach churned, knowing help was *not* on its way. Mr. Dao had more muscle than they'd anticipated.

This is not going well.

She knew Bo heard TOP, too, because his body became even more tense. His shoulders were a taught line, blocking her vision.

When Bo said nothing, Mr. Dao's tone went from conversational to dictatorial. "Move away from her, now."

"Not happening, asshole," Bo growled in response.

"So he does speak." She peeked again and saw Mr. Dao wearing the smile that made her whole body clench with fear. "If you refuse, these men will make you."

"You can shoot me," Bo sneered, "but I'm taking you down with me."

Mr. Dao didn't like that comment because anger twisted his features. "I've had enough of this." He stepped behind one of the men as if he planned to use him as protection from Bo's bullets. "Shoot him," he demanded.

Every cell in her body rebelled at the thought of Bo being shot. No way would she stand there and let that happen. "Wait!" Acting on instinct, she stepped out of Bo's reach.

He glowered at her, but she didn't take her focus off Mr. Dao. Edging toward the terrace door, she said, "This is what you wanted, right? Show me the terrace but leave him alone."

When no one moved, panic stole over her, squeezing the air from her lungs. Desperate, she squeaked out, "Don't hurt him! I'll do whatever you want, just let him go!"

She understood leverage and that she and Bo had none, especially as she'd just given away her feelings for him. But she'd had to do something. If nothing else, her plan was to stall because the rest of TOP would show up eventually. She had to believe that.

Mr. Dao's face held that sinister smile again. "Well, isn't that interesting . . ." His gaze shot to Bo, his demeanor shifting to anger. "Hand over your gun or they'll shoot Selene." To punctuate his threat, one of the suits aimed his pistol at her. The guy's face was stony, his eyes dead. She had no doubt he would shoot her if Mr. Dao told him to.

When Bo relinquished his weapon, she could feel him vibrating with tension. He didn't take his eyes off the man whose gun was trained on her, but she knew he was angry at her. He'd have to deal with it because she refused to let him die for her. Bo deserved to live. To have a life not haunted by his past. Even if that life wasn't with her.

Sadness crept through the fear, trying to smother what was left of her hope.

Two of the suits grabbed Bo's arms, then Mr. Dao turned his attention to her. "Let's finish our tour, Miss Coleman." He glanced at the men restraining Bo and ordered, "Bring him."

As soon as they stepped onto the terrace, the wind stole her breath. It was even stronger up here than on the street. Mr. Dao gripped her arm, and she stiffened, eyes scanning for a way out. The terrace was impressive yet terrifying. Everything had snow dusting it from the slate gray tiles on the ground to the pale patio furniture surrounding a concrete, bowl-shaped outdoor fireplace. She had but a moment to take that in before her gaze locked on the four-foot-tall glass safety wall surrounding it all. You could see right through it. The tops of the other buildings seemed so far away.

When Mr. Dao tugged her to the edge, she had a severe bout of vertigo. She reached out, gripping the top of the glass as the world spun.

"It's a long way down, isn't it, Miss Coleman?" He didn't hide his snicker at her reaction. "A fall from here . . . you'd have plenty of time to think about how much it's going to hurt when you hit the ground."

Oh, God. She clenched her eyes shut, but it didn't stem the nausea rising up her throat. She managed to swallow it down, but dizziness assailed her. That was his plan? To throw her over the ledge.

If she made it off this high rise, she'd gladly never step foot in one again.

Her ears rang, but when she heard Mr. Dao mention Bo's name her eyes flew open, and she struggled to focus on what he was saying, "Until you tell me where the microchip is, I can't toss you over, but him"—he waved at Bo—"he seems like the perfect incentive."

"No, please!" Her breath shallowed out in panic. She didn't have a microchip to give to Mr. Dao. She had nothing to save Bo or herself. Nothing.

"Do it," her boss said to the men already dragging Bo to the ledge.

She tried to run to him to help, but the other henchman grabbed her from behind. His hold was unbreakable. Still, she didn't stop struggling as she watched Bo fighting the other suits.

She gasped when, for a moment, it seemed he would get the upper hand, but then Mr. Dao took the gun from the man imprisoning her. To shoot Bo.

She screamed and fought harder against the man holding her as adrenaline surged in her system. His cursing barely registered, nor did the pain, as he squeezed her hard enough to crack ribs.

The first gunshot seemed to cause time to slow. In horror, she watched Mr. Dao shoot wildly. He managed to hit the glass behind Bo more than anything. One of the suits fell, a bullet leeching the life from his eyes.

Bo still struggled with the other one, and their bodies slammed into the damaged glass. Her heart leapt in her throat as it spiderwebbed, a powerful cracking sound piercing the howling of the wind.

Mr. Dao's laughter echoed all around her as the glass gave way. Bo and the other man tumbled through it.

"BO!" The name tore from her lips in a frantic shout as his body disappeared over the edge of the terrace.

Noooooo!

Tears flooded her eyes and spilled down her cheeks. The remaining suit released her, and she fell to her knees. A powerful, body-shaking sob ripped from her throat. Her heart flopped around in her chest like a fish out of water struggling to breathe because the man who kept it beating was dead.

Bo was dead.

* * *

Bo

The mirror-like finish on the glass building meant Bo could watch himself plummeting to his death. As he fell, the wind roared in his ears, tore at his clothes, and bit at his face. Even if his comms had been working, there was no way the team could've heard him over the powerful rushing noise.

He'd first noticed the damned thing wasn't transmitting, only receiving, after screaming at Selene not to get in the elevator with those two men, and no one responded. He'd nearly ruined the op before it really began by breaking his cover until Herc intervened and squeezed in with her. As if not being next to Selene hadn't been hard enough, the added comms issue had nearly sent him over the edge.

Things went downhill after that—literally, if you counted his current predicament. A laugh burst from his lips only to choke him as air rushed in.

Focus, Bo.

He wrestled against the wind, tugging off the suit jacket he'd borrowed when he'd taken out the mercenary who'd rough-handled Selene. As a SEAL, he'd learned to be prepared for anything. That was why he worked to free the parachute container strapped to his back.

While he struggled, his thoughts raced to how he could've done things differently. The outcomes burned in his gut. He'd followed Dao into the penthouse without a clear plan, waiting for an opportunity to get rid of the bastard. He hadn't wanted to chance taking out Dao in the living room and having the rest of the men in the apartment coming after him and Selene. Not before he could get her out of there and the rest of his team arrived.

He couldn't risk it with her in the crossfire, but he'd screwed up not taking the chance when he'd had it. He'd been ready to lock her on the terrace while he took care of business, but then the whole thing became a goatfuck.

Because now, she was up there alone with that sociopath, and he had no way to tell TOP. Someone better get their ass in there and fast. He trusted his team, but worrying they wouldn't make it to her in time almost made him lose focus.

Dao won't kill her.

Bo soothed himself by repeating it. As long as Dao thought she had a file with information on Sentient Shadow hidden somewhere, he'd keep her alive to find it.

When he was out of the jacket, he let the wind rip it from his hands. Bo blinked watery eyes. The objects on the ground were starting to look bigger. With a curse, he pulled his BASE-jumping chute and braced himself as it jerked, slowing his descent.

The whole process had taken a matter of seconds, but he'd had precious few left before he would've become a splatter on the ground. Where a month ago he might've hoped his parachute didn't open, now, all he could think about was staying alive—for Selene.

Gritting his teeth, Bo fought to steer against the power of the wind. When he nearly smacked into the side of the building, he let out a slew of curses worthy of a sailor.

"This isn't how it ends for you."

Bo blinked to find Nugg floating down next to him, dressed in a wingsuit. Despite not having his chute open, he fell at the same rate.

"I fucking hope not," Bo muttered.

Nugg sighed. "But you gotta let me go, man. Go live the life you deserve. Hell, go live it for the both of us."

The words resonated through Bo, making something powerful shift in his chest. Maybe it was the fall, but he felt as light as a leaf spiraling in an air current. "I know." He smiled sadly at Nugg. "Catch you on the flipside."

Nugg grinned back. "She's worth it, man."

Before he could respond, Nugg pulled his parachute and disappeared. Bo knew Selene was worth facing his demons for, and if he lived through this, he'd make sure she knew that he knew it, too.

He'd beg her for another chance because there was no way in hell he'd be able to walk away from her. Thinking he could was not only stupid, it was cowardly.

She'd risked her life for him. He might have wanted to strangle her for it, but if he needed a sign that what they had was worth living for, that was it. He wouldn't throw it away. Not if he could help it.

He might not deserve her, but he would damn well spend the rest of his life trying to. If she let him, he'd spend every day working to be worthy, to be a better version of himself, for her. He'd even see a counselor if that was what she wanted. Anything to help him cope with his past so he could have a future with her.

He loved her enough to try.

No. To hope.

That he could heal.

Glancing past his feet, Bo aimed for the avenue between the buildings. Thankfully, there weren't any trees on this side. There were a lot of people, though, crowded around what he could only assume was the body of the man who'd fallen off the roof with him. At least the crowd had stopped traffic.

Bo's boots hit asphalt, and he stumbled to a rough stop that shot pain up his left leg before the wind grabbed the chute, face-planting him hard enough to knock the breath from his lungs.

Fucking A!

Car horns and sirens blared around him as he

rolled to his back, trying to get air in. The blue and yellow colors of the parachute ballooned above his face, filtering the afternoon sunlight. When he could breathe, he took stock of his body. He didn't think he'd broken anything.

Then get your ass up there!

Concerned voices reached his ears, but his sole focus was getting back to Selene. He snapped off the rig, extricated himself from the chute, then ran into the building straight for the elevators. Waiting for one to open, he tried listening for his team, only to realize his comms device had come out in the fall.

Motherfucker!

Now he was deaf as well as blind.

Palming his SRK, he slammed his finger on the elevator button again. When he was ready to give up and run up sixty flights of stairs, the damned thing opened.

"Holy shit, frogman," Victor breathed, eyes widening. He and Romeo both held up a despondent Selene.

At the sight of her, his chest squeezed so tight he had to croak, "Is she okay?"

Her head snapped up at his voice. "Bo! Oh my God, Bo!" Selene ran out of the elevator and plowed into him.

He hugged her, catching her weight as she collapsed into his arms. She was crying and trembling so violently that he wanted to panic. He tried to run his hands over her to check for injuries, but her legs didn't hold her weight. Scooping her up, he held her bridal-style while looking to his team for answers.

"Dao?" Just saying the man's name made him glower.

"Eliminated," Victor stated.

Bo nodded. He'd wanted to be the one to end that fucker, but knowing he was gone gave him a measure of peace.

Romeo had a huge grin on his face. "Don't worry, Bo-man. We cleaned house."

"Let's move this reunion to the van before the local authorities show up," Victor directed, and led the way outside.

Bo followed, carrying Selene while Romeo brought up the rear. She'd stopped crying by the time they reached the florist van, but he could still feel her body shaking. The door swung out, revealing Herc inside, sitting with his leg elevated. Romeo hopped in while Victor took shotgun.

With a nod to his team, Bo shut the door without getting inside. "Can you stand, ocean-eyes?" he asked, desperate to set her on her feet and get a good look at her to ensure she was all right.

She nodded, so he let her down, but didn't release her arms. Those beautiful eyes met his and took his breath away. "How," she whispered, "how are you alive?"

Tears still glistened on her cheeks. He cupped her face, wiping them away with his thumbs. "I had a parachute. For BASE jumping."

She blinked at him a couple of times, then a laugh bubbled out of her mouth. "Just in case?" she asked before her laughter intensified, sounding hysterical.

Releasing her face, he ran his hands over her body, checking for injuries. He didn't see any blood, but he had to be sure.

She finally stopped laughing. "What are you doing?"

He cupped his hands around her waist. "You're not hurt?"

"No." She took a deep breath and ran a hand over her heart. "Not anymore. God, Bo. When I thought . . ." Her eyes filled as she trailed off.

"Shh, don't cry, ocean-eyes," he begged, brushing the hair from her face.

Her eyes were shiny but fierce as she said, "I love you, Bo."

His heart somersaulted as his chest filled with warmth. A smile stretched across his lips before he huffed out a laugh and pulled her lips to his own.

She tasted warm like the hope shining in his heart. Her soft sigh of contentment as their tongues twined flooded him with relief.

She was safe, and she was his.

He released her mouth. Lifting her against his chest, he squeezed her and told her, "I love you, too. And if you're willing to let me, I'll stay. I don't want to leave your side. Not now, not ever."

The smile on her face stole his breath. Setting her down, he lowered his forehead to hers. "You're my rainbow," he murmured.

He might've been fighting against the waves of a storm for the last few years, but she'd thrown him a life preserver and pulled him to dry land. The deluge had stopped, allowing the sunlight to shine through and create a beautiful, ocean-eyed rainbow.

"That's all I want." She cupped his face, her hands gentle against the scrape of his beard. "Forever with you."

Forever didn't scare him anymore. It didn't fill him with guilt or anger. Not when he couldn't face the alternative—not having her in his life. Taking her hand, he kissed her palm, promising, "Forever."

The van doors flew open, nearly hitting them. Duke yelled from the driver's seat, "As touching as this is, it's time to go, love birds."

Selene touched the comms device in her ear and giggled. It was adorable. "Oops."

When they climbed inside, everyone started to rib or congratulate him. For once, Duke's jabs didn't get on his nerves. Nothing they said could touch him. Not while he had the best part of his life snuggled in his arms. He didn't know if he'd ever been this happy. His chest had certainly never felt so warm. The pit lingered, but the sun shone on it, keeping the gloom at bay.

He hugged Selene to his side and nodded to Herc. "Glad you're not dead."

Herc's grin took in him and Selene, then he shifted with a wince, and Bo met him halfway, releasing

Selene to slap Herc on the back as they quickly hugged. "Likewise, man." The hug didn't just mean 'glad you made it out of there with only a graze.' It also conveyed his thanks to Herc for protecting the woman he loved.

Romeo said something in Spanish that Bo didn't catch, but Selene glanced at the SEAL and smiled, responding in the same language.

When Bo sat down, he pulled her close again and asked, "What did he say?"

Her head rested on his shoulder, so he felt the smile spread across her face. "Love is a rainbow with gold at both ends."

"What is that? A Spanish proverb?"

She chuckled. "I think it's a Romeo proverb."

"Yeah? Well, I don't need gold. I just need you." He kissed the top of her head, and her wildflower scent wafted over him. He was going to buy a case of her shampoo and shower with her every day. His blood stirred just thinking about it.

"Lucky for you, you have me." She lifted their joined hands and kissed the back of his.

He *was* lucky. Lucky to be alive. Lucky to have found her. Lucky to have a second shot at living. He'd spend the rest of his days being grateful for that.

She squeezed the hand she gripped. "I found my next adventure, Bo. It's you."

Words of love filled his heart. Before he could spout them at her, something vibrated against his leg. He grumbled when Selene shifted away, reaching into her pants pocket for her phone. "What is it?" he asked, trying to read the text.

"It's Yumi." Her head lifted to meet the stares of his team. "She found the servers."

CHAPTER 22

Sixteen Hours Earlier

Yumi

Yumi had gone dark. She didn't know whom to trust after her last conversation with her case officer. Other than Selene—the one friend she knew wouldn't stab her in the back or ever trade her loyalty. The night Dao had tried to kill her, Yumi had been sent on a wild-goose chase. After that, she'd blown up at her immediate superior over the agency's lackadaisical attitude regarding Selene's safety. Then, they'd fed her erroneous intel about Taipei, and when her case officer told her to retrieve the AI model, she'd sealed her fate by refusing.

Her life had become a sad state of affairs. Too many people wanted her dead, and that list would multiply after tonight.

When she destroyed Sentient Shadow.

She snorted, disgusted with herself. For the pity

party she seemed to be throwing, and for the alarm she'd nearly tripped.

Find your calm. Be like the water.

She cautioned herself as she stepped out of view of the guard she'd almost missed. Checking for an alternate route, she backtracked. For once, the water in her mind wasn't calm. It rippled with waves and crashed against the shore of a lake during a thunderstorm. She'd given the agency ten years of her life, and they'd turned their backs on her in an instant.

The CIA wanted Sentient Shadow. She refused to deliver it.

It would only be a matter of time before they sent someone in her place who didn't realize that anyone possessing that kind of weapon was a catastrophic idea.

World War III? Nuclear Armageddon?

Those were only a fraction of the potential horrors weaponized AI could produce.

Years of training meant she managed to keep the scowl from her face as she traversed the east wing of the Chinese Embassy in D.C. She nodded and smiled as she passed through the sea of people.

The embassy was hosting a cultural event that included traditional Chinese musicians, performers, and artwork. All were on display throughout the main visitors' spaces in the building. Their colors drew the eye in what was a naturally neutral design scheme. The muted French limestone on the walls seemed to bounce the lights and sounds of the celebration.

But she wasn't here for that. What Yumi sought lived in the basement.

Weaving past an ancient jade vessel, she kept her face down, away from the cameras in the ceiling. Like many in attendance, she wore red. Her dress was a bright, floor-length number with a slit up the left side. She would've stood out in any other environment, but tonight she blended in. Red flashed everywhere you looked. On the servers' vests, the performers' costumes, many of the women's dresses, and even the carpet under her feet.

She made a point of moving slowly, as if she were merely another visitor admiring the delights the embassy offered. When she reached the staircase to the lower level, her pulse kicked up, but no one stopped her descent. She gripped the metal railing softly, eyes flickering to the Chinese pine beyond the window wall that framed the stairs. Its evergreen boughs embraced an outdoor garden while moonbeams glanced off the needles. It was after eight p.m., and the sun had long set.

She took another step, then stopped, her skin prickling with awareness. Scanning the glass, she searched for who was watching her. In its reflection, her eyes caught on a tall, dark-haired man in the room above, whose shaven face sent a shock of desire burning through her. When he smiled, she dragged her gaze away from his tailor-cut dark suit and red tie, shaking off the strange pull she felt. She didn't have time for whoever that handsome stranger was.

Another step, and she took note of the camera in the corner. Averting her gaze from its lens, she pretended to brush lint off her gown. Putting the intriguing man from her mind, she continued. The stairs wrapped around to reveal a candle fountain at the bottom of the last flight. It gurgled quietly, a backdrop to the Chinese mandolin playing upstairs.

She swept her gaze across the room when she reached the lower floor. Fewer people had ventured down here yet, but the area was still open to visitors.

What Yumi was after hid another level lower.

She wandered past the Confucius Room, where a small crowd had gathered around a young Chinese diplomat as he explained the story behind the artwork decorating the walls. Her head shifted toward the sound of laughter. It bubbled out of the grand ballroom. Stepping inside the large open space, she smiled at the sheer volume of people. The number could easily create chaos, should she need it to escape.

She hoped her plan went smoothly, though, and she wouldn't need to set off the fire alarms—her backup. On the stage at the back of the room, Chinese performers acted out a play she had no time to indulge in. Hugging the blonde-wood wall, she kept her eyes on the geometric patterns in the floor, counting carefully until she reached the right spot.

Pausing, she took a moment to steady her breathing and sense if she was being watched. The door she planned to open remained out of view of the cameras in the room. She was more worried about being followed. When she verified she was in the clear, Yumi trailed her fingers along the paneled wall until she felt a groove. Pressing the lever she'd located, the door that had been hidden behind a hanging tapestry slid aside. Before anyone noticed, she slipped through, quickly shutting it behind her.

The hallway she entered was narrow and dark. She turned on her phone's flashlight to illuminate her path. The passage was a failsafe, a safety measure for the ambassador should he ever need it. From the schematics she'd studied, it branched into multiple tunnels leading to the building's lower levels, a safe room in case of a nuclear attack, or a little-known exit onto Van Ness Street. Judging by the stale air, no one had been in it in a long time.

Yumi trudged forward, trying not to sneeze as her nose twitched in revolt against the trapped particles of dust or who knew what. The easy part of the job was done. Where she ventured now, no guests were allowed to go. The server room was bound to be guarded when she reached it. She had to be on her game. The hallway came to a fork, and she branched off into the tunnel on the right. It would lead her directly to the servers.

When her light gleamed off a red door, she knew she'd found it.

Where are the guards?

Her eyes searched the blackness beyond the reach

of her phone while her ears strained for any movement. But there was nothing. Wary, her heart tripped into overtime.

She lifted her phone toward the digital lock when she reached the door. Using the bypass app she'd created, she had it unlocked in two-point-five seconds. Grinning at how easily they'd made it to access the room, she slipped her folding tanto blade from the holster on her right thigh. Gripping it in her free hand, she stowed her phone into the bust of her dress.

Yumi expected a guard inside since there'd been none at the door. Preparing for that, she turned the handle slowly so as not to draw attention. After she pried the door open just enough to squeeze through, she slipped inside. The room had been dark, but as soon as she took a step, a series of lights on the ceiling lit in succession, triggered by her movement. She cursed and jumped behind a rack of servers, ears straining. She'd already noted the camera in the ceiling and prayed it hadn't caught her entrance.

Adrenaline coursed through her veins, and her pulse raced with each pump of her heart. The room was one big open space, but row after row of server racks gave her cover to hide behind. She heard no footsteps. There was no sign that anyone had noticed her.

That's strange.

Frowning, she kept to the shadows cast by the eight-foot-tall racks. Green lights flickered on the drives in each one while cables in various colors snaked out of them like some kind of computer monster. Each row stretched twenty feet, but the individual racks were only three feet wide. She needed the third one on the seventh row.

As she crept toward it, she counted to ensure she ended up at the right one. When she reached number seven, she turned down the row and froze.

She was not alone.

Damn, this job just got harder.

A svelte blond man stood in front of the rack she needed. If she had to guess, she'd bet the agency had sent him. A guard slumped at his feet, either dead or unconscious. He must have taken care of the cameras, too, or else they'd have company by now.

She stepped forward, and the blond's head jerked in her direction when he sensed her movement. A slow smile spread across his face. He didn't shift his position as she kept advancing, but she detected the coiled tension in his body.

Holding her blade by her side, she asked, "What are you doing?"

"Yumi Nakano, I presume?" He quirked a brow at her.

She wasn't about to confirm that. "Answer my question first."

He smirked and shifted his weight. Her gaze caught on the knife he'd just pulled on her. Though the blade was a different shape from hers, it was the same length and just as deadly. "Should we do this the hard way or the easy way?"

Internally, she sighed. She'd hoped she wouldn't have to ruin this dress. "Step away from that server."

"The hard way, then," he taunted with a grin and lunged for her.

Expecting his move, she easily dodged the swipe he made at her, spinning in her high heels to keep him in her sight. Physically, he had the advantage in height and reach. If she wanted to survive this, she'd have to disarm him. When he lunged again, she gripped his arm and used it to toss him over her body.

She spun as he hit the concrete floor, his breath pushed from his lungs in a painful-sounding expulsion. While he lay stunned, she put her stiletto to use, stabbing it through the fleshy part of his hand and forcing him to drop the knife. With her other foot, she kicked the weapon away.

She didn't have time to celebrate that fact because she'd severely pissed the guy off. He ripped his hand away and jumped to his feet with a roar. Then he launched himself at her, throwing punches she had to work hard to block. Each time he connected with the outside of her arms, she felt the force of it reverberate through her bones. If she lived through this, she'd be sore tomorrow.

On the defensive, she didn't have an opening to use her blade. He'd nearly pushed her back to the wall. Wanting to avoid getting stuck, she tucked her shoulder and rolled forward.

Coming up behind him, she struck with her tanto

before he even had a chance to turn. She'd aimed for his kidney. Maybe he'd live, maybe he wouldn't.

As he dropped to his knees then tumbled forward, she tried not to think about the blood pooling underneath him. The important thing was that he wouldn't be coming after her. Using his dark suit jacket to clean off her blade, she strapped it back to her thigh.

Steeling herself, she checked the guard slumped in front of the server that held Sentient Shadow for a pulse. Nothing beat beneath the skin at his neck. He was dead. Shifting her focus, she pulled a cord from her holster. With it, she connected her phone to the drive and started to overwrite Sentient Shadow. The program she used would replace the entirety of the AI model with random ones and zeroes five separate times.

It was the surest method to ensure the weapon's destruction without physically destroying the server. An option she'd considered, but one that would draw way too much attention. What she was doing would render Sentient Shadow unreadable—useless. For good measure, she encrypted the overwritten information so that no one could access it.

It was an encryption of her own making. Only she had the key, and she planned to destroy that for redundancy's sake. If she were lucky, it would take Dao a while to realize the AI model had been tampered with. Although . . . she glanced at the blond man who was groaning and bleeding out on the floor. His presence would set off alarms.

With a sigh, she finished the encryption and disconnected from the server. The best she could hope for was to make it out of the embassy before that happened.

With that aim in mind, she stowed her equipment. The quickest way out of the room was to walk by the man she'd incapacitated. Giving him as wide a berth as she could in the narrow path between rows, she began to scoot past when she sensed movement from him.

Before she could react, a burn scorched across her leg. She hissed in pain. The man had found the knife she'd kicked and used it to slice her leg through the slit in her dress. Enraged, she dropped to one knee, grabbed the weapon from his weakened grip before he could use it on her again, and plunged it through his neck.

Gasping, she crawled away from him. When she was far enough to be comfortable, she took stock of her injury.

There was a deep gash in the back of her right calf. Knowing it would leave a blood trail, she ripped the ruffled trim off the bodice of her dress and wrapped it around her lower leg. At least the man hadn't cut *through* her dress. The length would hide the injury enough to get out of the embassy. With a grunt, she pulled herself to her feet and headed quickly back to the ballroom.

By the time she made it, she was limping. Her leg

throbbed relentlessly. It felt like blood streamed out of the wound with each step she took. She prayed it didn't drip and draw notice before she could properly tend to it.

Feeling the wall, she found the lever and pressed. The hidden door slid aside, allowing her to step back into the ballroom. Hearing the door latch behind her, she took a steadying breath, leaning so as not to put weight on her right leg. Music played softly from the stage while a din of voices and glasses clinking filled the air in between. No one noticed her slip from behind the wall hanging.

Or so she thought.

"Ah, there you are," said a voice she didn't recognize as a large hand closed around her right upper arm.

Her instinct was to make whoever thought they could touch her regret that decision, but she reminded herself she didn't need to draw attention. Gritting her teeth, she met the gaze of the man who'd stopped her.

You!

Her mind stuttered on the exclamation as her stomach jumped and her breath shortened. It was the man who'd watched her on the stairs. Mr. Handsome was even better up close. He had flawless skin.

Probably moisturizes.

She smirked at the thought. High maintenance was not her type. Even so, she couldn't stop staring. His eyes were a deep caramel color, he had a cleft in his chin, and a dimple winked in his right cheek when he smiled at her perusal.

Get it together, Yumi!

She blinked, breaking out of the lust filling her senses. "Let go of me," she told him in as stern a tone as she could muster with her breathing going haywire at his touch.

He released her arm and extended a hand, his smile never wavering. "Barrett Burkhart. And you are?"

She started reaching for his hand, but then her brain reminded her she needed to get the hell out. "Leaving," she huffed, then spun around.

She winced when she took a step too vigorously, the pressure sending a sharp ache vibrating down her injured leg. Burkhart noticed.

"You're hurt," he told her with a frown.

Ignoring him, she tried to keep her face in a neutral expression to hide it as she moved toward the ballroom exit. She made it a few steps, panting in pain, before Mr. Handsome lifted her off her feet. He carried her against his chest with one arm at her back, the other underneath her legs as though she weighed nothing.

"Put me down!" she hissed under her breath. People were starting to notice, and she wriggled in panic. "Now, dammit!"

Concern dotted his features, but he did as she asked. "Let me help you."

"If you want to help, let me lean on your arm," she demanded while surveying the ballroom. The people whose attention they'd drawn had returned to their conversations. Yumi breathed a slow exhale of relief.

When she glanced at Barrett Burkhart again—*What kind of name is that?*—he held his arm out, waiting. Sliding hers through, she leaned heavily into him with her left side.

"Okay, Barry—"

"It's Barrett."

The fact that she detected annoyance at the nickname almost made her grin. "Right. Let's walk naturally to the nearest exit. Please," she added through clenched teeth.

"Who are you?" he asked as he complied.

"Who are *you*?" she countered, hoping inane conversation would keep her mind off the burning pain.

"I'm a lawyer with the State Department. What brings you to this event?"

"You ask a lot of questions, BB."

"BB?" He shook his head, but she detected a smile in his voice as he said, "I'm a lawyer. It's my job to ask questions. You evading them only makes me want to know more."

"Hmm," she hummed a noncommittal response and steered him toward the elevator. No way would she make it up the stairs right now. The cloth around her leg had soaked through with blood, and she was afraid to look down to see if she made a trail.

"What happened to your leg?"

"Someone cut it."

"Are you serious?" His question sounded choked.

"Yep," she popped the "p."

Hitting the button to call the elevator, she turned to stare at him. His eyes were wide in shock. She arched her brow at him. He blinked, dropping to his knees in front of her. Then, he reached for the hem of her dress and started to lift it.

"Hey!" She swatted his hands away and stepped back. "What do you think you're doing?"

He blew out a breath, then ran a hand through his perfectly-styled hair, mussing it a little. "Do you need a doctor?"

"No. I just need to get out of this building." She glared at the elevator. The embassy didn't have that many floors. Why the hell was it taking so long?

"Who did that to you?" The fury shining in his eyes with the question made her own widen in surprise.

Seriously, who is this guy?

The elevator dinged, and she looked away. Wondering if he'd follow, she stepped into the lift.

Burkhart was right behind her. "Are you in some kind of trouble?"

Yumi almost snorted. The lawyer was trying to puzzle her out. Maybe she'd have been amused if she hadn't been in the worst kind of trouble. But the CIA wanted her dead. What she needed was to disappear.

When she said nothing, he lowered his voice. Sidling closer, he lightly touched the top of her arm. "I have a brother who . . ." he trailed off with a shake of his head. "He could help."

The elevator opened on the main floor, and she looked up at Burkhart, silently demanding he offer his arm. When he got the hint, she wrapped hers around him, asking, "Who's your brother?"

They exited the lift, and she leaned on him while steering around the crowd toward the main entrance.

"Miles, or I guess he goes by Crane? He works for Tactical Operations & Protection. They—"

"I've heard of it," she cut him off.

Well, that's interesting . . .

She hadn't met Crane, but she recognized the name. The rest of his team at TOP was very familiar to her. Maybe Barrett Burkhart might come in handy, after all.

They were nearly to the glass exit doors when she felt it. Blood trickled past the bandage on her leg. Gravity urged its flow down her skin, and soon it would leave droplets on the limestone under their feet.

"Shit!" she cursed softly.

"What's wrong?" Burkhart's question sounded far away.

Her heels echoed against the stone and the noise buzzed in her ears. She blinked as the lights in the hall darkened at the edges of her vision. Her head didn't feel right. Another step, and she stumbled, but Barrett's arm kept her vertical.

Damn. She must have lost more blood than she realized.

Clinging to him, she managed to mumble, "Take me to TOP," before her vision completely tunneled and she lost her grip on consciousness.

EPILOGUE

Bo

Bo and Selene walked into Tactical Operations & Protection's conference room in Charlottesville, Virginia. They were the first to arrive for the operation debrief. No bodies filled the matching slim black leather chairs surrounding the shiny silver tabletop, and the television hanging on the wood-paneled accent wall remained dark.

Bo hadn't been inside this room or TOP headquarters since he'd been hired three years ago. They typically debriefed in the field or via videocall, but Victor had insisted everyone meet here for this one. He mulled over why.

"Where do we sit?" Selene's question pulled him from his thoughts. She hovered in front of the windows, twisting her fingers together.

Clearly, he needed to make her relax. Grinning at how he planned to do that, he advanced on her.

Backing her into the corner, he boxed her in and leaned down to steal her lips in a kiss that he'd been waiting the last several hours to give her. After wrapping up in Montreal, they'd flown straight here. He was ready to get this over with and find a hotel room for some alone time with her.

She returned the embrace with fervor. Wanting more, he slid his hand underneath her shirt to trace the skin just under her breasts.

Her mouth popped off his with a gasp. "We can't do that here!" she cautioned with a smile that told him she'd like to, though.

His hand was still up her shirt. He was pretty sure they *could* do this here. He craved her enough to want to but . . .

He huffed, "Yeah, you're right. I'm pretty sure there are cameras."

"What?" she shrieked, head swiveling to look for them. "Bo!"

He couldn't help but chuckle at her panic. Removing his hands, he tugged at her waist. "Let's find a hotel before we give them a show."

She shook her head with a smile. "Afterward."

As much as he didn't want to wait, he figured walking out on his team after what they'd done for Selene wouldn't sit well. "Fine," he grumbled.

Reaching for her hand, he led her to the table. He chose the seat closest to the door and parked her beside him. She chuckled when he pulled her chair closer so that he could keep his hand on her thigh.

A smile made his lips twitch as he thought about how he planned to spend the time in their hotel room. It started with slowly undressing Selene, and then—

"Who are you and what have you done with Bo?"

Crane's humor-filled voice broke into his fantasy. He turned to see the newlyweds had entered the conference room. Pushing back from the table, Bo stood, offering his hand to the tall, dark-haired Marine. "Crane."

After a flicker of surprise flashed on his face, they clasped hands. Then Bo nodded a welcome to Rogue. The dark-eyed blonde seemed as confused as her husband. He knew he deserved their scrutiny after he'd been so reserved for years.

Clearing his throat, he gestured to Selene. "This is Selene Coleman." She stood and offered her hand with a friendly smile. He touched her arm and added, "Selene, this is Crane and Rogue. They were the ones watching over your parents."

Her eyes filled with tears at his announcement, but she blinked them back. Her voice effused gratitude as she clasped both of their hands. "Thank you so much! I don't know how to repay you, but if you ever need anything, I'm in your debt."

Rogue shook her head with a smile. "You're welcome, but we were just doing our job." With a glance at Bo, she added, "Besides, TOP protects its own."

The sentiment behind her words had regret knotting his stomach. She knew what it felt like to be desperate for someone to help the person you loved. Pushing past it, he scrubbed a hand over his beard. "I, uh, wanted to apologize for missing your celebration. I don't know if I said, but . . . I'm really happy for both of you." He shifted on his feet as Crane and Rogue's gazes locked on him and tried for another smile. "Congratulations. I'll be better about attending things like that in the future." Especially now that he had Selene to go with.

A deep rumble of laughter rolled from Crane's lips. With a grin, he joked, "Maybe the next occasion will be *your* wedding."

"Crane!" Rogue elbowed her husband in the side while Bo heard Selene gasp next to him.

He only shrugged. "May-be."

Duke strolled in and halted. Eyeing them all with his cocky smirk. "What did I miss?"

No one answered, but Bo couldn't take his eyes off Selene. A blush colored the apple of her cheeks. The look in her ocean depths . . . it made him want to drop to one knee right then and there.

If only I had a ring . . .

Herc broke the silence when he lumbered in carrying a basket filled with snacks he'd likely stolen from one of TOP's reception rooms. He munched on something as he set it on the table and mumbled, "Help yourselves."

Romeo followed, carrying coffees for everyone. Those were snatched up fast, and then they all settled into seats.

Glancing at Selene, Bo asked, "Do you want anything?"

She shook her head, still looking a little dazed. Because his stomach was growling, he snagged a protein bar and ate it while they waited for Victor.

Conversation buzzed around the table, but his thoughts strayed to how and when he could procure a ring for Selene. There was zero doubt in his mind that he wanted to marry her.

What kind would she like? Should I ask her?

Victor swept into the room, heading for the end of the table in front of the TV. "Okay, people, I know you're tired. I'll keep this short, then we can all take a breather for a few days."

Calls of "hallelujah" and "fuck yeah" filled the air. Bo frowned. He wanted more than a few days.

Victor raised a hand, and the room fell silent. "But first, we have a problem."

That tripped Bo's pucker factor. What the hell had happened from the time they'd touched down 'til now?

Victor pinched the bridge of his nose, then sighed. "The CIA blacklisted Yumi Nakano. She's currently MIA."

Selene jerked, sitting up straighter in her chair. "We have to find her!"

Hating her distress, Bo reached for her hand and held on. "We will," he murmured, stroking his thumb across her skin.

"Did she take out the servers?"

"What happened?"

As the questions started firing, Victor raised his hands again. "Here's what we know." He waited for quiet before continuing, "At twenty hundred last night, she infiltrated the Chinese embassy in D.C., breached their server room, then disappeared."

"But I thought she just found the servers? Her message was from a few hours ago." Selene frowned, and Bo squeezed her hand in comfort.

"Spoofing," Romeo blurted, then looked to Victor for confirmation.

"Yeah," his gaze returned to Selene, explaining, "that message wasn't really from her. Someone just wanted it to look like it was."

"Who would do that?" Selene asked, but no one had an answer for her.

Bo could hazard a guess, but he was shooting in the dark without knowing more about Yumi's background.

"Why wouldn't she tell us if she'd already found the servers? We could've helped take them out," Herc grumbled.

Heads nodded around the table in agreement. In the beginning, Bo had doubts about the agent, but she'd proven him wrong. She'd done everything she'd said she would—helped them find Dao, protected Selene, and if she'd found the servers, he'd wager she destroyed the AI.

Unless someone prevented her from doing so.

He didn't want to voice that option and make Selene worry more. With all of TOP searching, they'd find Yumi.

Rogue frowned, a thoughtful crease forming between her brows. "Maybe she didn't have time to, or she didn't have a secure way to let us know." She tapped a finger to her bottom lip. "The CIA dropped her, so she won't have access to their resources anymore. She won't be easy to find if she's gone dark."

Bo spoke up for Selene's sake. "We'll find her. Yumi's one of us now."

Victor's stern expression didn't waver. "TOP leadership wants confirmation Yumi succeeded in wiping Sentient Shadow from existence. If she didn't . . ."

Bo swore under his breath. *Not fucking good.*

"So much for R&R," Duke commented.

Crane's phone rang, breaking the tension in the room. "Sorry," he said before glancing at the caller ID. Wearing a slight frown, he silenced it only for it to ring again seconds later. Concern etched his features, and he lifted his head, probably to ask Victor to step out.

He didn't have to say the words, though. Their team leader gave a curt nod, then zeroed in on Selene. The intensity on his face had Bo shifting in his seat. "Selene, TOP would like to offer you a job as a translator. You could work remotely, and there'd be travel involved if your language skills were needed for an op."

Fear sweat broke out on Bo's neck, and he opened his mouth to demand, "Behind the scenes, right? No more playing bait or taking risks with her safety."

Victor smiled, but it was brief. "It'd be a strictly non-operational role."

When she shivered as if the mere idea of being in danger brought back unpleasant memories, Bo gripped her hand tighter. She closed her eyes, then opened them after blowing out a breath. "I'm good with that."

Bo squeezed the hand he held. "Then I'd love to have you in my ear."

A genuine smile spread across her lips. Relief that she'd be safe, and he wouldn't have to disappear on her for his job, made him return the smile. As the team congratulated her, she blushed at the attention.

Victor's commanding voice spoke over the celebrations. "Everyone take today but meet back here at zero eight tomorrow morning. By then, we should have a bead on Yumi's location."

Bo assumed that meant asking favors from contacts at the three-letter agencies, but he didn't need to know. All he needed was Selene.

He stood, tugging her to her feet. He could feel the stress weighing her down and wanted to ease her worries about her friend. "Yumi is smart and tough. I bet she finds a way to contact us before we even find her."

She smiled at his words, but it looked forced. "I know you're right. It's just hard not to worry."

Hoping to lighten her mood, he cupped her face and lifted an eyebrow. "Then it looks like I've got my work cut out for me."

Her chuckle rewarded him as she caught his meaning. Brushing her hair over her shoulder, he let his palm linger on her skin. "Let's get out of here."

Thirty minutes later, they entered their hotel room. It wasn't as grand or eclectic as the place they'd stayed in Montreal, but it had everything they needed— namely, a bed. His thoughts kept ending up there despite Selene being on the phone with her parents. Now that they were safe, she'd called to catch up, which meant letting them know about quitting her job at Saber Tech and starting a new one. She fudged over some of the details, likely so they wouldn't worry.

Unable to not touch her, Bo wrapped his arms around her from behind. Leaning in, he rested his chin on her shoulder while she spoke to her parents about a vacation they wanted to take together. "Yes. As soon as I have time on the books, we'll travel to Barcelona." There was a pause before she added, a smile in her voice as she tilted her head to meet his gaze. "Oh, and I have someone I want you to meet."

When she hung up, he grinned and said, "Say Barcelona again."

With a smile, she obliged him.

His dick twitched as his gaze fell to her mouth. "That's so sexy. I could listen to your voice all day, ocean-eyes." He twirled her around and kissed her. When she moaned, he trailed his lips across her jaw to her ear. "It's the first thing I want to hear when I wake up in the morning and the last thing I want to listen to before I close my eyes at night."

The sound she made in response shot straight to his groin. Kissing down her neck, he found the spot on her collarbone that turned her on. When she gasped, he walked her backward to the bed. He was going to spend his time on that spot, then go searching for more that would drive her wild.

* * *

Selene

Selene had never been so thoroughly pleasured. Bo had teased her with his hands and mouth for what felt like hours. Her body hummed with all the force of an electrical storm, and she didn't know how much more she could take before she erupted.

"Bo-o-o-o," she moaned as he scraped his beard across her inner thigh. When his tongue teased her slit, she panted. "I can't," she gasped, "I'm going to—"

Instead of giving her what she wanted, he pulled away. "Yes, you can, ocean-eyes."

She glared at the gleam shining in those umber depths when she met his satisfied gaze. She'd lost count of the number of times he'd driven her to the brink of orgasm, only to deprive her of that blissful fall. Well, she was done waiting.

Making sure he watched her, she trailed her fingers up her thigh until she found her center. When she dragged them through her wetness, his eyes widened, and he let out a sharp exhale.

Next, she dipped her fingers inside. A grin spread across her face as he swallowed hard, his Adam's apple bobbing. She started to move them slowly in and out to tease him, but her own needs made her groan and pick up her pace. She lost sight of Bo as her head fell back, her body bowing off the bed.

Before she could find her release, his hand tugged hers away. A whimper escaped her lips. "Bo, please," she panted.

But he was already moving on top of her. His mouth claimed hers in a rough kiss as he pushed inside her body. She wrapped her arms around his powerful back, gripping and scratching with her nails while he thrusted.

When his mouth left hers, he rasped, "I'm so fucking in love with you."

His words and his dark mineral scent surrounded her, bringing her a sense of safety, security, and immense and overwhelming love. She gasped for breath as their bodies moved in unison. "I love you, too!" She pushed the words out as pleasure roared through her.

The intensity of it burst in her heart, traveling through her entire body like a tidal wave of warmth. When her orgasm hit, her shout was one of pure bliss. Bo froze, and his arms shook as his head dropped back with the force of his own release.

The electrical storm he'd built within her left her trembling with aftershocks. She barely registered him collapsing on top of her. Her molecules were scattered and took their sweet time coming back together. When they did, a laugh bubbled up her throat until she shook with the force of it.

Bo pushed up on his arms and shook his head as if to clear it. "Can't think," he mumbled, making her laugh some more.

She smiled and reached up to rub her hands over the beard she loved so much, up his rugged face, and into the soft auburn waves on top of his head. "That was . . ." She paused, unsure she had the words to describe how amazing it had been.

A slow smile softened the hard lines of his face. "World-shaking."

She chuckled. "Yes." Lifting up, she placed a soft kiss on his lips. "Thank you."

He shook his head with a growl. "No, ocean-eyes." After pressing a firm kiss on her mouth, his forehead lifted, and the gold and red facets in his chocolate eyes swirled with emotion. "Thank *you*." His expression softened as he said, "My heart was meant to love you, and yours was meant to heal mine."

His statement touched something deep inside her. Her eyes watered as her throat choked with love for him. Awestruck, she could only stare, trying to take everything in. Somehow, they'd managed to survive the ordeal with Mr. Dao. She had a new job with people she looked forward to working with, and she had Bo.

Before she could pull herself together to respond, he lifted her into a sitting position, then climbed off the bed to kneel in front of her.

A gasp pulled from her lips.

"Will you marry me, ocean-eyes?"

Words burst out of her. "Yes. Oh, Bo! Yes!" Her heart ricocheted in excitement. Now, she wasn't sure if she was laughing or crying or both. This felt surreal. Like she was dreaming and feared waking up.

He rose, then cupped her face with one hand. "I'm going to get you a ring at the first opportunity. Would you, ah"—he scrubbed at his beard with the other—"would you want to pick it out?"

She'd honestly never thought about it before, but her heart filled with warmth at the idea of doing it together. "I'd love to."

His smile seemed relieved. "Okay, yeah, good. We'll do it together."

She couldn't stop smiling. "Together," she agreed, then kissed her fiancé.

My fiancé.

She giggled against his mouth. The word filled her with so much joy that she felt like she could light the room with the glow beaming out of her.

They might not make sense on paper, but if recent events had taught her anything, it was that life was meant to be lived. Risks were meant to be taken, or you'd never reap the rewards. Her gut had trusted Bo to protect her, but her heart trusted him to keep it safe.

She knew he still had some healing to do, and she'd be there for him every step of the way. He'd promised her forever. No matter how rocky their path might be, she looked forward to traveling it. Together.

A NOTE TO READERS

If you enjoyed this book, please consider leaving a review. They help spread the word about my books through the recommendation process and help new readers decide if my books will be a good fit for them. Reviews contribute to rankings on sites like Amazon, making my stories more visible to new readers. Even a one-line review makes a difference!

If you can't get enough of grumpy former military heroes, try my book, *Blaze of Glory*. It features a grumpy heroine who is a former Army pilot. She butts heads with a cocky hotshot firefighter which leads to hate sex in a closet. When a disaster pits them together, they have to rely on each other to survive. As flames threaten to consume their animosity, will they surrender to the blaze of passion, or will their fiery clash extinguish any chance at love?

Check it out and follow me on social media for updates, teasers, and more.

Thank you for reading!

xoxo,

Blye Donovan

ACKNOWLEDGMENTS

Thank you to every single reader who read *Going Rogue* and wanted more of the crew from Tactical Operations & Protection. You guys push me to keep writing. Yumi's book is next in the series if you haven't guessed. Her hero is none other than Crane's brother, Barrett. I've got plans for the remaining Burkhart sibling, too. Ali will be paired up with a member of the team, but I'll let you wonder about who that might be . . . for now.

Getting a book ready for release is far from a solo job. I know I'll forget some people, but I want to say a big thank you to M.K. for continuing to put up with me. You are an invaluable critique partner. I don't know what I'd do without your comments and suggestions.

Angela Haddon, I am in awe of your book covers. Thank you for bringing Bo to life for me.

Charissa, thank you for helping me navigate Bookfunnel for ARCs. I'd have for sure messed it up without your wisdom!

Speaking of ARCs, thank you to every member of my team. You help more than you know. I couldn't do this without you. Your reviews keep me sitting in front of my computer every day.

Finally, thank *you* for buying this book! I hope you enjoyed Bo and Selene's adventure!

ABOUT THE AUTHOR

Blye Donovan is a military brat and a veteran who resides in the Lowcountry of South Carolina with her husband and fur-child, Maximus. Besides books, she's addicted to coffee, peanut butter, and shoes. When she's not feeding these addictions, she writes books that are romantic suspense stories featuring strong heroines and alpha protector heroes overcoming dangerous villains. Her books are  often set in small towns because she loves the atmosphere associated with them, especially when they have historic architecture. She was supposed to become a historic preservationist, but . . . writing has always been her passion. You can check out her current series, follow her on social media, and more all at this link: https://linktr.ee/blyedonovan.